BROKEN

Karin Fossum began her writing career in 1974. She has won numerous awards, including the Glass Key Award for the best Nordic crime novel, an honour shared with Henning Mankell and Jo Nesbo, and the *Los Angeles Times* Book Prize for *Calling Out For You,* which was also shortlisted for the Crime Writers' Association Gold Dagger Award.

Charlotte Barslund translates Scandinavian novels and plays. Her recent work includes *Broken* by Karin Fossum, *Machine* by Peter Adolphsen and *We, The Drowned* by Carsten Jensen.

ALSO BY KARIN FOSSUM

Don't Look Back

'Fossum's characters are painfully real. Sejer belongs alongside the likes of Adam Dalgliesh and Inspector Morse'

Boston Globe

He Who Fears the Wolf

'In spare, incisive prose . . . she turns a conventional police procedural into a sensitive examination of troubled minds and a disturbing look at the way society views them'

New York Times

When the Devil Holds the Candle

'As always Fossum gets right under the skin of her central characters . . . An engrossing psychological thriller'

Sunday Telegraph

Calling Out For You

'Karin Fossum proves once again that she's one of the very best of the new wave of Nordic crime writers'

Independent on Sunday

KARIN FOSSUM

Broken

TRANSLATED FROM THE NORWEGIAN BY
Charlotte Barslund

VINTAGE BOOKS
London

Published by Vintage 2012

2 4 6 8 10 9 7 5 3 1

First published with the title *Brudd* in 2006 by
J. W. Cappelens Forlag, AS, Oslo

First published in Great Britain in 2008 by
Harvill Secker

Vintage
Random House, 20 Vauxhall Bridge Road,
London SW1V 2SA

www.vintage-books.co.uk

Addresses for companies within The Random House Group Limited
can be found at: www.randomhouse.co.uk/offices.htm

The Random House Group Limited Reg. No. 954009

A CIP catalogue record for this book
is available from the British Library

ISBN 9780099565536

This edition has been published with the financial assistance of NORLA

Printed and bound by CPI Group (UK) Ltd, Croydon, CR0 4YY

To Herdis Eggen, my editor

CHAPTER 1

I see them in the porch light.

A long queue of people waiting on the drive outside my house; on closer inspection they turn out to be a mixture of the old and the young, men, women and children. They are patient, their heads are bowed, they are waiting for their stories to be told and it is I who will tell them, I am the author. I watch them for a long time, partly hidden behind my curtain, all the time thinking about the challenge ahead of me. But I am tired now; it is midnight, tomorrow maybe, I think, yawning. I need a few hours' sleep, it is hard work to give life to new characters every single day, it is not as if I am God, I am just a tired, middle-aged woman trying to keep going.

I watch the ones whose faces are in the shadows. There are so many of them, they are hard to count, and what happens to the ones whose stories I never get to tell, who will look after them? I press my nose against the window, my breath makes the glass steam up, I draw a little heart. At the front of the queue is a young woman cradling a small bundle, it is a baby swaddled in a blue towel. She clutches the baby to her chest, her face is racked with guilt. What can be haunting her so terribly? She is awfully young, emaciated, early twenties probably. She is wearing a dark coat with a hood and she wears high-heeled ankle boots. She stands as if rooted to the spot, with the baby in her arms and her head bowed towards her chest. Behind her stands a man. He looks somewhat puzzled, his hands are folded. An unassuming man in his early forties, thinning hair, he stoops slightly. He is not a religious man, though he might be praying to me; it seems as if he is beckoning me, that he has attached himself to the fringes of my consciousness. Behind him stands a very old man, scrawny and withered. There is no glint in his eyes, he has one foot in the grave and nobody notices him. But God knows he needs to be noticed, I think and scrutinise him. Inside his concave chest beats the noblest of hearts. Behind him is a woman, a little thin, greying hair, could she be me, will I tell my own story one day? I realise that it is midnight and I make an effort to tear myself away. I have to turn my back on them, I'm exhausted. I have drunk a bottle of burgundy and I have just taken a Zyprexa for anxiety, a Cipralex for depression and a Zopiclone to make me sleep, so I need my rest now. But it is so hard to turn my back on them, they continue to disturb me. At times they stare at my window in an intense and compelling way. How many of them are there? I lean against the window and try to count them. More than eleven, that means it will take me at least eleven years to get through them all. At the same time I know that as soon as I have dispatched the young woman with the baby and the man with his hands folded, new characters will arrive in a steady stream, I don't believe it will ever stop. This is how my life has turned out. I walk down the stairs every morning, then across the floor to the computer; I delve into the fate of a new character oblivious to everything around me. Time stands still, I feel neither hunger nor thirst, I am fixated by the blue glare from the computer. After several hours' work I finally resurface. The telephone rings and brings me back to life. It is busy outside, a real world with laughter and joy, with death, misery and grief. While I am absorbed by fiction, I pull the strings like a puppeteer; I make things happen, it's a passion and a lifelong obsession.

My cat appears on the veranda; I let him inside where it is warm. This agile grey animal is one of the most beautiful creatures in the world, I think; he walks across the parquet floor silently, softly and elegantly.

'Are you sleeping on my bed tonight?' I ask.

He fixes his green eyes on me and starts to purr. Then he heads for the stairs. Together we walk up the fifteen steps to the first floor and into my bedroom. It is small, cool and dark. There is my bed, my bedside table with the blue lamp. An alarm clock, an open book. I open up the window completely, the cool November air wafts in. By the bed is an old armchair, I place my clothes on the armrest. Then I slip under the duvet, curl up like a child. The cat jumps up, settles at my feet, a warm, furry ball of wool. For a moment everything is wonderfully quiet, then faint noises start to come through the window. Rustling from the cluster of trees outside. A car drives by; its headlights sweep ghostlike across my window. The house sits solidly on its foundation, resting like an ancient warrior. I close my eyes. Normally I am asleep the second my head hits the pillow and I remember nothing else. But now I am disturbed by a sound. Someone is trying to open the front door; I'm not hearing things. My eyes open wide and I struggle to breathe, fear surges through my body because this is really happening. The sound was very clear, it could not be misinterpreted. Did I forget to lock the door? Frantically I look at my alarm clock, the green digits glow, it is past midnight. The cat raises his head and I sense his movement through the duvet, this means the noise is not a figment of my imagination because cats are never wrong. What happens next is terrifying and eerie. The stairs creak; I hear slow, hesitant steps. I lie rigid in my bed. Then all goes quiet. I'm breathing too fast, my fists are clenched, I brace myself, I lie still, listening to the silence, praying to God that I'm hearing things. It could have been the trees outside, or a deer, perhaps, stepping on dry twigs. I calm myself down and close my eyes. Finally the sleeping pill kicks in; I drift off and only a tiny fragment of my consciousness is present. That is when I awake startled. Someone is in the room; I sense another human being. A pulse, a smell, breathing. The cat arches his back, he sniffs the darkness and in the dim, grey light from the window I see the outline of a man. He takes a few steps towards me and sits down on the chair next to my bed. I hear the creaking of the chair and the rustle of clothing. For several long minutes I lie very still under the duvet; the situation is bizarre, every single cell in my body is trembling. Neither of us speaks or moves, times passes, my eyes acclimatise to the dark.

'Turn on the light,' I ask him softly.

He does not reply, does not stir, his body is still in the chair. So I raise myself up on my elbow and turn on the light. I stay in this position watching him in amazement. He sits with his hands folded. The light causes him to blink fearfully, his grey eyes avoid looking at me.

'You've jumped the queue,' I say.

He bows his head in shame. Nods his heavy head.

'I recognise you,' I say. 'You're second. There is a woman with a baby in front of you.'

'I know!' he groans, his face contorting with pain. 'There's always someone ahead of me, I'm used to that. But I can't bear it any longer, I'm exhausted. You have to tell my story now, you have to start this morning!'

I sit upright and smooth my duvet. I lean against the headboard. The cat jumps up and listens, his ears perked up, he does not know how to react either.

'You're asking me to make you a promise,' I say, 'I can't. The woman has been waiting too, she has been waiting for many years and she is deeply unhappy.'

He rocks restlessly in the chair. Moves his hands to dust off something from the knees of his trousers, then his fingers rush to the knot of his tie, which is immaculate.

'Everyone is unhappy,' he replies. 'Besides, you can't measure unhappiness, the pain is equally great in all of us. I have come forward to ask for something, to save my own soul. I'm using the last of my strength and it has cost me a great deal.' And then in a thin voice: 'Should that not be rewarded?'

I give him a look of resignation; I'm filled with conflicting emotions. I'm not a naturally commanding person, but I try to be firm.

'If you have been waiting that long,' I say, 'you can wait another year. The woman with the baby will be done in twelve months.'

He is silent for a long time. When he finally speaks, his deep voice is trembling.

'This assumes that you live that long,' he says eventually. His voice is very meek, he does not look me in the eyes.

'What do you mean?' I ask, shocked.

'I mean,' he says anxiously, 'you might die. Then I'll have no story, I'll have no life.'

The thought that I might die soon does not upset me, I live with it daily and every morning I'm amazed that I'm still alive. That my heart beats, that the sun still rises.

'But then that applies to all of you,' I reply in a tired voice. 'I can't save everyone. Have you seen the old man behind you in the queue? He is way past eighty. He is valuable to me. The very old know more than most people, I want to hear what he has to say.'

He gives a heavy, prolonged sigh. Glances at me, a sudden touch of defiance in his grey eyes.

'But I've summoned the courage,' he says, 'I've come all the way to your bedroom, I've taken action. I'm begging you! And I want you to know something; this is terribly difficult for me. It goes against my nature, because I'm a very humble man.'

I watch him more closely now. His eyes are downcast once again, his face tormented. His hair is thinning and a little too long, it sticks out inelegantly at the back, he is wearing a slate-grey shirt, a black narrow tie and a black jacket. Grey trousers, black well-polished shoes with even laces. He is very clean and neatly groomed, but old-fashioned-looking, a man from another age.

'A very humble man,' he repeats.

I exhale; my breath turns into a sigh.

'I'm completely awake now,' I say. 'I won't get any sleep tonight.'

Suddenly he cheers up. The pitch of his voice rises.

'Well,' he says excitedly, 'if you make the decision now that you will get up in the morning and start my story, then you will be able to sleep, I'm certain of that. You need structure and I can give you that.'

'And what about the woman with the child?' I ask. 'She's first in the queue, you know, and has been for a long time. It's extremely hard to pass people over, I can't handle that.'

At that he looks me straight in the eye. It comes at a price, his breathing quickens.

'I think it is too late for her anyway,' he says quietly.

I reach for the cat, draw him to me, hold him tight.

'What do you mean, too late?'

He nods his heavy head.

'I think the child is dead.'

I shake my head in disbelief.

'Why do you say that? Have you spoken with her?'

Once again he brushes his trousers, I imagine it is a kind of reflex, which he cannot suppress.

'You write crime novels, don't you?' he mumbles. 'So the child will have to die. Her story is about the child's fate, about what happened to it. Did she find her child dead? Did she kill it herself? Was the child killed by its father, was it ill? Things like that. She would get picked by someone else anyway. Whereas I'm not interesting like her, no one else would pick me. Do you see?'

His voice is timid and pleading.

'You're wrong,' I state.

'No, I'm not. Please don't tell me that I have to go outside again, please don't ask me to go back to that wretched queue!'

His voice falters.

'I know lots of people who would pick you if you came their way,' I say, 'greater writers than me.'

'But this is where I've come,' he says, hurt.

'Why?'

'Why?' He shrugs. 'You must have summoned me, I was driven here, it's already been three years. For three long years I've been waiting under the porch light.'

'I never summon anyone,' I say in a firm voice. 'I haven't invited you. Suddenly you appeared as number two in the queue. And yes, I've known you were there for a long time, I've seen you very clearly, but there needs to be some sort of system, otherwise I lose control.'

The cat has curled up once more in my lap and is purring unperturbed.

'What's the cat's name?' he asks suddenly.

'Gandalf,' I reply. 'Gandalf, after Tolkien's wizard.'

'And what about me?' he goes on. 'Give me a name too, please, if nothing else.'

'What if I have a cruel fate in mind for you?' I ask him. 'Painful, difficult? Filled with shame and despair?'

He juts out his chin. 'I thought we might have a little chat about that. And agree the bigger picture.'

I narrow my eyes and give him a dubious look.

'So you're going to interfere too?' I shake my head. 'That's not going to happen, I'm very sorry, but I'm in charge here. No fictitious character ever stands by my bed telling me what to do. That's not how it works.'

'All the same,' he pleads, 'hasn't it occurred to you that I might make your job easier?'

'How?' I reply sceptically.

'There will be two of us making the decisions. If you get stuck I can tell you what I would like to happen; don't push me away, think about it, please.'

'I never get stuck,' I declare. 'I need to sleep now, it's night-time and I need to get up early.'

'A name, please!' he begs. 'Is that too much to ask?'

'Right, I'll name you,' I say, 'and before I know it, you'll want something else. A profession. Somewhere to live. A girlfriend.'

'No girlfriend,' he says quickly.

'Really? Why not?'

He becomes evasive once more. He falters. 'I don't need one, let's keep it simple.'

'So you're already interfering?'

Suddenly he looks wretched. 'I'm sorry, so sorry, I didn't mean to, but I'm scared! If you die soon, I will be lost for eternity.'

'I'm not going to die,' I comfort him.

'You are! All of us out there are worried about it and for good reason. Several members of your family have died from cancer. You smoke forty cigarettes a day, you drink too much red wine in the evenings, you're addicted to millions of pills, you eat too little, you work too hard, so you're clearly not going to live to be an old lady.'

I ponder this. 'Very well, you may be right. I can only do what I do and death is never convenient. However, I'm only fifty-one and you are second in the queue.'

'Name me,' he pleads again.

I pull up my knees. My shoulders are freezing cold, and my temples are starting to throb.

'Come closer to the light.'

He gets up and lifts the chair; he moves closer to the bedside table. He sits down again and folds his hands.

'You have a sensitive face,' I say inspecting him. 'You're gentle, poetic with a tendency towards melancholy. You come from a small, unassuming family of hard-working people. They all have this humility, this awareness of nuances, with the exception of your mother, perhaps, I'm not quite sure about her. I can picture them, they are fair-skinned and you can see their veins like fine, green threads.'

He pulls up the sleeve of his jacket and studies his wrist.

'You have large grey eyes,' I go on. 'However, your gaze is often defensive; if anyone talks to you, you'll look away. Your hair is thinning; it bothers you because in your own way you're vain despite your self-proclaimed modesty. You have dreams, they will never come true. Yet you're patient. You've always been patient. Right up until now.'

'And my name?'

'Give me a little time. Names are very important. If I rush, it will be wrong and I doubt that you'll be content with just anything.'

'I'm sorry I interrupted you,' he says, 'please continue, I'm listening.'

'Your hands,' I state, 'are really quite small. Your shoe size is thirty-nine, which is small for a grown man. You're clean, you watch what you eat and you're good at saving money. You're never ill, and you drink moderately. You have a green thumb, you're very fond of music. You notice how the light changes outside your window, you watch people and they fascinate you in a way you don't understand, yet you don't feel connected to them. You never approach anyone, you live your life without involving anyone else. You never complain, you don't shout, you never object to anything, you never get stressed; you make yourself go on like a carthorse. What do you think of Torstein?'

He gives me an uncertain look. 'It's not terribly poetic.'

I think again. Names fly through my mind and with each one I observe him closely. I hold the name up to his face, trying to make it fit.

'I would have to agree with you. Besides, Torstein is a strong man's name, resourceful and decisive. And I don't want to hurt your feelings, but you're a bit spineless.'

He bows his head and blushes scarlet in the light from the lamp on the bedside table.

'You must forgive me,' I say, 'but it was your idea to enter my house and I'm in charge here.'

'I know, I know. I will take what I'm given, I mean that from the bottom of my heart.'

'Then let's continue.'

I think again, I close my eyes.

'You sleep well at night, you sleep like a baby. You get up early and are always equally content with each new day. However, this serenity of yours, this meticulousness is actually very fragile. No one is allowed to disturb it, enter into it or distract you. You need to be in control and have a clear overview of absolutely everything that will happen.'

New names fly by. Names full of gravity and poetry.

'How about Alvar?' I suggest.

'Is that a name?' He looks at me quizzically.

'Of course it's a name. Though better known in Sweden than here in Norway. Attractive, too, in my opinion. Think it over.'

'I am. What about my surname? I suppose I'll be given one of those too?'

'Of course. Personally I favour monosyllabic names. Like Krohn. Or Torp. But I want to give you more than that.' I close my eyes again. Search through a myriad names.

'Your surname is Eide,' I say with absolute conviction.

'Alvar Eide,' he says quietly. 'That's good, I'm very grateful.'

He straightens his back and smiles.

'So you'll be starting tomorrow?'

I rest my head against the headboard, I shrug with resignation. Never, in all my life, have I experienced anything like this.

'Because now that I am visible to you, you won't be able to wait. I'll have a word with the woman holding the dead child, I'm sure we can come to an understanding.'

'Well, if you've been reassured now, would you kindly leave and find your place in the queue? I need some sleep, it's very late now.'

'Yes!' He nods adamantly. His grey eyes have lit up. 'There's just one small thing.' He raises his hand, he is begging. 'Am I a good person?'

I smile and shake my head at this. The way he is looking at me makes me laugh, and I concede that he has won.

'Of course you're a good person, Alvar Eide, you're as good as gold. Now leave me alone, I'm tired.'

Finally he gets up; he carefully puts the chair back in its place. Turns off the light, bows politely and exits. I hear his footsteps on the staircase, I hear the door being closed. I put my head on my pillow, I feel dizzy.

'Goodness gracious me,' I say out into the darkness. 'What do you make of this, puss?'

The cat is asleep, his paws twitching, he is hunting.

'Gandalf,' I whisper, 'listen to this. There is mutiny in the queue outside the house!'

The cat sleeps on determinedly. I turn on to my side and pull up my knees. What does it mean that I no longer have an orderly system? This has never happened before. What will happen in future, if they start arguing about the sequence? Is there a moment far into the future where this flow of people ends? Where will I turn then? Will I have to settle for people who have created their own lives, real people? Lives I have no control over, lives I cannot shape the way I always have? I can find no peace. I don't like this night, this turn that my life has taken, I'm used to a certain amount of control, a certain order. But now Alvar Eide has wedged himself into my life. I turn to the wall and I want to go to sleep, but I'm troubled by words flying through my head. I want to enter the room where Alvar lives, but the door is shut and locked. I don't find the key until the early-morning hours.

CHAPTER 2

I'm a good person.

So thought Alvar Eide, just as he was putting on his coat. He stood in his hall studying his face in the mirror. This thought, that he was a good person, seemed to comfort him, as if he had suddenly realised that he had not amounted to much else in this world. He had never distinguished himself, never caused a stir. Not that he had wanted to either, but the years were mounting up, he had started to think about the end. At the age of forty-two he was thinking about the end. Perhaps because his father, Emmanuel Eide, had only lived to fifty-three. Then without warning his heart had stopped beating never to start again. Alvar found it hard to believe that he himself would live past this age; he imagined his death was programmed into his genes like a time bomb and that it would go off in eleven years. But there was now one thing to comfort him, one cool morning in November just as he was about to walk the two kilometres to his place of work: I have never achieved anything major, I have never distinguished myself, but deep down I know I'm a good person.

He stuck his arms through the sleeves and reached for a camel-coloured woollen scarf he liked to wear wrapped around his neck. The scarf lay beautifully and neatly folded on the chest of drawers beneath the mirror. His gloves lay in a drawer; he pulled them on, they were slightly too big. He knew they kept his hands warmer that way. On his head he wore nothing. Even so, he glanced at the mirror to check that his hair was in place, gently combed over from his right temple and all the way across to his left. There was no breeze outside.

He grabbed the door handle. Pushed it down and went out into the cool air; it felt clean and fresh against his cheeks. The light caused him to squint. Alvar Eide lived in the upstairs flat of a house in Nøste outside Drammen; his neighbours, the Green family, owned the ground-floor flat. He did not know them very well. They came and went and he nodded briefly by way of acknowledgement; but he did everything he could to avoid having to make small talk. Alvar Eide was a shy man. Green, however, could be intrusive; sometimes he would linger downstairs by the letter boxes wanting to chat about everyday matters. The weather, the price of petrol, interest rates, the new government. And as Alvar liked to think of himself as a good person, he was never curt so that his behaviour might be interpreted as frosty or arrogant. Yet he kept Green at arm's length, gave monosyllabic answers to every question, while smiling politely the whole time and speaking in a low, educated voice. But is that goodness? he suddenly started to wonder and felt upset. Am I really a good person after all? I have never hurt anyone, but does that make me good? Surely you're meant to do good deeds, go the extra mile, make sacrifices in order to earn the label 'a good person'.

He struggled with these questions as he walked down the steep hill into town. The fjord gleamed metallically in the low sun. He felt weighed down by gloom. How impossible it was to know anything about yourself, something you could be certain of. And he had never been severely tested. Of course he donated to charity, modest sums. It never occurred to him to refuse. The thought of this brightened his mood instantly. Many people said no. They said, no, actually I wouldn't dream of helping, the hungry will just have to fend for themselves, the same goes for drug addicts. And cancer, well, that's never affected our family, I'll probably be struck down by other things and when the time comes I will make my contribution to whatever charity will benefit me and my own health. It's everyone for themselves. It's not my fault that people starve in Africa, that there's a war in Iraq. Maybe that's what they said holding their heads high, looking right at the face of the child with shiny eyes, perhaps, who might be standing outside their front door holding out a sealed collecting tin. Some, possibly, said nothing at all, they simply slammed the door with a bored look. Or even worse, they never even bothered to open it. He always opened the door whenever someone rang the bell even though he found it very difficult. Not a great deal happened in his life, he saw no one and had no family, no friends, no wife and child. So he went to the door when the bell rang even though it made his stomach lurch. He became very nervous when the shrill tone of the bell rang out through the rooms, at the mere thought that someone might want something from him. Might demand things, beg. Break into his neat, ordered world. On one occasion he had happened not to have any money on him; he had found that terribly embarrassing. Having to close the door without having helped, to close the door with downcast eyes and flushed, burning cheeks. Had they even believed him when he said he was out of cash? Or had they walked off, angrily denouncing him as a skinflint? The very thought of it tormented him because he regarded himself as generous, if only people would give him the chance. He usually found some kroner in a pocket or the bowl in the kitchen where he would store excess change from his wallet. Heavy wallets ruined the cut of his clothes, his mother had taught him that. He continued walking into town feeling troubled. He no longer felt good about himself. He gave money because it was embarrassing to say no. He never went back into his living room with the feeling of having contributed something, it felt more like a game and he was simply playing by the rules. Perhaps it's because I don't give enough, he thought. If I gave a thousand kroner, I might feel differently. But that would be too much. Surely there was something ostentatious about giving one thousand kroner? The whole point of charity appeals was that many people donated and everyone gave a small amount.

A cool gust of wind from the fjord hit his face. The comb-over, which lay loosely across his scalp threatened to fly up. He braced himself against the wind and hoped for the best. He looked down towards the light-bulb factory with its giant dome, which was lit up at night. The dome with its bright yellow glow was a landmark.

Often in the evening he would stand by the window staring at its strong light. He saw the busy port, the silos belonging to Felleskjøbet, the bridges and the trains with their green and red carriages. Now he was turning left, reaching Engene. He would walk along until he had Bragernes church on his right, then he would pass the grandiose old fire station, past Harry's Café before reaching Albumsgate. And Gallery Krantz, where he worked. The time was a quarter to ten. Now it was the wind from the river which nipped his cheeks; he kept on walking, swinging his arms rhythmically.

Whenever anyone came walking towards him on the pavement, he would make way for them in plenty of time. I enjoy walking through the town, Alvar thought, I like watching other people and wondering about them. Many walked around in pairs. Sometimes three or four walked together, some formed small groups on corners where they would chat. Voices and laughter flew through the air. Alvar Eide observed this phenomenon with a certain degree of bemusement. People had an indefatigable urge to socialise. It was something he personally had never done, he had gone through his life alone. But it was not a nagging loneliness. It was the life he preferred, because it gave him clarity and control. On top of that it was convenient, no demands, no unpleasantness. No agreements to fulfil, no promises to keep, no intrusive questions, how are you, Alvar? How are you really? It seemed that friends had some sort of right to know how you were. Consequently he never had company, it just so happened that he was perfectly happy minding his own business. He liked the peace and quiet of the flat, he enjoyed listening to Bach's 'Toccata and Fugue', quite loud, if he wanted to. He liked sleeping on his own. He considered sleep to be something terribly intimate and he shuddered at the thought of another person being able to watch him in this condition, as he lay curled up with his eyes closed and his mouth open. There had been times when he had considered getting a cat, but it had remained a thought. Cats probably needed all kinds of things, food, vaccinations and a tag, and even neutering if he chose a tom or contraceptive implants if he chose a female. He would have to take the animal to the vet's and deal with all of these things. Not that he would be incapable of that, he was a very competent man and he had a way with words when it was required of him. After all, he dealt with customers in the gallery. But still the thought of having to sort all this out, everything he would have to remember and take care of, had so far prevented him from getting a cat, even though he did, in fact, really want one. And it might get ill as well, it might come home with worms. When he was a boy, their neighbour had a cat. A heavy, tabby tomcat without a tail. One day it came into the living room and started vomiting violently. And the pile on the rug had started to squirm. Inside the revolting mess there was twitching and writhing. Alvar had been sent next door by his mother, holding a cup with no handle to borrow some sugar, and the sight of worms in the vomit had haunted him from that day on. That's just what cats are like, the neighbour had assured him, Alvar, don't worry about it. But Alvar knew that he would not be able to stomach an experience like that. And then there were fur balls, which they kept bringing up. So no cat.

Alvar kept on walking. He knew every courtyard, every street, every single shop in the heavily trafficked road. He returned to the question of being good. He had always believed that he was a good person. So how come this doubt had appeared like a bolt out of the blue and why would it not leave him alone? He realised that he had never, ever in all his life done anything which could be considered a good deed. He had never saved anyone's life, never intervened, never made the first move. Well, apart from the spare change he handed out whenever the doorbell rang. Or, preferably, to the Salvation Army officer who often stood outside the entrance to the shopping centre, silent and dignified, his uniform immaculate, holding a tin. Sometimes he had pushed a fifty-krone note through the slot and felt very pleased. Pleased, but not good. In a way the officer did the work for him. If I had stood there myself holding the tin, Alvar thought, then I would have felt better, that could have been deemed an active contribution. And I have a lot of my life left to live, or eleven years at any rate, and I can continue doing good work. Sponsor a child in India, perhaps, in Peru or Zimbabwe? He dismissed the thought instantly. A sponsored child would want letters and presents and he did not know how to relate to a foreign child in a country far away, a country he would know nothing about anyway. He had no experience of foreign cultures. But it would have been a good thing to do. Perhaps he would receive a photo of the child which he could hang on the wall above the fridge, a beautiful brown child with white teeth. Suddenly another thought cropped up, it came out of nowhere, like a bolt of lightning, possibly because a man was coming towards him, a very obese man struggling to walk, his cheeks flushed with exertion. What if this man collapsed from a heart attack right there and then on the street, what would he do? Stand there petrified, unable to move? He did not know first aid, he did not own a mobile phone, he would not even be able to phone for help. He visualised the grim scene, him standing there paralysed, his arms hanging limply. Others would come running and deal with it. The image instilled profound despondency in him. A sensation of worthlessness. The feeling was so painful that it stopped him in his tracks. He stood there, still staring at his newly polished shoes, as a car raced past, causing his coat to flap; it billowed like a sail. And then his tuft of hair stood up, something which always sent a shiver down his spine. A feeling of having been revealed as a fraud. For a long time he stood like that, but snapped out of his trance as a lady passed him on the outside of the pavement. Quickly he averted his eyes.

He walked on thinking, once I get myself to the gallery and the paintings then I'll be myself again. Because the paintings, these frozen moments, always filled him with serenity. Finally he could see the front of the stately building where he worked. A three-storey, twentieth-century villa, very well maintained and exclusive, painted a warm, creamy shade of yellow with a few details in red. Columns fronting the entrance, large arched windows and a double, reddish-brown oak front door with magnificent carvings. He did not earn a huge salary from his work there; however, he could manage on very little. He had inherited the flat in Nøste from his mother and the mortgage had been paid off ages ago. In the yard behind the house stood an old Mazda, which he would use if the weather was awful or if he fancied seeing a little of the surrounding countryside. He was very good at saving money and he had no expensive habits.

The owner of the gallery was an art dealer called Ole Krantz. He had run it for years and had many regular customers. Then suddenly at the age of fifty he had started to paint himself. It was going surprisingly well, he painted with latex on thick, high-quality watercolour paper. Decorative, colourful, easy-to-sell pictures. The subject might be the wing of a bird, a pansy, a bowl of strawberries, the kind of images people like having on their walls. Ole Krantz had become a child again following the amazing discovery that he had a talent for painting. Though, when discussing his own work, he said that it hardly counted as great art and this was consequently reflected in the price, which was moderate. The pictures went for anywhere from five to ten thousand kroner. Alvar truly felt at ease in the gallery. He enjoyed visual art, it was a subject he was well versed in and comfortable with, and he was a good salesman. He was patently good because during his long career there had not been a single instance where a customer had regretted a purchase and had come back to return a painting. Ole Krantz had a different sales technique, however. He sold huge quantities of paintings, but had to accept that several would be returned. He sold by seducing the customers, by stressing the rise in value, the unique features of the painting, the beneficial influence of a particular shade of blue, how this very picture would fill a void and, yes, it was pricey, but you can always pay in instalments. And so on and so forth in a steady persuasive stream. He was quick to spot what the customers wanted and roughly what they could afford. This one can stretch to a Willibard Storn while that one over there will probably have to make do with a Halvorsen. However, when Alvar sold a painting it was always based on mutual understanding and profound respect. The customer should always be left with the feeling that he had made a choice he would not regret.

Even though he was only an employee in the gallery, no sooner had he entered and disabled the alarm by pressing three-three-four-two, than he felt he owned the whole building. This was his castle, his kingdom, his undisputed domain. He instantly took in the smells, the familiar aroma of oil and turpentine and the meticulously washed stone floor. Yes, this was his territory, he revelled in the feeling and he was the master of this house. Alvar Eide was a man of few words. However, when it came to art he was practised at expressing himself and he was confident, he knew the terminology. He had long conversations with the customers and it was no effort at all as long as there was a painting between him and the other person. A kind of wall that he could hide behind. He never spoke about personal matters.

Now he switched on the light on the ground floor before going upstairs to the first floor. Onwards into the kitchen which doubled up as the break room. There he switched on the monitors; the cameras were aimed at the important areas of the gallery, primarily the ground floor where the most expensive paintings were hung. He had an Ekeland, a Revold and a Gunnar S. downstairs, and from time to time a Weidemann or a Sitter. They usually hung there for a while, the price tag was high. He poured water into the coffee-maker and measured coffee into the filter, seven level spoonfuls. It was two minutes to ten in the morning and the gallery closed at five in the afternoon. They were comfortable working hours with a free Saturday every other week when Ole himself staffed the gallery and handled any sales. He did not want to lose contact with his customers altogether. Alvar found a mug in the cupboard and sat down at the table. He stared at the three monitors. They showed the gallery in black and white, and while the images were not particularly sharp, at least they gave him the chance to keep an eye on things. There was no denying that the building contained pieces of staggering value. On a few occasions people had popped their heads round the door to inspect the gallery, then noticing the cameras attached to the ceiling, had spun round and disappeared. He did not know what that meant. Perhaps they had just dropped by out of sheer curiosity and then realised that the prices were too high. Though sometimes he entertained the notion that they were casing the place, planning a raid. The thought of this sent a chill down his spine. However, nothing serious had ever happened during the time he had been working there and he always felt safe and contented throughout the whole day.

Every day he spent some of his time framing pictures. Not the major paintings, not the ones by Knut Rumohr or Nerdrum, Ole Krantz dealt with those as he was a trained frame maker. But other things, smaller items. He cut the glass and the passepartout, he brushed dust and grit off the surface of the painting, he cut lists and joined them with tags, he made the fixings. There were small lithographs, which sold for a thousand kroner, or paintings, which people had handed in for framing. Drawings or photos, or something they had bought on their holidays abroad. It was pleasant work and he felt at ease in the framing workshop, which was at the back of the gallery on the ground floor. It smelled of wood, cardboard and glue. He had a radio in there, which was always tuned to P2, the arts channel. By now the coffee had filtered through and Alvar poured himself a cup. Ole Krantz had spared no expense when it came to the kitchen, it was equipped with a fridge, dishwasher and a microwave. In the fridge were several bottles of sparkling white wine; whenever he made a good sale Krantz was in the habit of opening a bottle so he and the customer could toast the painting. Alvar never did that. Partly because he was shy. One glass of wine could lead him astray. Also he would rather that the customer left with the painting, went home, hung it on their wall and then had a glass of something to savour the moment and their own excellent choice, their own good taste. That was how he thought it ought to be. Alvar could tell immediately if Ole Krantz had sold a valuable painting on one of his Saturdays because there would be two wine glasses standing on the worktop.

Alvar drank his coffee and kept an eye on the monitors. The big building was very quiet, there was not a sound to be heard, only his own slurping as he drank the strong coffee. This wasn't a place people flocked to, sometimes one, two hours passed between customers. Then he would sit and ponder, ponder life and himself, and at regular intervals he would take a walk through the building. He would start on the second floor, which housed all the foreign art, names unknown to most people, but the paintings were of a high quality. Prints were on the first floor, some of them French, but mainly good, Norwegian prints. The Norwegian paintings were lined up on the ground floor; most were oils, but every now and again an artist would experiment with acrylics, which created a rather bold and vivid impression. There was something about acrylics, they commanded your attention more than oil did, Alvar thought, shuffling from picture to picture, his hands folded behind his back. He had a personal relationship with each and every one of these paintings, he made sure to develop that as soon as they arrived at the gallery. So when a customer's attention was caught by a painting, a Ruhmor for example, he could find the right words instantly. Words which would guide the customer inside the painting, help the customer understand and respect the work. If they asked whether it would increase in value, he deftly avoided the question by asking, what is important to you? Why don't you simply buy the painting because you like it, because it gives you something unique? Why don't you simply buy the painting because you think it was meant for you?

He knew that Ole Krantz appreciated him and his contribution, he knew that his job was secure. A better person could not replace him; he was absolutely convinced of that. Pleased at the thought of this he went down to the workshop to check out what was lying on the worktop waiting to be framed. A photo of giggling, chubby toddlers. Their father had taken the photo, he regarded the result as particularly successful and had decided to have it enlarged and now framed. He has asked for a red passepartout, something which vexed

Alvar. The way he looked at it, one should never, ever, regardless of what type of picture it was, choose anything other than an off-white passepartout. Only the picture should speak, not its frame. The red passepartout would sap the photo of its strength. But the customer is always right, he thought and calmly began his work. He lifted up the sheet of glass and placed it carefully on the worktop. Found the cutting diamond and the ruler and started cutting with a steady hand. He liked the sound of the hard stone, he enjoyed snapping the offcuts, the crispy sound, like brittle caramelised sugar. He worked slowly and with concentration. But all the time parts of his mind were preoccupied with other things. He was alone, no colleagues disturbed him and his thoughts freewheeled. Was he really a good person deep down? Why was it starting to haunt him like this? Selling art to people was a fine thing to do, it was honest work, he did it diligently, he did it with conviction, respect and love. He was doing well in life, he donated to charities. He led an orderly life, he did not hurt anyone. So why had this strange feeling come over him?

CHAPTER 3

I turn off the computer and go into my kitchen.

The cat follows and starts to beg; he is hoping for a prawn, perhaps, or a bowl of tuna. He pleads silently with his green eyes. I give him pellets and fresh water. I hear his sharp teeth crunch the dry feed.

So, I think, he's really got to me, Alvar Eide, indeed he has. I have taken off and I'm in the air. I need a bite to eat before I go back to work; I open the fridge and look inside, spot a scrap of salami, a curled-up piece of brown cheese, four eggs, a tube of mayonnaise. And a wheel of Camembert cheese. I take an egg and the Camembert from the fridge, find a bowl and a fork. Crack the egg on the rim of the bowl and whisk it forcefully. I find some stale bread in the bread bin. I crumble it on the breadboard and unwrap the Camembert. Then I hear footsteps in the hall, soft, cautious steps. Alvar enters my kitchen. He stands in the doorway with his hands folded across his stomach watching me with meek, apologetic eyes.

'I'm sorry to disturb you,' he says and looks down.

'What is it?' I ask him, surprised. I lean against the kitchen counter and look at him with curiosity.

'Just wanted to stop by,' he says shyly.

He spots the cheese and the egg. Chews his lip. His voice is a mere whisper. 'Shouldn't you be working?'

I let my arms fall and give him a stern look.

'You won't even allow me to stop for lunch?' I reply. 'I can't think when I'm hungry. Don't you understand?'

He slumps on a kitchen chair. Dusts off the knees of his trousers even though they are immaculate.

'Of course,' he says quickly. 'I didn't come here to make a fuss, I don't want to cause you any trouble. Really, I don't.'

He looks at my food on the breadboard. The cheese, the bowl with the beaten egg, the breadcrumbs.

'Why don't you just wolf down a sandwich? You normally do, you stand by the counter when you eat. This is going to take time. But, don't get me wrong, I'm not telling you how to organise your day, I'm just very keen to get started.'

I cut two thick wedges of cheese with a sharp knife. Find a frying pan in a cupboard, put it on the cooker.

'Now calm down, Alvar,' I say, 'you're inside now. Right inside as a matter of fact,' I say, tapping my temple. 'Besides, you're only forty-two. Think about the old man; I do.'

I put a lump of butter on the pan, immediately it starts gliding towards the edge; the cooker tilts slightly towards the wall.

'And I do, I really do,' Alvar says. 'He's really very patient, he stands there like a post, waiting. No one in the queue minds that I jumped it. You must believe me.'

I dip the wedges of cheese in the beaten egg and coat them with the breadcrumbs.

'What about the woman with the child?' I ask. 'What does she say?'

He bows his head, I see his chest heave.

'It was like I said. She is unable to say anything, because the baby is dead.'

I look at him and sigh. 'She's just standing there with a dead child, waiting?'

'Yes. She's incapable of action, I presume. It upsets me, really it does. I feel it here.' He places a hand on his chest.

'So it should,' I say, placing the cheese wedges now coated in egg and breadcrumbs in the frying pan. The butter is golden yellow, it sizzles temptingly, the smell of melting cheese begins to fill the kitchen.

'It upsets me too,' I say. 'And I have thought a great deal about this. Whether it's acceptable to anticipate events in this way.'

Slowly the wedges of cheese turn golden. I go to the fridge for cranberry sauce, find a plate, a knife and a fork.

'Well, I stand by my decision. But nevertheless something about it troubles me. Now take it easy, Alvar, and don't put too much pressure on me.'

I turn the cheese over, the wedges are perfect.

'I do like my flat,' he says. 'I'm very pleased about my job at the gallery. It's almost more than I dared hope for, I could have ended up in a dirty workshop with a gang of noisy, crude men, I would not have enjoyed that.'

'If you're so pleased,' I say, 'why are you here? I think you're too quick to interfere, I've only written one chapter.'

He squirms a little on the chair. I look at his black shoes, they are so shiny you can see your face in them.

'The thing is, I'm worried,' he says. 'I'm forty-two years old and I am starting to question my own worth. My goodness, which I have always taken for granted. And pardon me for mentioning this, but from what you've written so far it's starting to look suspiciously like a midlife crisis.'

I stop what I am doing and my eyes widen.

'Surely I'm not destined for that kind of story?' he asks nervously. Then he smiles apologetically and lowers his head.

I lean back and fold my arms across my chest.

'If this is going to work at all, we have to trust each other,' I say. 'Last night you said that you would accept whatever fate you were given. Do you stand by that?'

Alvar is embarrassed, but he nods. I look at his folded hands, they lie like a knot in his lap.

'Why do you always sit with your hands folded?' I ask him out of curiosity.

'I can't put them in my pockets,' he says quickly, 'it ruins the cut of my trousers, my mother taught me that.'

I nod and I understand. I remove the wedges of cheese from the frying pan and slide them onto my plate, arrange the cranberry sauce next to them and carry everything into the dining room. Alvar follows me softly. He pulls out a chair.

'You will go back to work when you've finished eating, won't you? There's still much of the day left.'

I rest my chin in my hands. 'Would you kindly let me eat in peace?'

He falls silent. His grey eyes flicker around the room, he looks at the pictures on my walls.

'Death,' he says all of a sudden. 'You have a picture of Death on your wall.'

I nod and spear a slice of cheese with my fork.

'Why is that?'

'He's an old friend.'

He shakes his head at this. Gives me an uncertain look. 'What's that supposed to mean? An old friend?'

I cut a piece off the melted cheese and dip it in the cranberry sauce.

'Well, how can I put it? He feels familiar, like an old, faithful friend. When I can't manage any more, he comes and takes me away. Maybe he'll put me on his lap, just like the picture.'

'It's a drawing by Käthe Kollwitz,' Alvar says. '*Death with a Maiden on his Lap.*'

'That's right. It's beautiful. Look how gentle he is, see how delicately she rests against his chest. Sometimes when I work, Death comes into my room. He places a hand on my shoulder.'

'That would chill me to the bones,' Alvar says. 'Doesn't it frighten you?'

'No. It's more like a gentle caress. Not now, I tell him calmly, not now, I'm in the middle of a book and I have to finish it.'

'There's never a good time for dying,' Alvar says. 'We know that we all have to and it's a fate we carry with dignity as long as it doesn't happen today. Or tomorrow, because there are a few things we were hoping to do.'

'That's how it is,' I reply. 'However, I prefer to maintain a degree of contact with Death. It's an exit, which is always open. At night I play a game. I go to bed and feel my sleeping pill wash over me like a wave. Suddenly I'm on a beach and a man dressed in black comes rowing. I stand completely still waiting while he moors the boat. The water ripples over the stones, the old wood-work creaks.'

'Do you get in?' Alvar asks me earnestly.

'Yes, I do. The water is like a mirror. Death turns the boat round and rows with steady strokes, he knows where we are going, he knows these waters and he is confident.'

'Is it night and is it dark?' Alvar wants to know.

'No,' I say. 'It's twilight. And Death rows until we have reached the middle of the fjord; then he places the oars at the bottom of the boat and looks at me firmly. "Tomorrow is another day," he says. "Do you want it?" I think about this for a long time. I have been in this world for over fifty years; I suppose I can manage one more day. So he turns the boat round and rows me back, and I disembark. Back on dry land for a new day, which was never a certainty. Because every night I have to choose.'

Alvar is silent for a long time. Again he looks at the paintings on my wall.

'You also have a Lena Cronquist,' he enthuses, pointing to a painting above the television.

'I do. Do you know her?'

'Of course. I pride myself on being well informed when it comes to modern art.'

I eat more cheese, it tastes delicious. And while I eat, my thoughts are drifting. What do we people have in common? I wonder. Well, we're born. Not because we want to be, but because someone else wanted it. We grow up and we don't know where we're going or what we'll get. We think we can make our own decisions, that we can plan things. And so we can to a certain extent, but fate can be very capricious. A late-running bus can change a whole life, it can steer us towards another fate. We stumble on the kerb, someone rushes to our aid, we catch someone's eyes for a brief second and lightning strikes. A glance can lead to marriage and children, suddenly we've ended up in a totally different place from what we imagined. Alvar doesn't have much, not at the moment. A flat, a job, and a very sensitive personality. This sensitivity, I decide, watching him secretly, that will be his fate. He wants to be a good person; however, we don't live in a world where good people are rewarded, but he doesn't know that.

Alvar follows each mouthful with his eyes. I finish eating and clear up after myself, then I sit down in the living room, I light a cigarette; Alvar follows me. He comes into the room hesitatingly and finds a chair for himself.

'Please don't let anything happen to Ole Krantz,' he says out of the blue. Again he looks down as if every time he says something he instantly regrets his words.

I blow a column of smoke across the coffee table, it hovers there swirling in the light from the lamp.

'I'm not allowed to let anything happen to Krantz?'

'No, because he's a fine man, he doesn't deserve it.'

'My dear Alvar,' I say in a patronising voice, 'there can be no dramatic tension if I'm not allowed to make anything happen. I would have thought you understood that.'

Again he is embarrassed. There are red patches on his throat and his grey eyes blink.

'You're mine now,' I continue, 'you're not responsible for the other characters. I'm the one who'll be taking care of them, it's a matter of honour with me.'

'That's your twentieth cigarette today,' he points out shyly.

'So you're keeping count?'

'I don't have any bad habits like that.' He says this with pride.

'I'm sure you don't. But we all have our crosses to bear. You can die from so many things. Perish for any number of peculiar reasons.'

29

CHAPTER 4

The oak door opened and the bell rang out.

The bell had a fragile and wistful ring to it, which Alvar really liked. It announced that someone had arrived, someone who needed his expertise and his always impeccable service. He was sitting in the gallery's kitchen with a list of names. Krantz wanted to arrange a special exhibition in the new year, the preparations were underway, brochures would be printed and sent out to all their regular customers. Alvar looked through a pile of colourful photographs. The artist's best painting would adorn the cover together with a brief biography about his achievements so far. In this case, the artist being Knut Rumohr, these comprised fifteen large paintings, which were all outstanding. Alvar looked closely at the photos. He felt he could vouch for every single one of them and this was not always the case. Most artists were inconsistent. Rumohr, however, never disappointed and every painting was unique, there was strength and radiance in all of them. Besides, he was an unassuming man, private and polite, friendly and modest, a man after Alvar's own heart. He often visited the gallery wearing green wellies and with a sturdy sheath knife hanging from his belt. A craftsman, almost a labourer.

However, the bell had rung and Alvar looked up. On the left monitor he could see a woman entering. She was tall, slim and wore a dark coat. He let her wander around, it was not Alvar's style to charge in, the customer needed to be given time. His coffee had gone cold so he poured it into the sink. He went over to a mirror on the wall to check that his hair was in place. He looked at himself for a long time. His head was heavy, he took after his father. His features, however, were clean and fine, his dark brows strong and straight. He arranged his thinning hair across his scalp and then he went slowly down the stairs to the ground floor. She noticed him as he took the last few steps, nodded and smiled at him. A minute elegant nod of her head. She was an attractive, well-groomed woman, a little older than him, and, judging from her clothes, she was well off. She probably owned some works of art already. Alvar greeted her in a friendly manner, but remained standing, a little defensive, with his hands folded across his stomach. He did not recognise her, perhaps she had only recently moved to the town, or she might be passing through, he was not sure which, but he had a number of regular customers whose names he knew. Or the artists themselves popped in to see if anything was going on. He enjoyed talking to the artists. He had quickly made the discovery that the vast majority were down-to-earth, hard-working people.

However, here was a woman in a dark coat. She wore a foxtail around her neck and gloves of fine brandy-coloured leather. She wore boots with buttons. Alvar became almost besotted by them, they were black and pointy with high heels and, like his own shoes, polished to a shine. She continued to wander around; Alvar stayed in the background. It was easy for him to spot whether the customer had any knowledge of art. This woman stopped in front of a painting by Axel Revold, to Alvar's intense joy; however, the painting was so expensive that it was unlikely that she would be in a position to buy it. You do not sell a Revold just like that, a Revold is an event. So Alvar thought while he watched the woman furtively. She had moved on to a painting by Gunvor Advocat. An Advocat would be a respectable choice, too. But no, she carried on and after a few minutes she disappeared up to the first floor to the prints. He followed her, but went into the kitchen, he did not want to pester her with his enthusiasm. Because that was what he experienced at every sale: enthusiasm, selling a painting was like finding a home for a stray dog. A work of expressive art would finally find its place and give daily joy.

The woman seemed self-assured as well as determined. He could tell from looking at her that she wanted something specific and he felt quite sure that he would shortly secure a sale, because of the purposeful way she was moving around. While he waited, he followed her on the middle monitor. She walked from picture to picture, came back again, took a closer look, read the artist's signature, leafed through some brochures which lay on a table. Then she straightened up and approached a picture, stood calmly in front of it. At this precise moment Alvar got up from his chair and joined her. She had stopped in front of a work by Jon Bøe Paulsen. A small picture modestly priced. Alvar sold a great deal of Jon Bøe Paulsen, people liked his beautiful lines and a few even said, I like Bøe Paulsen, because at least I can see what it's meant to be. The pictures could resemble photographs; they were darkly lit and full of atmosphere. The print depicted a svelte, but graceful woman seen from behind. She had lifted up her long hair and was piling it up on the top of her head, so that her body arched and all her curves and muscles were clearly and attractively displayed.

He stopped behind her and cleared his throat.

'The appeal of Bøe Paulsen,' he said, 'is his gentleness. His delicate hand, his light strokes. No strong expression, but softness.'

She nodded and smiled at him.

'Yes,' she said, 'it's lovely. But it's not for me,' she added, 'I'm looking for a present for a friend who's turning fifty. She'll probably like this.'

She said this in a tone, which clearly indicated that her own taste differed. She did not dismiss the print, but it was not her type of art.

'Personally I prefer a somewhat stronger expression,' she admitted.

Alvar nodded.

'Have you seen the paintings by Krantz?' he asked, thinking that she might enjoy the strong latex pictures.

'Yes, they're impressive,' she said, 'but they won't last.'

Alvar agreed completely, but he did not say so. Ole Krantz's painting got your attention instantly, but what they had to say, they said in a moment.

She had made up her mind and decided on the print. As the picture was a present he took it downstairs to the workshop to gift-wrap it. He cut a piece of corrugated cardboard and folded it around the picture, then he wrapped it in tissue paper. Finally he covered it in wrapping paper and made a rosette from some gold ribbon. She paid with a credit card as people always did, then she said goodbye and Alvar was once more left to his own devices. If only Ole Krantz had heard that, he thought, that he won't last. On the other hand it was unlikely that he would have been offended, because Krantz did not consider himself to be a proper artist, more a decorator. Alvar poured himself another cup of coffee and pondered his lack of goodness once more. The thought kept returning and had now begun to torment him in earnest. Here he was sitting by the kitchen table enjoying a cup of coffee, he was at work, he performed his job well in every way, so why would he reproach himself on account of his absent goodness? He who had never hurt a fly.

He drank big gulps of coffee as his brain began to spin. Was there anything he could do about it? And if he were to do something, would that make the thought go away or would it grow worse? You could never be certain when it came to human psychology. After all, weren't there stories about aid workers who became totally caught up by all the misery they witnessed in foreign countries? They ended up consumed by despair at the world's bloodthirsty injustice and when they returned to Norway developed huge problems just eating a meal without feeling racked with guilt. He did not want his life upset like that.

He got up and decided to start work on some frames. He left the kitchen and went down to the workshop, to the little pile of small pictures. The chubby children were ready and he thought the photo was good, but not striking. The children had round cheeks and large soft mouths. He had never understood the appeal of children or why people became so fascinated by them. Children always made him feel anxious and awkward and they had a habit of gawping at him in a cannibalistic manner. When it came to children he felt as if they shone a spotlight directly at him and they stared with large, bright eyes right into his soul. Obviously he did not believe that they had this power, but that was how they made him feel. He preferred adults, if he was forced to deal with other people. But most of all he preferred the elderly. The secretive, wrinkled faces, the slow movements. Nothing unpredictable ever happened in their company. That in turn made him relaxed and calm, it meant he was in control.

He selected another picture. It was a drawing, made by an amateur, who clearly felt that he had surpassed himself given that he had asked for the drawing to be framed. The subject was a very muscular horse. And it was presumably these muscles which had inspired him to make the drawing to begin with, perhaps it was his own horse, or his daughter's, because in the bottom left-hand corner he had written in pencil underneath his signature 'Sir Elliot, 4 June 2005'. The paper had a faint yellow tint, which meant that it was good quality, and the drawing was not at all bad. However, the actual soul of the animal was lost in the formidable mass of muscles and that was the proof that he was, in fact, not a good artist at all. Alvar cut glass and cardboard for the picture. The customer had requested a gold frame. Alvar was not a huge fan of gold frames, personally he would have chosen a narrow black or grey list for the picture. However, he always sided with the customer and would give him what he had asked for. He finished framing the drawing and returned to the kitchen. He felt like having his packed lunch now, it was half past twelve and he had not eaten since breakfast. He had three open sandwiches with slices of cold cuts and slivers of cucumber wrapped in greaseproof paper. He made another pot of coffee and found a plate in the cupboard, placed his sandwiches on a chopping board and halved them. Just then the downstairs bell repeated its fragile and wistful greeting. A young man entered. Alvar saw him on the left monitor, he was wearing a fashionable light-coloured coat. Once more he left the kitchen and went downstairs.

The man had stopped in front of a painting by Reidar Fritzwold. He was looking at it closely now, his hands in his coat pockets, leaning slightly forward, eager. The painting was challenging: it depicted a roaring waterfall with chunks of ice and snow in the surrounding landscape. It was magnificent, Alvar thought, impressive and grand in every way, but it needed a lot of space. As a result it had been in the gallery for a long time. The man appeared to be in his early thirties. He had taken a few steps back and placed his hands on his hips. Now he was standing with his legs apart inspecting the painting.

'Quite overwhelming, don't you think?' Alvar nodded, indicating the foaming water. You could almost feel the spray from the waterfall in your face. The colours were extraordinary, all shades of blue, green, turquoise, purple, yellow and white.

'Is it by a Norwegian artist?' the man wanted to know. He filled out the light-coloured coat. He had broad shoulders, a trendy short haircut with a few blond highlights in it. Alvar nodded.

'Norwegian born and bred,' he said. 'Name's Fritzwold. He paints landscapes. This is one of his most dramatic paintings. He usually paints mountain scenes, calm, blue paintings with a great deal of harmony.'

'I'm buying a painting for my living room,' the man said, 'and I would like the painting to be a good investment. My point being that if it's not going to go up in value, it's of no interest.'

Alvar moved forward very cautiously. He recognised the man's attitude and prepared for battle.

'But you like it?' he said lightly.

'Christ, yeah,' the man said, moving closer. 'Very, very good,' he muttered, nodding to himself. His eyes grew distant as if he had disappeared into another room and Alvar understood that he had mentally gone to his own living room where this painting might hang one day. Now he was trying to visualise it. The ice-cold torrents of water cascading down his wall.

'There are times when it is very important to make a good

investment,' Alvar said in that light, amiable voice he always used. 'However, it's terribly important that you like the painting, that it gives you something unique. Always follow your heart,' he said, 'don't intellectualise the process. Remember it's a relationship for life, it might even be passed on to the next generation.'

'It's huge at any rate,' said the younger man, 'it's bound to create a stir.'

Right, Alvar thought to himself. He wants attention, possibly from the guests, who would enter his living room and see the roaring waterfall, clap their hands with excitement, as they toasted their host's exquisite and dramatic taste.

'Surely it's possible to buy with your head as well your heart,' he ventured, giving Alvar a challenging look. His eyes were blue and sharp.

'Indeed it is,' nodded Alvar. 'But the fact is that this painting is not primarily a good investment.'

The young man fell silent for a moment and his brows contracted while he thought hard. His eyes, however, could not bear to leave the colossal water masses on the wall.

'So why isn't it a good investment?' he demanded to know. His voice had acquired a sulking touch, he hated that things were not going his way. He had taken a fancy to the painting now and it felt like his living room would be nothing without this work of art.

'It will most certainly increase in value,' Alvar stated, 'but not to the same extent as other paintings. Partly because it is not an oil painting,' he continued. 'It's an aquarelle and it has been painted using an opaque technique.'

The man was taken aback, but did not want to admit to his ignorance when it came to the visual arts.

'I see.' He hesitated. 'I was wondering why the painting was behind glass.'

'Plexiglass,' Alvar said. 'Regular glass would have been too heavy. And watercolours need more protection than oils.'

'Watercolours?' He gave Alvar a confused look.

'They're sun-resistant,' Alvar said quickly, 'but the painting ought to hang on a wall which is never exposed to direct sunlight.'

Once again the man visualised his living room, as if to check out the light conditions.

'A picture with glass is difficult to hang,' Alvar said calmly, 'precisely because of the glass. I'm only telling you this now so that you have all the information.'

The man had fallen silent. He squirmed a little and seemed troubled at his own indecisiveness.

'Why didn't he paint it in oil?' he asked as if Alvar would know.

'Fritzwold has always worked with a range of techniques,' he explained patiently. 'Many artists do. And this is a very successful piece of work, in my opinion.'

The waterfall continued to cascade in front of them. Suddenly the man started to walk backwards. He walked almost as far as the opposite wall.

'You can't tell that it's not oil,' he argued, 'even from a short distance.'

Alvar could easily tell that it was, but he did not say so.

'I mean, it's not as if I have to tell anyone.'

Alvar had to smile at this so he bowed his head to conceal his reaction.

'It's a very fine painting indeed,' he said. 'Its surface is more delicate than an oil painting's, but you have nothing to fear. The waterfall will last,' he smiled, 'the waterfall has timeless appeal.'

Once again the man walked up close to the painting. He had reached the most important point.

'The price?' he said softly. Alvar could see he was nervous now.

'Thirty thousand,' Alvar replied. 'Plus the usual three per cent, but I'm sure you're aware of that.'

The man breathed a sigh of relief.

'I can afford that,' he said. 'I could actually do this.' He stood there admiring the painting a little longer. It did not lose its impact, it went on roaring, he liked the forces and the play in the torrents of water. He liked the fact that the painting was huge, almost overwhelming, as he had never seen a watercolour of this size, and in his living room the painting would almost reach the ceiling. Everyone who entered the room would instantly be met with all this force.

'But,' he then said, 'why isn't it primarily a good investment?' He had wanted to make a good investment and he was annoyed that he couldn't have everything his way.

'For several reasons,' Alvar said. 'It's not an oil painting and it's not a typical Fritzwold. Fritzwold's forte is calmer landscapes than the one he has painted here. In some respects this painting is an exception to his style. As though for once he wanted to go to town. Indeed, he normally paints far smaller paintings. His paintings sell quickly, but this one needs a special buyer. If you like the painting then you will form a special bond with it and thus you will have made a good emotional investment. That's valuable too.'

The man exhaled and took a few steps back.

'Yes,' he said. 'I'll go for it. Why the hell not?' He laughed and seemed instantly happy as if he had finally come out of the shade and ended up in the sun. 'But how am I going to get it into my car?' he wondered, looking at the parking bay outside the gallery. A dark blue Audi, the latest model, was parked there.

'Mr Krantz, who owns the gallery, will drive it home to your house,' Alvar said. 'He has a Blazer Chevrolet and it'll take most paintings. However, I can't promise you that it'll be today. It depends on how busy he is, he does all sorts of things. If you would like I can call him and find out right now.'

The man nodded enthusiastically even though the light in his eyes went out because now he could not wait to have the painting in all its glory up on his wall. He paced up and down restlessly while Alvar ran upstairs to telephone.

'Krantz,' Alvar said down the receiver, 'you won't believe this, but I've sold the waterfall!'

'Really,' said an elated Krantz down the other end, 'I have to hand it to you, Eide, I really do. Let me guess. It's a man. He's under forty. Wants to show off.'

'Correct.'

'Ask him if he works in advertising. Or, he might be an estate agent.'

Alvar could not help but smile. Krantz had a good nose after all his years in the business.

'And I'll bet he frequents some gym or other. And I'm sure he's the type who likes to do a line of coke or two at the weekend.'

'Is there anything else?' Alvar asked him, still smiling.

'He prefers red wine to beer.'

They chatted for a few minutes then Alvar went downstairs again.

'He'll deliver it tomorrow,' he said cheerfully. 'That's not too bad, is it? After all, you'll need to make room for the painting or do you have a big empty wall just waiting to be filled?'

'No,' the man had to smile, 'I don't,' he admitted. 'I have some old photos and other stuff that I need to take down.'

'And you need to get a very strong hook,' Alvar said. 'It's a heavy painting; the frame alone weighs a good deal. Please make sure that you buy the right fixings or the waterfall will land on your head.'

He nodded and followed Alvar to pay for the painting. As he took out his card, Alvar detected the minute hesitation, which occurred from time to time. However, a moment later the man seemed content once more.

'Are you local?' Alvar asked.

'Yes, I live out at Bragernes,' he said. 'Do you want me to write down my address?'

He found a pen and a piece of paper and wrote the address in very neat handwriting. He was a little edgy, the way people are when they have spent a considerable amount of money, or what they would regard as a considerable sum. A thirty-thousand-krone painting was still a modest sum in Alvar's eyes, he had sold paintings worth two hundred thousand.

'So, tomorrow afternoon it is,' he said smiling to the younger man. 'Go home and make room for the magnificent painting.'

Oh yes, he would go home immediately and make some room. He thanked Alvar for his help, and went on his way happily; he even threw a pining glance at the painting as he went out to the Audi. Alvar heard him rev up the engine. He returned to the kitchen on the first floor. He felt very pleased with himself. He had sold a huge Fritzwold and he had been honest the whole time. He immediately sank his teeth into a sandwich. He was now so hungry that his stomach was rumbling. He ate slowly as he listened to a radio programme. Half the day had already gone. Life's not too bad, he thought, I enjoy it here, I do. I haven't achieved a great deal, but then again not everyone does. Some stick their necks out, they choose to take risks, others seek the path of least resistance. He was suddenly reminded of his parents and how they had lived their lives. It's none of our business, his mother always said, whenever anything happened. Her attitude to life was that people should take care of themselves. She did not want her life upset.

His father had been a silent and shy man who never showed any initiative; Alvar had barely known who he was. And thus I became a decent, but very defensive man, he thought, and that is fine. It makes life simple, no conflicts, no unexpected events. A little flat, perhaps, a little dull. But comfortable. In the evening I can relax with a good book and sometimes I treat myself to a sherry. Only one, but it's a large one. I sleep well. I have no friends, but then again no enemies either. He swallowed coffee in between mouthfuls of sandwich and looked out of his window onto the street below. A steady stream of cars was heading for the town centre. Having finished his lunch, he returned to the workshop. He wanted to frame a few more pictures, he enjoyed tinkering downstairs.

On the wall hung a picture by Danilo. The painting was in the gallery's workshop as it was still drying. Krantz had been visiting the artist in his studio, he had bought it instantly and brought it to the gallery to allow it to dry. Danilo was easy to sell. It was quite a charming picture, not one of his more impressive ones, but nevertheless, reasonably well executed and it was priced at ten thousand. Alvar went over to the picture, stopped, legs apart. The subject was a bowl of strawberries. It had been tipped over, the red glistening berries had rolled out onto a rustic wooden table. The berries were so ripe, so juicy that you felt like sinking your teeth into them. Alvar stood there looking at the moist, shiny surface. And then suddenly, like a bolt from the blue, he raised his right hand. Then he planted his thumb right in the middle of a strawberry. The paint smeared. He quickly withdrew his hand and jumped as if he had received an electric shock. What kind of behaviour was this? And his thumb covered in red paint. Terrified, he moved closer. He could clearly see the lines of his thumbprint. For a moment he was paralysed. Where had that impulse come from, and what did it mean? He was not someone who felt the need to draw attention to himself in any way, surely? Baffled, he went looking for a bottle of turpentine. It was easy to remove the paint from his finger. He stared at the painting once more. Look, there was the Danilo with his own thumbprint. Someone would buy that painting and hang it in their living room, but they would never know about this print, Alvar Eide's secret signature. He began cutting glass, cardboard, he sawed lists. He tagged and he glued. He hummed to himself, but he was disturbed. It was only a sudden impulse, he thought, trying to reassure himself and calm his pounding heart.

Nothing to fret about.

CHAPTER 5

It was five in the afternoon when Alvar left the gallery.

First he checked in the mirror to make sure his hair was in place. He put the plate and his mug in the dishwasher, he checked that every room was clear of customers. He locked the door and activated the alarm. He took the first right and wandered down towards Albumsgate, came out at Bragernes Square and strode purposefully across the large open space. Pigeons were sneaking around hunting for crumbs. He noticed the old man who always sat on a bench with a bag of stale bread, leaning forward, his hands trembling and a confusion of birds between his legs. He saw several of the town's homeless people stagger around, their eyes vacant. The sight of them made him feel despondent, they were so pathetic and shabby, every single one of them pricked his conscience. He sneaked past them averting his eyes, turned into the pedestrian area and headed for the Cash and Carry; he wanted to get himself something quick and easy for dinner. Something simple, something from the deli counter he could reheat in his microwave. The store was big, he preferred the smaller shops, but they didn't have a deli counter like the Cash and Carry.

He took a number and queued patiently and quietly. When it was finally his turn, he hesitated. Hotpot, lasagne or casserole? He opted for the lasagne, he knew it was good. He bought a large piece and had it wrapped in foil before moving on with his basket. He found a bag of ground coffee and a half-litre of milk. That was everything he needed, the modest shopping basket of a bachelor. He went to the checkout and joined another queue. And it was while he was waiting that he started to look at the trolleys around him. People shopped to excess, the trolleys were loaded. He looked at his own purchases and felt how sad they looked, surely anyone would guess that he lived alone. That no one was waiting for him, that his flat was empty. He did not mind living on his own, but right now he minded that it was so obvious to other people. That man over there, they might be thinking, he's never found someone, there's probably something wrong with him, a loner, an outsider. Finally it was his turn to be served and he placed his modest purchases on the belt, paid and left the shop. He turned left, passed the light-bulb factory and began the long, slow ascent to his home. The Green family in the ground-floor flat had two teenage children, a boy and a girl. He would sometimes see them in the morning on their way to school. They were both laden down with heavy rucksacks as they walked out through the gate, and every time he saw them it struck him that it was hard to tell them apart. They were wearing the same type of clothing, they were exactly the same height. Perhaps they're twins, it suddenly occurred to him, he had never thought of that before.

He walked calmly and contentedly up the hill and arrived at the front garden. Let himself in and carefully hung up his coat in the hall. He went into the kitchen. He unwrapped the lasagne and put it in the microwave, then he laid the table in the living room for dinner. He placed the newspaper he had just bought next to his plate and poured water into a jug. Three minutes later the microwave emitted a ping and he burned his fingers as he lifted out his plate. He ate extremely slowly, alternating between reading the newspaper and looking out of the window. The large room had four windows, which let in plenty of light, and he had several green plants, they were lush and verdant. The furniture was the same as when his mother had been alive, it was heavy and solid and he would never manage to wear it out. It didn't bother him that it was old-fashioned. It was comfortable to sit in and he thought it was nice. There was also a large fireplace made from soapstone. On the mantelpiece stood seven crystal trophies, which his father had won at bridge. They were not particularly attractive, but he could not make himself

44

throw them out, in some way they were a family heirloom. A family which would cease to exist when he himself died. In eleven years' time when the bomb went off. As he was sitting there quietly minding his own business, he heard a sudden bang. Something had happened in the street outside, glass was shattering, metal screeched and he jumped out of his chair and ran to the window. Two cars had collided. He stood, as if nailed to the spot, staring at the accident. The cars had come to a stop diagonally across the street; the tarmac was covered with shards of glass. A distressing silence followed. A couple who had been walking on the pavement now came rushing across the street to help. One of the car doors was opened and an elderly man staggered out. He supported himself against the car, slumping helplessly against the metal. Then the other driver stepped out. He, too, just stood there looking lost and cradling his head with both hands. For a while they remained there staring at one another, incapable of action. Alvar's heart was pounding and suddenly the memories came flooding back. They knocked him sideways and he staggered across to the sofa, collapsed onto it and leaned forward over the coffee table. He sat there breathing heavily, trying to pull himself together, but to no avail.

His cheeks were scarlet with shame. The shame that was the reason he would never be able to connect with another human being. To him this shame was visible, his eyes glowed with it and that was why he always averted his eyes whenever anyone looked at him. Even now, after so many years. As the memories overwhelmed him, something inside him ripped open and began haemorrhaging. They had gone for a drive in his father's lemon-coloured Anglia. A Sunday one spring. How old was I then, he thought, seven, maybe eight years old? He was sitting alone in the back looking out of the windows. He could hear his mother chatting in the front. His father drove and said nothing.

'Look at that garden, Emmauel,' he heard, 'look at those roses. They must be Nina Weibull, they're thriving. I think we should consider planting Nina Weibull around the house, they're so hardy.

It's some house, I must say. Why do people need so much extra space? I'm so glad I'm not living in a tower block, those flats look like nesting boxes, don't you think? Look at that awful plastic pool in those people's garden. It makes you wonder what people are thinking, it looks so tacky. Oh, a whole wall of clematis! I've often thought that we ought to plant clematis on the west wall, Emmauel, what do you think?'

His father was still silent. He leaned forward and hugged the steering wheel. By now they had reached the countryside and the houses were fewer and far between. The landscape glided past. Alvar sat in the back quietly enjoy the reassuring hum of the engine. He sat with his hands folded and stared; here were some chubby-looking sheep, over there a herd of fat, red cows. From time to time, but not often, a car coming from the opposite direction would pass them.

'Those people have a double garage, would you believe it?' he heard his mother say. 'I can't imagine how people can afford to have two cars. But I suppose they have to. And look, there's also a rusty old wreck blighting their farm. I don't know why people don't have their old cars towed away.'

'Perhaps they need it for spares,' his father mumbled from behind the wheel.

His objections were meek and drained of strength. Alvar's ears pricked up. His parents did not seem aware that he was present in the car, they were in an adult world of their own, and if he wanted to snap them out of that, he would have to ask them something. He did not do that, he was a polite child, he sat very still watching everything they drove past. Some people were out walking their dogs, he saw a couple of cyclists.

After they had been driving for a while they spotted something ahead of them on the road. Alvar sat bolt upright, craned his neck trying to get a good look. It was a car crash. It must have just happened as there were neither police nor ambulances in attendance. One car was lying off the road on its roof, another was crushed and had ended up diagonally across the road. His father slammed on the brakes. The Anglia swerved to the right and came to a halt. People were standing around the wrecked cars screaming. One man had blood pouring from his forehead, another was still in his car, slumped across the wheel. A woman spotted them and came staggering towards them, blood gushing from her head.

Then something happened that Alvar found utterly incomprehensible. His mother started screaming.

'No, no!' she cried. 'We're not going to stop, I'm sure they've already called an ambulance, there's nothing we can do, Emmauel, drive on. Drive on right now!'

Her voice was so panicky that Alvar's heart froze. All three of them remained in the car staring, horrified, at the injured people and the damaged vehicles. The woman with the head wound was approaching the Anglia, Alvar could hear her pleading voice, he curled up on his seat in a foetal position. Again his mother screamed that they should drive on, she was banging the dashboard with one hand; he had never seen her so frenzied. His father clung to the steering wheel struggling with his conscience, torn between the urge to help and the strong woman in the passenger seat who had such power over him. Alvar was now pressing his face against the rear window staring at the injured woman. She stared frantically back at him and stretched out her white hands as if trying to get hold of him.

'Drive on, Emmauel, now!' his mother screamed again.

'But,' his father stuttered, 'they're badly hurt!'

She spun round in her seat. 'So you're a doctor now, are you? Do you know anything about what to do in an emergency situation? No? Now drive! The ambulance is on its way, I'm sure I can hear it coming! I want you to drive now.'

His father put the car in gear; Alvar held his breath. The woman had now reached their car, she was still staring at Alvar with pale, frightened eyes and blood was pouring down her cheeks. Alvar stared back horrified because his parents were running away from it all and he felt a sudden pang in his chest as if a cord had been severed. The magnitude of their betrayal nearly knocked him unconscious. He buried his face in his hands and huddled in a corner, he felt a shame so great that his entire body burned with it. The woman had seen him. He knew he would never forget her eyes and her white outstretched hands, hands he never got to take. His father pushed the accelerator and changed into second gear, the car leapt forward.

'Someone else will deal with this,' his mother shouted, 'it's not our problem!'

'But,' his father said in his meek voice, 'running away like this –'

'We're not running away,' his mother interrupted him, 'we realise that there's nothing we can do. Do you know how to do chest compressions, can you stop bleeding? No, you can't and neither can I.'

'All the same,' his father stuttered, hunched over the wheel, 'perhaps we could have helped them in some other way.'

'And what way would that be? Can you do mouth-to-mouth resuscitation? No, you can't. And we don't even have a first-aid kit in the car, not as much as a single plaster, so how would we be able to help them?'

Alvar held his breath. His mother had become hysterical, she was rocking backwards and forwards in her seat, there were red patches on her cheeks.

At that moment they finally heard the sirens, faintly at first, then they grew stronger.

'I told you so,' his mother said triumphantly. 'Someone's on their way who'll know how to deal with this; we're ordinary people, Emmauel, we can't get involved with such terrible things, we would only make it worse. You're not supposed to lift an injured person, they could become paralysed. Do you hear, Alvar?' Suddenly she turned towards the back seat and looked at him, her face was flustered. Alvar kept silent, he was terrified. His father gritted his teeth and drove on. At a slightly lower speed now, shaken by what had happened.

Alvar sat on the sofa remembering this incident. And it occurred to him that he had inherited his mother's cowardice. It was linked to an inability to take action and it was sown in him at that very moment. The moment when the woman staggered across the road stretching out her hands and his father had sped away. And Alvar felt that something inside him had been snapped clean off. That was why as an adult he was incapable of connecting with another person. Why he discreetly, but at the same time very efficiently, blocked any attempt at conversations with others. He hated using the telephone, for example. He could barely manage to make a call should a situation arise which he could not manage on his own. Whenever the telephone rang his heart leapt into his mouth. It was ridiculous, and yet it was real. He just wanted to be alone in his own universe, without having to deal with anything. He got up and returned to the window, peering out nervously. A police officer had arrived; he was making notes on a pad.

Later, as Alvar sat in front of his television watching the news, he pondered this cowardice again. It was mankind's worst feature. Everyone sat, like him, watching misery on a global scale while they all thought that somebody else ought to do something about it. His thoughts made him feel depressed and he found a book on the shelf, turned off the television and made himself comfortable. Reading was always comforting. He instantly disappeared into a world of fiction and everything around him was forgotten. He read for two hours, then he went to the bathroom and had a shower. Afterwards he made his packed lunch for the next day, put four shirts and some underwear in the washing machine and returned to his seat in front of the television. He watched a programme until the washing machine had finished. Then he hung his shirts on hangers, turned off all the lights in the living room, cleaned his teeth and went to bed. His eyelids began to close. He thought about this day which was now over. The crash outside his window, the disturbing memories. Nevertheless, he thought, quietly contented, no big, nasty surprises, no situations he was incapable of dealing with. No great joys either, but he was okay, in good health and sleepy. He had sold two

49

pictures. And tomorrow would come and it would be exactly like today, filled with the same activities in the same order. The years would pass and the days would remain the same, broken into short segments, which he would live through one by one. In time he would start to slow down, become more sluggish. His vision would deteriorate, as would his hearing. So his life would proceed until the fifty-three years, which he believed he had been allocated, were up.

Suddenly a thought struck him like someone throwing a spear at his chest. The feeling made his eyes widen. What was this? A distressing feeling of panic. Surely he was not going to start having trouble sleeping now? He had never had any problems with that. Perhaps it was his age, was he about to go through a midlife crisis, like some men did when they reached their forties? He turned over onto his side and pushed the spear away. He felt as if it had scratched him. He exaggerated his breathing, making it deep and even and felt how tired he was. Of course, it was naive to think that nothing would ever happen to him, something happened to most people, surely he was no exception. But what would happen to him? He sensed unease, a touch of dread. But he could see nothing in his future to fear. He sat upright in bed. Went out into the bathroom and drank a glass of water. That was it, he thought, it was thirst, nothing more. He returned to his bed and lay down, closed his eyes. Surely there was an interference in the silence, which he had never been aware of before? Why had he suddenly started noticing things? Perhaps there's something missing in my life? A distraction. He kept thinking about the cat. He wanted a grey one. He wanted a tom. He could put an ad in the paper, or he could think about it, at any rate. Again he turned over in his bed. It was strange. Something in his life was upsetting him, he had a premonition of upheaval. And he could not understand it.

However, the next morning everything was as it always had been. He contemplated the night before and remembered his uneasiness, but it had passed. He shaved in front of the mirror in the bathroom. The growth of his beard was exceedingly modest, but he enjoyed the ritual even though strictly speaking he could get away with shaving every other day. He used a razor. He liked going out into the fresh air and feeling the unique sensation which newly shaven skin always gave him. The weather was a little overcast and he walked along easily and contentedly. A steady flow of people was heading for the town centre. Big wheels turning, he thought, we keep this machine in motion, we don't give up, it's touching. What if we all were to lie down and give up? It was inconceivable. It was a question of keeping death at arm's length. It will come to us, but we pretend it won't, because it's obviously not going to happen today, and probably not tomorrow either, and definitely not next week. That too is touching, he thought. He was not scared of dying. But on one occasion he had articulated the following thought to himself: the last thing you lose is your hearing. So it was possible that he could be lying in a bed and someone would be sitting by his side checking that his breathing and heartbeat had ceased, someone who would then say: he's gone. That he might, in fact, lie there for several seconds knowing that he had just died. What would that be like? Was it the case that some people experienced such a moment? A moment they could never tell anyone about? As far as his own death was concerned he had few wishes, but he hoped that he would be lying in his own bed when it happened. It was less important to him whether he was alone or might have a carer sitting beside his bed. Many died alone.

He walked on and began to wonder why he was so preoccupied with death. Perhaps it was the previous day's uneasiness manifesting itself after all? No, he was in the midst of life and that was the time when such thoughts arose. Children and the young are immortal, he thought, and that is their privilege, but in the end it comes to us all. I'm of an age where I start to reflect and it is a good age. I'm better off now as an adult than I was as a child. Not that I had a bad childhood, not at all. My parents were kind and loving. True, they were shy bordering on awkward. He could find nothing to reproach them for, yet something had been missing. A sense of belonging. He remembered Magnus, a friend from his childhood, who had moved

51

away the summer they both turned thirteen and whom he had never seen again. After Magnus he never made another friend. But he managed fine on his own. Again he thought about other people and how they sought each other out. Not to mention men and women and their eternal search for love. He did not comprehend that either. Did they consider themselves incomplete without a partner? And then there was sex. He realised that he lacked something that many others had. However, many people went without sex, it was perfectly possible to live a celibate life. What if I tried sex, he thought, blushing instantly, would I then start to need it? Maybe. Perhaps it was something you could become addicted to, like food and drink.

He had reached the church and he looked up at the cemetery. This is where I'll end up one day, he thought, and it's beautiful. On a hill above the town. He had put money aside for his funeral and he also had some savings. Seventy thousand kroner. He was a regular saver. He was not saving up for anything in particular, but it was always good to have something set aside for a rainy day. During the time he had worked at Gallery Krantz he had bought some prints and a few drawings. Not expensive items, but pictures that he really appreciated. He had often dreamt of finding the one painting that was destined for him. Because he believed it existed, he had seen it happen many times in the gallery. A customer would enter and stop in their tracks in front of a picture mesmerised. And they would be rooted to the spot, they would be incapable of returning to their home without this painting. The painting was something they had been searching for, something they had been missing. He never thought it was an act, but a precious moment. A unique meeting between the artist and the spectator, a singular language, which would be understood by a chosen one and would seduce him. Personally he had never encountered such a picture.

He greatly appreciated the coal drawings of Käthe Kollwitz, but Kollwitz was out of reach both in terms of price and in other ways. But something along those lines, he thought. In fact, the artist's name was less important; however, the impact had to match that of

Kollwitz if it were to move him. Few artists had such an impact. But if he were ever to spend his seventy thousand kroner on anything it would surely have to be a painting. He had often thought that he might do a bit of travelling, but it had remained a thought. Although he fancied a trip to Copenhagen at some point, a weekend break perhaps. Potter about in the friendly Danish atmosphere, eat warm open sandwiches with liver pâté and crispy bacon, have a Tuborg and a snapps or a 'lille en', as Danes called it. However, he preferred his flat, and from this base he went for walks in the town and surrounding area. For example, he often drove up to Spiralen and went for long walks through the forest. There were people and dogs he could watch, there was nature with its smells and mild breezes. There was a view. And last but not least a lovely café where he would buy a roast beef sandwich with remoulade. On a few occasions someone had struck up a conversation with him and he had stopped and replied politely, but he never encouraged a lengthy conversation. He went to the cinema from time to time. He studied the film reviews in the newspaper and whenever he came across something interesting, off he would go to buy a ticket. He had seen many excellent films. He liked sitting in the dark cinema with all the other people he would never have to talk to. And munching some chocolate, a Cuba bar perhaps. He even liked the adverts, he found them entertaining. He liked going out into the street afterwards, filled with this experience, if the film had been a good experience and it had been on some occasions. He never got tired of playing Mozart's Requiem on his stereo. He thought the best paintings were good enough to hang on a living-room wall a whole lifetime, and would last into the next generation. Though if he were to buy a picture there would be no one to leave it to; however, this did not worry him unduly, after all, when you are dead you are dead and he was not troubled by how strangers might dispose of his property. A retirement home? he thought next. No, not a retirement home, not at any cost. True, his mother had spent three years in a retirement home and been looked after very well, but there was no way he was

CHAPTER 6

'I'm starting to feel a little worried,' Alvar says, stopping in the middle of the floor. 'I didn't mean to disturb you, you know it's not in my nature; but as I said, I'm worried. I have trouble sleeping. I can't handle that. Suddenly I'm lying in my bed overcome with panic.'

His voice is troubled.

I am sitting in front of the computer, my fingers skate quickly across the keyboard. There are times it becomes flexible like a ribbon in my hands and I can bend and twist the language any way I please. Alvar comes up behind me, shifting nervously from one foot to the other.

'Are you really going to burden me with your sleeping problems and anxiety?'

I turn round and give him a somewhat patronising look.

'Everyone struggles with anxiety,' I say. 'Can you feel how it eats away at you? In here, behind your ribs?' I tap my chest with my finger. 'A cowardly rat sits in here gnawing its way through your ribs. It hurts.'

'But I'm a decent man,' he says, 'I always keep my affairs in order.'

I turn off the computer, turn round in my chair and look at him again. 'Yes, that's true. At the same time you're all alone. It's dangerous to go through life without someone you can lean on. In certain circumstances it might well prove to be extremely dangerous for you.'

'In certain circumstances,' he echoes, 'that you are about to put me in?'

I get up from my desk and go to my armchair, sit down and light up a cigarette.

'What will be will be,' I say to him over my shoulder. He follows me. He stands with his hands folded. It is grey outside the windows. Heavy and wet, no hint of wind or movement.

'That rat,' I continue, 'which gnaws at us all, it never feels satisfied. We constantly seek relief in every way possible. And on rare occasions it allows us a brief respite. Do you know what it's like when everything suddenly falls into place, when that feeling floods your body? It's like taking off from a great height. We float through the air and everything around us is warm. For a few brief seconds we think how great life can be. You'll have such moments too, I promise you.'

He sits down on the sofa, on the edge as usual.

'Are people supposed to settle for a few brief moments of happiness?' he asks, dismayed.

'That's a good question. It's up to each and every one of us to decide. The majority spend most of their day looking for some kind of relief. A cigarette, a bottle of red wine. A Cipralex, going for a run. I won't deprive you of sleep, Alvar, I promise you. But you have come to my house. I have seen you close up and some events are inevitable. At this point in the story I'm no longer free, there is a clear structure and I have to work within it.'

'That doesn't make any sense,' he says. 'You can use your imagination. It may not be boundless, but you have artistic licence.'

'Think of my imagination as a lake with a thousand outlets,' I say. 'Rivers, streams and waterfalls. I flounder in this lake while I look around for an outlet. If I drift in a certain direction then I am swept along by the current. It may carry me towards a waterfall or towards a peaceful pond. The point I'm making is that as I'm drifting I cannot turn and choose another route. From then on all I can do is describe what I see on my way. That particular landscape, the vegetation and the people I pass.'

'So you're drifting?' he says anxiously. This revelation makes him blink.

'Yes,' I say. 'I'm drifting. But I do have some tools. Because other people have an ability to intervene, interfere or cause change. Someone might build a dam and divert the river. A waterfall is directed through pipes. Farmers discover the stream and use it to water their fields. So I might end up somewhere completely different from where I had imagined.'

'Nevertheless, you can choose to give me a happy ending,' he pleads. 'You can determine in advance that everything will turn out all right. All this talk of drifting is making me nervous.'

'There are many things which are hard to accept, Alvar. And true, there are people who are masters of their own destinies. But you're not one of them. You're not a proactive person. Neither am I.'

'But you work several hours every single day,' he objects. 'You make things happen. You can dole out love and happiness.'

'Yes,' I reply, 'it's like blowing on embers in a fire, they flare up instantly. But I am watching you from a distance and I describe what I see. It's rare for me to act. We are very like each other, you and I. And that's why it's possible for me to tell your story. In some ways you live your life through the pictures in the gallery. You live in a fictitious world of people and landscapes. I live my life through all the characters I invent. If it's any comfort I do know how you feel.'

He buries his head in his hands. 'No, there's no comfort in the fact that others feel the same way, it's no consolation that others are worse off. I watch people as I walk through the town, they drift around Bragernes Square. Drug addicts. Stiff-legged and pale with glassy eyes. I see that they are in pain, but they're none of my business. The strength I have I need for myself. To live a decent life that no one can find fault with. People come into the gallery every day, they chat to me, but these are brief conversations and then they leave; I have no need to expose myself, I don't want to get involved with them. I don't want to know if they are feeling bad. I am probably selfish and it troubles me. Why did you have to mention that rat? Now that image is in my head for ever. Now it's gnawing at me too.'

'Perhaps it's a sign of things to come?' I say. 'Now, try to take it easy. You're at the front of the queue now, it's finally your turn. You have questions and they will be answered. Consider yourself privileged. I can delete unpleasant things as well. If only you knew what I would give to erase certain chapters from my own life.'

He gets up from the sofa and paces the room restlessly.

'Please may I ask you a question?' he says.

'Feel free.'

'When you're in bed at night, I mean before you fall asleep and everything in the house is quiet, do you think about me then?'

'Every single night,' I reply. 'I follow you with my mind's eye.'

'How much do you see?'

'Everything.'

'So you're inside my very home?'

'Further than that,' I say. 'I follow you into your bedroom, I watch you when you sleep.'

'And you have your own ideas?'

'Yes, I have my own ideas. Every day I notice something new. A minor observation that tells me something about who you really are and what is going to happen. For example, I see you turn off the lights in your flat. You carry your coffee cup to the kitchen, or your glass if you have treated yourself to a sherry, you rinse it under the tap. Next you go into the bathroom where you brush your teeth and wash your hands before turning off the light in there as well, you like saving electricity. You continue into your bedroom and you undress. You fold your clothes neatly and place them on a chair. I watch you slip under the covers and set your alarm clock. Then you allow yourself to sink into the mattress as you give yourself a few minutes to think about the day that has just gone. You're about to turn off your bedside lamp when you notice that you did not fold your trousers properly, they will crease in the wrong place, so you get out of bed to refold them. As you have got out of bed anyway, you go over to the window. You look out into the street, which lies so silently outside, perhaps you see a lonely person wander by in the darkness and you count yourself lucky that you can hide behind the curtain and won't ever have to know how it feels to be the person wandering in the night on his own. You go back to bed, you always lie on your side with your knees pulled up. You don't pray because you know no God, but then again you feel no emptiness either. The alarm clock ticks. You like the silence and the darkness and your thoughts move on to the next day. You trust that everything will be fine, that you will be able to do everything which is expected of you. Your eyes glide shut, your breathing slows down. At that moment I always feel a great sense of calm. I let you rest for a long time and when I feel my own strength returning I wake you up to a new day. Then I take your hand and we continue the journey together.'

He lets the air out of his lungs.

'Do you see anyone else apart from me?' he asks shyly.

I smile a little. 'How do you mean?'

'I mean it's a long queue outside. Your computer is full of drafts, unresolved fates hanging in the air. Does it ever happen that your eyes are drawn in another direction? Might you follow someone else and forget about me?'

'That would be such a relief,' I admit, 'if I could forget about you for one moment. But you're very persistent, you don't make it easy for me, and that surprises me because you're a mild-mannered person. However,' I add, 'we all wish to be seen. Even a lone wolf hungers for a brief glance. He only shuns other people because he has abandoned all hope that they'll notice him, but the longing for a warm hand on our shoulder is there all the time. Someone who stops you in your stride and asks how are you, do you need anything, anything I can give you? You think of yourself as a man of few needs. You make no great demands, all the time you take what you're given and that's not a lot. But you've shown your true colours by stepping out of the queue, Alvar, because you do need something and that requires a certain amount of courage. Now I'm rewarding you just like you asked me to. And now I'm asking you to leave so I can think in peace.'

But he does not leave, he lingers. He examines the objects in my living room, the angel on the bookshelf with its wings outstretched, the icon on the wall, my pictures. The small wooden casket on the top of the chest of drawers.

'That's a beautiful casket,' he says stepping forward to study it more closely.

'Yes,' I say. 'Hand-carved. From Indonesia. I'm fond of that casket, it's important.'

'What do you keep in it? Letters?'

I shake my head. 'The casket is filled with worries.'

His eyes widen. 'What do you mean? Bills?'

His literal thinking makes me laugh.

'No, it's like I say. The casket is filled with worries, all kinds of worries. I write them down and place them in the casket and then I slam the lid shut. So they can lie there in the darkness and never materialise.'

'May I take a look?' he asks cautiously.

I shrug in resignation. 'If you want to. Even though I think worries are very personal.'

He lifts up the lid. Looks at the little heap of white scraps of paper. Picks one of them up. Reads it.

'"This novel won't be good enough. I'm going to get slaughtered."'

'Precisely,' I say earnestly. 'That's how it is. That's what I think.'

He takes another one, holds it up.

'"I probably won't grow very old."'

'That's something I've always known,' I explain. 'And I can live with that, it's fine.'

'"Alvar Eide won't make it."'

He shudders and looks at me in horror.

'There, there,' I say, 'it was just a spontaneous outburst. As I told you, I follow the current and I promise you that I will use all the literary skill I possess to save you from destruction.'

But now he is deeply worried. He slams the lid shut, goes to the window. Stares out at the azalea by the entrance.

'Not a single leaf is moving,' he says, 'even though there must be thousands of them, gossamer-thin leaves on stems as delicate as silk. Not one movement, not a tremor. Where is nature's overwhelming force?'

He turns round and looks me in the eye. 'Is it the calm before the storm, I wonder?'

CHAPTER 7

The waterfall was swiftly replaced by a merry-go-round.

Ole Krantz had hung it in the space that had belonged to Reidar Fritzwold, and the change in the room was striking because the painting was smaller and darker. When Alvar let himself into the gallery, he stopped short, took it in. The painting was unusually detailed. One metre square, with an extravagant gilded frame. Thin layers of paint, fine brushstrokes and gaudy colours. Alvar stood still, staring at the painting with one hand under his chin, leaning forward slightly with squinting, peering eyes. A big, old-fashioned merry-go-round from a fair, with black-and-white horses, snorting, galloping on shiny hooves. There was a rider on each horse, dressed in bizarre clothing. The picture lacked a focus, a centre that the eyes would be drawn to; he felt how his eyes flittered, jumping about looking for something, a point, a revelation. On his journey around the painting he noticed all the details, the reins of the horses, a boot with a shiny buckle, a broad-brimmed hat with a feather. A glove-clad hand, a whip, a spur, a velvet jacket with gold buttons. The canopy above the merry-go-round was beautifully decorated; there were red and green lanterns, an elegant cast-iron structure which held it all together. His eyes kept jumping about looking for somewhere to settle.

Finally, after a very long time, he made an unexpected discovery. It made him step back. The riders sitting on the horses were all dead. He had not spotted that at first, all he had seen was the merry-go-round, the horses and the long, colourful garments. Now he could see that the riders were ghosts, they grinned at him with yellow teeth. Their eye sockets were black holes and they cracked their whips and rode the horses in ecstasy and with malicious joy. He stepped back a bit further to get a better perspective. What was there to say about this picture? he thought perplexed; someone might want to buy it and it was vital to have some observations ready. A skilled art dealer would never stand dumbfounded in front of a picture. Well, he could highlight the element of surprise, that the merry-go-round was ridden by ghosts, that at first sight they looked as if they were enjoying themselves, a colourful experience, until the truth was brutally flung in your face. Death rides a merry-go-round, he thought, how disturbing. Once this discovery was made the picture became more of a clever display. Painted with a confident hand, that much was true, with a precision bordering on photographic, but apart from that the picture lacked soul. He narrowed his eyes and considered it. Many years in the gallery had turned Alvar into a connoisseur.

The picture was priced at eighteen thousand kroner and was likely to be sold quickly. To someone with little knowledge of art. Someone young. A man. No more than thirty-five years old. Someone it was easy to impress, someone who enjoyed gimmicks. Here I will need to highlight the painter's striking technique and the fine strokes, Alvar thought. The richness of detail, the colours. As he leaned forward again he noticed to his amazement that a few of the skulls had tiny white dots in their sockets. You had to be very close to detect them and it required a great deal of light. This was something he would need to mention to the future buyer. This painting needs a picture light above it if you are to see all the details, he would have to say. It varied from painting to painting. Some lit up all on their own, such as those by Advocat or Sitter. He went upstairs to make coffee. The merry-go-round haunted him for a few minutes; he started to think it might be an omen. After all, death had been on his mind a fair amount the last few days and now it had followed him into the gallery. But he dismissed it. No, it's only human to ponder death. They always had pictures with elements of death in them, this was merely a coincidence. Slowly he drank his coffee while he leafed through the local paper. Every now and again he looked up at the monitors.

The first customer arrived at eleven in the morning and entered briskly and purposefully. A woman of about fifty wearing a sea-green knitted coat. She smiled softly and in recognition as he came down the stairs; she had been there often, he knew her well. No, not *knew*, because he knew no one, but he was aware of how she behaved and this gave him a sense of calm. She was one of those mature women who were at ease with themselves and their lives, and Alvar could relax. Now she took off her gloves and looked around the gallery. Took a few steps forward and stopped.

'What a ghastly picture,' she laughed, taking in the merry-go-round. 'Who painted that?'

'An Englishman,' Alvar replied. 'His name's Wilkinson.'

He suppressed a comment to the effect that he did not like it either; it was a risk he could not afford to run, his primary purpose was to sell it, after all. But the way he saw it, it was vital that it was sold to the right buyer and this woman was not the right one. Although she might not like the picture personally she might want to give it to someone else; he always had to bear such things in mind.

'I don't like it,' she admitted. 'There's something wrong with this picture. Don't you think?'

Alvar exhaled deeply. Now he could relax and answer her question honestly.

'It doesn't come alive,' he explained. 'The painter wants to depict a jarring moment, but his expression is frozen, almost stylised. This subject should be generating a great deal of noise, but notice how silent it is.'

'But it's a picture of ghosts,' she smiled, 'they're not meant to be alive, are they?'

'No, perhaps not,' he smiled back. 'But there's something about this painter, he's missing something. The way I see it it's nothing but a clever display.'

She agreed with him, yet remained standing in front of the merry-go-round for a long time.

'Some yuppie will come along and buy it,' she stated.

'Yes, that was my thought too,' he admitted. 'Someone who likes to show off a bit.'

He looked at her politely. 'So what can I do for you today?'

'Nothing at all,' she said. 'I just wanted to pop in to see if you had anything new. Something exciting.'

'I've sold the waterfall,' he told her.

'Yes, of course, it's gone!' She spun round and stared open-mouthed. 'I'll really miss that,' she said. 'That waterfall was here for a long time.'

'Two and a half years,' he said.

'Who bought it?' she wanted to know.

'A yuppie,' Alvar smiled and they both laughed conspiratorially at this. Afterwards she wandered around for a long time visiting all three floors and Alvar left her to it. He returned to the kitchen and watched her on the monitors every now and again. She probably knew that he was doing this, but it did not bother her, she moved around confidently and calmly and gave herself plenty of time for each picture. At half past twelve he ate his three sandwiches. Up until now my life has been fine, he thought, once his hunger had started to abate. Nothing unforeseen has happened. No big surprises, no unexpected turns. Other people are struck down by all sorts of things and here I am eating my lunch without a care in the world. He thought that it would last. He was once more lost in his newspaper when he heard the bell downstairs. He raised his eyes and looked at the right-hand monitor. Something resembling a grey shadow had entered the gallery.

A grey shadow.

Alvar remained sitting staring at the monitor as he watched it slip quietly through the door. Then it stopped and stood immobile on the stone floor. A shadow, strange, blurred. He narrowed his eyes in order to get a better look and it occurred to him that it was obviously

65

a person. A small person, he thought, as she glided towards the wall. A woman. He thought it was a woman, but could not understand why she moved so oddly, she was rigid and fluid at the same time. Something told him instantly that this was no ordinary customer. He straightened up, scratched his cheeks nervously. But the shadow did not appear to be interested in the pictures. It was supporting itself against the wall and now it stood there motionless. The seconds ticked away and she did not move. Alvar left the kitchen and went quietly down the stairs, his heart beating faster. When he reached the ground floor she came into focus. A young woman, skinny and dressed in grey clothes. She wore tight, pointy ankle boots with incredibly high heels. A grey jacket, which came down to the middle of her thighs. It had a trim of filthy, tatty fur. Her legs, too, were very thin. Her hair was blonde and matted, wisps of it hung over her cheeks and her roots were dark. Her eyes were heavily made up. Her doll-like face was pinched and pale and all he could see were these panda eyes. They were staring at him. He stopped. What was it about her eyes? Her pupils were as tiny as pinheads. And how she trembled, she was actually shaking, as she stood there slumped against the wall. Alvar had never in all his life seen anyone as cold and translucent as this young woman. He stopped some distance away and kept watching her. His heart was pounding as he tried to get a grip on the situation.

'It's bloody cold outside,' she said feebly.

He nodded automatically. At the same time it began to dawn on him what kind of creature she was. She was a drifter, there were so many of them in this town. They normally hung out around Bragernes Square where they wandered about aimlessly. But this one here had found her way to Albumsgate and the gallery.

'Just trying to warm up,' she whispered.

She seemed both lethargic and excited at the same time. Trembling and quivering, yet she spoke slowly, slurring her words, and he realised that she had to be on something, he did not know what, but she was only partly present. Her eyes were distant, they rolled and then she closed them. She leaned upright against the wall next to the merry-go-round and she had clearly forgotten all about him. Alvar did not know what to do. He saw her thin, narrow hands and the pointy ankle boots and thought that she ought to be wearing thick-soled boots and thick woollen socks and a padded jacket and a woollen cap rather than wander around in such thin clothes, after all it was November and very cold. He saw her tiny mouth and her pretty snub nose and thought that she was in fact quite nice. And yet so incredibly ravaged. She had dark circles under her eyes, her lips were drained of colour. And she was just standing there, far away in her own world and not even aware of him. What was it Ole Krantz had told him again and again? If any drug addicts come in here, you've got to get rid of them straight away, Eide. Sometimes they come in here to shelter and you just can't trust them. Don't start talking to them, just show them the door. But she was not doing anything. She was just standing there borrowing a little of their central heating. In his head he could hear the three words he needed to say to get rid of her. Please go away. However, he was unable to open his mouth and say them. He had never ever said anything so dramatic to another human being. And as far as he was concerned she could stay there. There were no other customers in the gallery, no one who might take offence at this wretched creature.

He moved away and headed for the workshop; he could stay in there and watch her from a distance. Krantz was undoubtedly right: people like that could not be trusted. But he found it hard to imagine that she might suddenly stir, snatch a picture off the wall and then push open the door as she escaped. She doesn't even look as if she could lift a carton of milk, he thought. She was only just managing to remain upright. Suddenly he was frightened that she might collapse. He had heard that they often did that. In which case he would have to call the police. But it seemed to him to be quite ridiculous that he, a grown man, would need help to get rid of a young woman, that two broad-shouldered police officers would have to turn up to remove a girl weighing forty kilos. And even to ring a public authority would be beyond his capabilities. She looked to be less than twenty years old and her skin was transparent like delicate paper. When he had been standing in front of her, he had noticed the veins in her temples, a delicate blue-green web. At least there was real blood coursing through her body, he thought, though she looked like a zombie. Her skin was waxen. And cold. He stood in the workshop watching her through the doorway. No, she could stand there. And if a customer were to enter, he would just go over to her and politely but firmly escort her to the door. He doubted that she would resist, she seemed without a will of her own. Alvar reached for a bottle of glass polish and started polishing some graphics, which strictly speaking were in no need of being polished, but at least it gave him something to do. He kept looking at her furtively. He wanted to leave her alone. After all he was a good person. But if it had been Ole Krantz who had been working in the gallery that day she would have been turfed out instantly, Alvar was sure of that, and probably been given a piece of Ole's mind as well. There would have been swearing. Krantz was not known to be merciful. Alvar kept on polishing the pictures.

The young woman kept leaning against the wall, but suddenly she squatted down on her heels. She started blowing into her hands. Oh, dear God, how cold she is, Alvar thought, he could hardly bear to watch her. And there was the familiar nagging of his conscience again. He remembered that he had some coffee left in the coffee machine upstairs in the kitchen. Quietly he walked up the stairs and when he reached the top step he turned round and looked at her again. Some coffee. A warm mug to hold in her hands. It was a tiny gesture, it cost him nothing and after all he was a good person. He found a clean mug in the cupboard and filled it right up to the brim. He went back down the stairs. Hesitated. When he stood in front of her she looked up at him indifferently. She spotted the mug and took it without thanking him. Perhaps he had been expecting a small word of thanks, yet at the same time he understood that she had very little surplus energy for good manners. She drank the coffee greedily.

He thought that she would burn her tongue. But she did not, she carried on drinking until the mug was empty. He had never seen anyone drain a mug of hot coffee so quickly. When the mug was empty she held it out to him. A big blue mug.

'Feeling better?' he asked cautiously, taking it from her. Then something strange occurred. She held on to it. One of her fingers was hooked around the handle and a strength he would not have credited her with prevented him from getting hold of it. He stood there desperately trying to snatch the mug. Her eyes fixed him with sudden lucidity and just as he was about to let go, she released the mug and he took an involuntary step backwards. This manoeuvre wrong-footed him. She put her hands, which had now been warmed up a little by the mug, on her cheeks. Her white, cold cheeks. He thought, you have to go now. You've been here a while, someone might come. But she did not go. She stayed squatting with her hands on her cheeks and Alvar stood there utterly helpless. She's almost like a child, he thought, even though she was eighteen, yes, she had to be eighteen and thus of age. An adult. But incapable of looking after herself. So why had she come? Was she homeless? He could not imagine that she might not have a room or a home somewhere, after all she was so young. Homeless people were older, at any rate he thought so.

'Thanks,' she said suddenly. He was startled, her words were so unexpected. She had thanked him after all and he felt a tiny warm spark of joy inside.

'It was nothing,' he said softly. And then after a while: 'Are you starting to warm up?'

She looked up at him again and he noticed that her make-up-smeared eyes were actually very pale. They were bluish, like thin ice.

'I'll be gone in a minute,' she said, lowering her head again. He stared down at her dark roots. He wanted to say that she was welcome to stay, but that would not be entirely true. Besides, he was feeling rather pleased with his efforts. He was not a man to turn people away, he had a heart. And this much he knew: that many businesses in the town would not even hesitate when it came to people like her. He looked at her and said: 'I've got some work I have to do.' Then he returned to the workshop. He polished more glass. He kept glancing furtively out of the door the whole time. After fifteen minutes she got up. She staggered for a while trying to find her feet. Then, as she turned round, she noticed the paintings. It was as if she had not seen them until that moment. She'll go now, he thought, and she did. She shuffled towards the door. He had never seen a young body as ravaged as hers. She was like a doll, fragile and slender as a reed. She leaned all of her forty kilos against the door and slowly forced it open. Then she was gone.

Alvar rushed out of the workshop and over to the window. From there he watched her stumble down the street on her high-heeled ankle boots. He guessed she was heading back down to Bragernes Square in search of more drugs. That was how it was for those wretched creatures, they had to have drugs all the time. As it left their bodies, the hunger for more returned. He stood there watching her for a long time. Then she turned left and disappeared at the crossing and he lost sight of her. The large room was empty once again. He returned upstairs to the kitchen and sat down, contemplating what had just passed. How would she spend the rest of her day? And night? Did she have somewhere she could sleep? Perhaps she was a vagrant who would eventually collapse somewhere, on a bed he hoped, where she would sleep a dreamless sleep. She had to have someone. Parents or brothers and sisters. He sincerely hoped that this was the case.

He tried to read his paper again, but was unable to concentrate. He kept thinking about the kohl-black eyes, and the thin fingers, frozen blue like icicles. How do such people make it through the winter, he wondered, being outside freezing like this month after month? He was able to return to a warm flat, a hot shower. A fireplace and a bed with a feather duvet. He could not get her out of his mind. People visited the gallery, they admired all his pictures, the hours ticked away.

When the working day was over and he had tidied up after himself and locked the door, he crossed Bragernes Square to look for her, he could not help himself. To his great surprise he spotted her outside the Narvesen kiosk. She was with a man and counting coins, which she held in the palm of her hand. He did not want her to recognise him, so he walked past her at a distance. He wondered what her name might be. He wondered about the man standing next to her, he was older, thirty maybe. Scruffy and dishevelled. He hoped that she was not a prostitute, but did not want to be naive either. Addictions cost money. A lot of money. Once again he went to the Cash and Carry, as always he went to the deli counter, and bought a meal for one. A heat-and-serve casserole. God only knows when that girl last had a decent meal. Alvar walked home slowly. He heated up the food and sat down by his dining table; he felt terribly privileged. Yes, he really did. He was all alone in the world, but at least he was able to take care of himself. Not everyone was. However, it did not follow that she was a bad person, that much he understood. At the same time he was a little nervous. She had unsettled him. She had clung on to the blue mug and her glance had demolished his defences.

He thought about her a great deal in the days that followed.

Not all the time, but in brief snatches he remembered her frozen body and her kohl-black eyes. The spiky, thin fingers, the pointy ankle boots. Every time the gallery bell went he would glance quickly at the monitor, but she did not return. It was not that he hoped she would come back, but he was unable to forget her ice-blue eyes. She looked like a fallen angel, he thought, with her blonde strands of hair and her frail shoulders. She had to belong to someone. Surely someone as young as her could not be all alone in the world, he refused to believe that. Every day when he left the gallery he looked out for her on Bragernes Square, but it was as if she had vanished into thin air. Other lost souls wandered restlessly around begging alongside the pigeons. From time to time they managed to get a few crumbs too, a five or a ten kroner. In the course of a long day it probably added up to one shot of relief. A miserable but simple existence, Alvar thought, with only a single aim: more drugs.

Alvar was getting ready for Christmas. He always spent Christmas on his own and he knew how to pamper himself. He bought ribs, sausages and sauerkraut. He placed poinsettias on his windowsill, he lit candles. He burned incense; he enjoyed its sweet smell. On his door he hung a wreath of the kind normally placed on graves, they were his favourite kind. He enjoyed listening to Christmas carols on the radio; he liked the lights and decorations in town. Christmas never highlighted his loneliness, he simply pampered himself with a little extra. Sometimes he bought a chocolate yule log, cut it into thin slices and placed the slices in an elegant fan shape on a plate. He also made glühwein for the customers in the gallery. Sales increased dramatically. In fact, the last two days before Christmas were usually their best days in the whole year. When people came at the last minute they parted with their money more easily. Ole Krantz had invested in some beautiful shiny wrapping paper and the small lithographs sold like hot cakes. Life's good, Alvar thought, I can't complain, I'm doing fine. I'm a very contented man.

The new year brought cold temperatures and an abundance of fireworks over the town. Even the dome of the light-bulb factory paled in comparison with the colourful visions in the night sky. He went to bed at half past midnight. A new year had begun. He did not think that it would bring any exciting changes as far as he was concerned, but on the other hand he was not looking for exciting changes. Though minor, unexpected events were not to be sniffed at.

You never could tell.

CHAPTER 8

'Hello, it's me again, sorry to disturb you. Shouldn't you be working?'

I nearly jump out of my chair. Alvar appears behind me. He leans forward and reads a few lines on my screen.

'I'm writing a letter to a good friend,' I reply tartly. 'Is that all right with you?'

He nods, a little contrite.

'Just wanted to drop by as soon as possible to say thank you,' he says politely.

I turn round and look him in the eye.

'Thank me? For what?'

'For the girl. The poor freezing girl you sent me.'

I feel a prickle of guilt and look away.

'I mean,' he says enthusiastically, 'I got the chance to do a good deed. Of course, there is no reason to make a song and dance about a mug of coffee, but afterwards I was pleased that I did what I did.'

'That's good, then,' I say and look at the screen again.

'I'm not one to start chatting to people like that,' he goes on, 'in fact, I'm quite surprised at myself. But my own circumstances became so clear to me. How lucky I really am. And as you know, if you're well off, you have a duty to do good. Don't you think so?'

'Alvar,' I make my voice firm. 'I need to finish this letter, it's important to me. It needs to be posted today and the last post is at three thirty this afternoon.'

He folds his hands and shifts from one foot to the other. 'You're starting to get a little cross, aren't you? I spot things like that straight away. But I just wanted to mention something: I've always considered it a matter of honour to be respectful. Or to have good old-fashioned manners, if you like. But the thing is that we have a relationship, you and I, and you can't expect me to just sit back and wait when it concerns my own fate; you know I'm someone who needs to be in control.'

'Yes,' I say drily, 'I've noticed that.'

'And that's why,' he carries on, 'I must admit that I was terribly upset when this girl came into the gallery.'

'Whatever for?'

He coughs nervously covering his mouth with his hand. 'Well, we've talked about relationships. For one awful moment I thought you were going to turn us into a couple.'

I give up trying to finish the letter. I fold my arms across my chest instead and study him.

'My dear Alvar,' I say in a kind voice, 'I'm well aware that you prefer men.'

I am totally unprepared for his reaction. He flushes deeply all the way from his throat and up his cheeks. He takes a step sideways to recover his balance. Then he buries his face in his hands.

'You thought I didn't know?' I ask softly.

He does not reply, he groans. Frozen in this desperate position with his hands over his face. He wants to speak, but cannot find his voice.

'Please don't be so upset,' I comfort him.

He exhales deeply and gasps. Turns away in shame.

'Do you have to tell them that?' he whispers.

'You mean, do I have to include it in the story? We can talk about it. I obviously know more about you than what I put in the book. However, we can't prevent those who meet you from speculating. Don't underestimate people. You will never be able to control their thoughts.'

Finally he straightens up, but he finds it difficult to look me in the eye.

'I'm begging you on my knees,' he stutters. 'Please, please cut that bit, it's not as if it's important.'

I ponder this. Reluctantly. 'No, I'm not going to cut it, but I can treat it with respect.'

He begins to relax a little. He breathes a sigh of relief. 'I want to put the record straight,' he says suddenly. 'I have no such feelings for Ole Krantz. Just so you know.'

I have to smile. 'I know.'

'So we understand one another,' he says, reassured. 'And please forgive all my interventions, but I'm very shy, you know that. The idea that people can read me like an open book is unbearable.'

'It's not as scary as you think,' I reply, 'people knowing who you are. Wasn't that why you jumped the queue? You jumped the queue because you wanted to be noticed.'

'I did,' he admits instantly. 'But they don't need to know everything.'

'True,' I concede. 'Of course I make choices. But readers can be very perceptive, they add to the story and complete the picture. Ultimately you're protected by the boards of the book.'

Again he looks relieved.

'Will my story be several hundred pages?'

'Oh, no,' I reply immediately, 'it will be a modest story about a modest man. As I said before. If you're looking for volume, you'll have to go elsewhere.'

He runs his hand across his head, but takes care not to disturb the comb-over, which does not move. 'In other words: you don't think I'm very important? What about the woman and her dead child? They'll get more space, won't they?'

'Perhaps. I don't know yet, I've got my hands full with you. And my head,' I add, 'and my heart.' I place my hand on my chest. He smiles bashfully and looks at the floor.

'That's almost more than I had hoped for,' he says, 'that I can truly move another person. You. It's a wonderful feeling!'

Again I have to smile.

'But I'm not funny,' he warns me. 'Don't add humour to this story, it wouldn't work.'

'I don't have a sense of humour,' I confess, 'so you have nothing to fear. I'm looking for depth and drama.'

'Drama? That sounds disconcerting. Why do you have to have so much of that?'

'Drama makes the blood run faster through your veins. When the story reaches its peak that's when I feel most alive. You could do with a shot of adrenaline, you know, it's a fantastic high and totally addictive.'

'I think I'll stick with sherry,' he replies and smiles. 'There's something else. Where did you find the girl?'

'On Bragernes Square. There were several of them, all I had to do was choose one. And the one I picked stood out. She was so skinny and pale and translucent that she appeared to be almost ethereal. Did you notice her eyes? They're like ice. Her hair is like cotton grass. Her skeleton as fragile as a bird's. I felt I could snap her in half with one hand like a twig. I was taken with her frailty. She reminds me of Royal Copenhagen china.'

'That was beautifully put,' Alvar says.

'Thank you, I do try.'

'But she should be wearing something else on her feet for this time of year. Did you see her ankle boots? I've never seen such high heels, she could barely walk in them. And those boots aren't terrible warm either, did you know that? I'm sure they're synthetic, only plastic. What do you think?'

'Mm. They're plastic.'

'I mean, they must be very uncomfortable, on top of everything else. For example, she can't run in such boots, should she have to.'

'Heroin addicts don't run, Alvar, in fact they're very, very slow.'

He looks at me for a long time. 'So if something were to happen to her, she wouldn't be able to escape?'

I do not reply. I look at the screen again and my half-finished letter. I rest my chin in my hands.

'You've suddenly gone very quiet,' Alvar says. 'I'm convinced that you've thought of something, that you've just had an idea of what's going to happen.'

'That's correct. And I can't tell you what it is, I'm sure you understand.'

I look at him, he is twisting his fingers. There's something very virginal about him. A man of forty-two with his innocence intact. A man who has hidden himself away his whole life. It feels as if I'm about to throw him to the wolves. His unease is totally justified, he senses that something is about to happen. I force myself to be tough and push ahead with my plan even though I know I will cause him a great deal of pain.

'What are you thinking about?'

He looks directly at me.

'I'm thinking of everything we humans have to suffer. Restless hours filled with anxiety and distress. Sleepless nights, pain. I'm thinking of the bravery dormant in us all. How we grit our teeth and carry on. Some go with God. And those of us who don't have that option, those of us who don't lift our heads towards heaven, we walk on all the same with our heads bowed, right until our own end.'

'I can visualise what you've just said,' Alvar says. 'It's a powerful image. If I were a painter that is the very subject I would have chosen. Two people going to their deaths, one with and one without God.'

'Have you ever dreamt of being a painter?' I want to know.

'Oh, no, not ever, I don't have the talent. I'm perfectly happy just admiring the work of others. Whenever I stand in front of a painting, I can always find the words. Then I'm able, despite my shyness, to have long, in-depth conversations with another human being. However, when I'm outside on the street and someone stops me to ask directions, then I'm helpless.'

'Because there isn't a painting between you?'

'That's right. Of course, I give them a reply, but only a very brief one, and then I hurry on as quickly as I can. But in the gallery I can stand in front of a painting and talk for an hour.'

'You're an enigma,' I smile.

'Perhaps I'll surprise you along the way,' he says, looking terribly pleased with himself.

No, Alvar my dear, I think to myself, you're the one who is going to be surprised.

I turn my back on him so I can finish my letter. He stands behind me for a few minutes; I sense his presence like a shadow and I find it hard to concentrate.

'Do you ever dream about me at night?' he asks out of the blue. I sigh deeply, save the last sentence and turn round again with resignation.

'No, never. I dream vividly every single night, but I have never dreamt of you.'

He looks disappointed.

'May I ask you what you dreamt about last night?' he asks cautiously. 'I mean, if you don't think I'm being too forward?'

I lean back in my chair. I recall last night's events and the very unpleasant dream which still haunts me.

'I dreamt I was living in a city with narrow streets,' I tell him. 'I was drifting around this city; I had no mission, no purpose. Everyone was busy doing their own thing, but I wandered through the day with nothing to do. Then an important delegation came to the city, five grave-looking men dressed in black. They walked in procession through the streets carrying their heavy suitcases. One of the men was carrying a small bundle, but I couldn't see what was in it. They soon spotted me. They stopped and looked at me solemnly.

' "We have an important task for you," the man with the bundle announced. "We're here for five days, we have something very important to discuss and during those five days you must take care of this." He passed me the bundle, which was wrapped in a piece of filthy cloth. I unwrapped it and inside I discovered a baby.'

Alvar listens attentively, never taking his grey eyes off me.

'It wasn't a normal baby,' I say, 'it was the tiniest baby I'd ever seen. Three pounds at most and stark naked. Baffled, I looked at the child and the man fixed me with his eyes, then he said in a stern voice, "This is your responsibility. We will come back to collect it in five days." Then they left with their suitcases, they disappeared into the town hall and I lost sight of them. I was left standing on the cobbled street with the baby in my arms. And it wasn't just any baby, Alvar, it was slippery and smooth like a bar of soap and it immediately started to squirm, you know, like a cat struggles when it no longer wants to be held. I tried to tighten my grip on it, but despite my best efforts, it slipped from my hands and hit the cobbled street head first. I felt a sudden attack of dizziness as if I was about to pass out. Strange gurgling sounds were coming from the child's mouth, and its head on its fragile neck looked sickeningly as if it was loose. I felt nauseous with fear when I bent down to lift it up. But it was alive. It had shrunk a little, but I could see from its tiny chest that it was breathing. I started walking to a small hideaway with a simple bed and a blanket. I went inside still holding the baby and quickly lay down on the bed. There I felt safe in the knowledge that nothing would happen. We lay there until the next day. From time to time the baby made sucking noises and I realised that it needed food. I got out of bed. Very carefully I held the naked baby and went over to a bench where I had access to fresh water. I found a cup, filled it halfway and tried to pour the water into its tiny, tiny mouth; it didn't go very well. The baby began to squirm and wriggle again and in an unguarded moment it hit the ground for the second time. I heard its tiny skull smack against the floorboards. My heart skipped a beat. There was no doubt that the child had been injured, and it was as if its neck had been stretched into a long thin thread; its head was barely connected to its frail shoulders.'

I look at Alvar; he returns my gaze breathlessly.

'Again I lay down on my bed. But I understood that you can't spend your whole life in bed, you have to get up and face the world and thus risk exposing yourself and those you love. So I went out into the streets clutching the baby, pressing against the walls, looking left and right. Again the baby started to squirm, again it hit the cobbles, and when I lifted it up I thought it was dead. But I detected a weak pulse, and its head was still hanging by that thin thread that its neck had become. I crossed the square, ashamed because I had failed this simple task entrusted to me. Another four days passed and I knew that the important delegation would soon come out of the town hall to collect the child. I stared at it and could see that it had shrunk a great deal. For the fourth time I dropped the baby and I felt that hope was fading. Finally I slumped against a stone wall, leaned my head against it, clung on to the child, closed my eyes and just wanted the time to pass. And it passed, and the delegation came walking down the street with their black suitcases. I felt relieved that everything would be over soon and I could hand back the uncontrollable baby that kept squirming. They stopped a metre away from me, formed a semicircle and watched me with their black eyes.

'"The child," they said gravely.

'I handed them the bundle. My hands were shaking; I couldn't give it back soon enough. One of the men reached out to receive it. At that very moment it began to squirm violently; it shot out of my hands like a bar of soap in the shower and smashed against the cobbles. It lay there and did not stir; its neck was now as thin as a nail, and its head partly bashed in. They stood there looking at me accusingly and I was at my wits' end as to what I should do. I was weighed down by guilt and despair.

'"We gave you a simple task," they said. "And you failed."

'I could give them no answer. The baby had been in my care and I had failed. Suddenly they vanished and I was left alone.'

I stop speaking. Alvar is gawping.

'And then?' he asks eagerly. 'What happened next?'

'I woke up,' I reply. 'And thanked my lucky stars that it was only a dream. But that sense of failure has haunted me the whole day.'

I turn to the computer again; I want to finish my letter.

'But what does it mean?' he insists.

I shrug. 'Perhaps it is about you after all. I'm scared that I won't manage to hold on to you. Scared you'll slip out of my hands, that we won't make it to the end.'

'I won't squirm,' he says quickly.

I have to smile at this. 'That's true. And you're not slippery and smooth either. But you're a lot heavier than the baby. I have to carry you for a whole year and that's hard.'

'No one has ever held me like you,' Alvar says.

CHAPTER 9

January and freezing cold.

It was five to ten in the morning when Alvar let himself into the gallery. He walked across the room, stopped and looked around. He immediately made a breathtaking discovery, as if he had unexpectedly reached a hilltop and a new and unknown landscape had opened up inside him. Ole Krantz had acquired a new painting. Alvar felt a chill down his spine. Suddenly he was gripped by a force field. The painting had not been hung yet, but was propped up against the wall, beautifully lit by the big arched window in the middle. A large oil painting, strangely dark and powerful. Alvar stood as if struck by lightning while his eyes took in the subject. At first all he could see was the faint outline of a building in a dark fog, something black slowly emerging from a deep canyon. He felt the hairs on the back of his neck stand up. Now what was this? He moved closer, shaking his head. A bridge, he realised, a heavy bridge. A bridge, which disappeared into murky darkness. But it was not just a bridge. It was an unfinished construction; it ended abruptly, halfway across the void, as if the project had been halted. The bridge did not reach the other side. Or, it struck him, it had been severed; he could make out some jagged beams jutting into the fog. So the bridge led nowhere. Alvar gasped. It was a huge and violent painting and he surrendered to it. The bottomless void, the steep mountainsides, the mysterious, hazy light. This severed bridge, so majestic. But a beautiful construction, nonetheless, he could see that, simple but ingenious, beautiful and arched, delicate yet strong. But also amputated. He stood as if paralysed, staring at the bridge. Who had painted this picture? Which artist had had the idea of painting a severed bridge? He walked closer, but he was unable to read the signature. He got hold of the top of the painting and tried to tilt it. Perhaps its title was on the back? The painting was heavy even though it was as yet unframed. He leaned the painting forwards and wiggled behind it so as to get a better look. And there was the title scribbled with a charcoal pencil. *Broken*, 1997. He put the painting against the wall and once more took a few steps backwards. It certainly was broken. Perhaps a ship had miscalculated the height of its masts and torn the bridge in half, that had to be it, he understood it now. But what was it about this bridge, why was he drawn towards this painting as if by an inexorable force? Because it's my painting, Alvar thought, I've been looking for this, this is the one for me. It speaks to me in all its gloomy silence. He turned away for a moment because it was all becoming too much for him. He stood there with his back to the painting while thoughts welled up in him, wild and raging. He must ring Ole Krantz instantly; he had to know who the painter was. What if it turned out to be a commission, imagine if the painting was not even for sale? he thought, with something bordering on desperation. The picture had not been hung, or priced. It's expensive, Alvar thought, this is a fairly expensive painting, not everyone will be able to afford it. I have a chance. I have seventy thousand in the bank. He tried to tear himself away. He went upstairs to the kitchen and made coffee. Then he had to go back downstairs for a second look. It probably would not have the same powerful effect on him this time, some of its force would diminish, since he had studied the painting in depth once already. But when he came downstairs the picture took hold of him with the same violence. It drew him in, he was swallowed up by the fog, he saw the broken surfaces, the severed bridge, beams and wires bristling in the darkness, and he gasped for air. He ran up the stairs and called Ole Krantz.

'Happy New Year,' he croaked into the receiver.

'Have you caught a cold?' Krantz asked. 'It sounds like you've lost your voice.'

Alvar shook his head. He cleared his throat. 'No, I just had something stuck.'

A moment's silence followed while they waited for each other. Alvar checked the monitors, he did not want any customers now, he had to find out about this picture, this violent force on the ground floor. He struggled to control himself, he wanted to come across as professional and mature, but it was impossible, he was quivering with excitement.

'Did you see the bridge, Eide?' Krantz said out of the blue.

Alvar jolted. 'Yes,' he stammered, 'and it's overwhelming, Krantz, utterly overwhelming.' He could not help it, his voice was falsetto. 'Don't you think?'

At the other end Krantz chuckled. 'I suspected that you would like it.'

Alvar held his breath. Focused and took off.

'Where does it come from?'

'An unknown chap,' Krantz said. 'His name's Lindstrøm. I came across the painting in Stockholm and had it sent back here. I'm sure we'll be hearing a lot more about him.'

An unknown chap, Alvar thought. Perhaps the painting won't be so expensive after all. Unknown painters could not expect high prices, there were rules for these things which had to be respected, it took a long time before they finally made it. The breakthrough that they all dreamt about. *Broken* could be such a breakthrough, literally.

'If anyone happens to ask,' Alvar said, trying to keep his voice at a steady pitch, 'what kind of price are we talking about?'

Again he held his breath. Krantz thought about this for a long time.

'I'm thinking seventy thousand.'

Alvar reeled. He felt like giving up. Seventy thousand kroner. All his painstakingly compiled savings, his entire life insurance. For an unknown painter. How could he even contemplate something like that?

'Did you say the painter was an unknown?' he stammered, clutching the handset. His ear flattened against his temple.

'He is, he is. But what a picture! It's monumental. It's worth seventy thousand.'

Alvar pondered this amount. This bizarre coincidence. Could it be a sign from above?

'We'll have it in the gallery for a long time, then,' he said out loud, nursing a faint hope, because he needed time. He was not an impulsive man and he was not used to feeling spellbound as he did today. He was composed, measured. A man who always thought before he acted.

'Let me put it this way,' Krantz said, 'if anyone makes us an offer, we'll consider it.'

I want to make you an offer, Alvar thought, but he did not say it out loud. He wanted to hang up, he wanted to return to the picture, stand in front of it and feel the strange sensation that the picture portrayed him, his very core. This was how he had always felt, he had never connected with other people, something inside him had been severed.

'Someone will be completely smitten with this picture,' Krantz went on, 'and this one person will be prepared to pay the price. Just you wait and see. I'm right about this, mark my words.'

I already know you are, Alvar thought. He managed to conclude the conversation. He went back downstairs, walking hesitatingly down the steps, and over to the picture. He remained in front of it for a long time. He was scared that someone might come. He was scared that someone might appear in the doorway, spot the picture, fall completely in love with it and take it away from him. He was overcome by a childish urge to hide it in the workshop so that no one would ever see it. There is no other way, he thought, I'll just have to buy it, it's that simple. And I must buy it now. There is no time to lose. If I don't buy it, someone else will and this picture was meant for me. But it costs seventy thousand; it's everything I have in the bank. It'll clear me out. Poor as a church mouse, he thought, and shivered at the thought. On the other hand, he argued, money is there to be spent. And I'll never find a picture like this ever again. But seventy thousand kroner. Then he would have nothing put by for sudden expenses and that in itself was extremely risky. On the other hand he was a good customer at the bank, so if any unforeseen expenses were to crop up, it was likely that the bank would offer him a small loan. If he were to dent the car or break a tooth. Anything could happen, Alvar thought; he was a man with a lot on his mind. Right now he was infatuated by the picture. He felt quite faint. He was experiencing a dizzying joy. This was art at its best, this was happiness. At that very moment the doorbell rang. His heart leapt to his throat. Was it happening already? Was someone coming to take the picture away from him?

He recognised her instantly.

The young woman in the high-heeled ankle boots. She stopped in the open doorway and looked at him. She looked better than last time. Her eyes were brighter, she was composed and her movements were steady, she was not staggering as before. She let the door close behind her and took a few steps across the stone floor. Looked at him with her ice-blue eyes and said, 'Hi, only me. Could you spare a cup of coffee?'

Alvar gawped. He had almost forgotten her, no, not forgotten her, but she had been out of his thoughts for a long time. It had never occurred to him that she might come back, not after all this time.

'Coffee.' He hesitated. Right away he experienced a deep, disconcerting resistance. If he were to give her a cup of coffee, what would happen then, where would it lead? But it was hard to say no to such a simple request. How could he suddenly be mean when he had previously been so compassionate? That would not look very good and he was a decent man.

'Very well,' he mumbled reluctantly, 'I suppose I could.' He turned round mechanically and went up the stairs. She followed him. In the midst of it all he experienced a bizarre sense of relief. She was not here for the picture, she just wanted some coffee. She stood in the opening to the kitchen and stared at him while he complied with her simple request. He found the same blue mug from before and filled it right up to the brim.

'It's cold outside,' he said, watching her white fingers. She took the mug and drank. Her lips were thin and bluish white, but her eyes, which he recalled as being dull were suddenly as sharp as glass. 'Bloody cold,' she said, looking at him over the rim of the mug.

No, it struck him as he watched her, she had to be older than he had first assumed. She was probably in her early twenties, he detected some fine lines around her eyes. She was wearing the same clothes as the last time. Perhaps she had never taken them off. It horrified him that a young person could look so dreadful, but of course her body was totally ravaged by drugs.

'Where do you live?' he blurted out.

'Here and there,' she replied indifferently. 'It's not very strong your coffee, is it?'

'Oh.' Alvar was disappointed. He had always believed that he made a decent cup of coffee. He could not allow this; he would have to do something about it later.

'You here every day?' she asked, looking around the large building. Her question made him smile.

'Yes, every day. Year in, year out,' he replied.

'That sounds utterly boring,' she stated.

'Oh no, not at all,' he assured her, folding his hands across his stomach as was his habit.

She kept hold of the mug and started wandering around the rooms on the first floor. He followed her. She looked at the pictures. Shook her head, screwed up her eyes. I don't suppose she knows much about art, Alvar thought.

'Is that expensive?' she asked, pointing at a picture.

'Terribly,' he admitted. 'Well, some of them are, not all of them. But that one, however, by Nerdrum, that's expensive, you wouldn't be able to afford it.'

She laughed a delicate and tinkling laugh, the way little girls laugh.

'You don't have anyone to talk to in here,' she pointed out, and he stared down at the toes of his shoes as if she had humiliated him. 'Or perhaps you talk to the pictures?' she teased.

She looked directly at him now, and he tried to meet her eyes, she was only a girl and a cheeky one at that.

'I don't have a great urge to talk,' he explained and cleared his throat. He was thinking about the bridge. If you had a painting like that on your wall, it would no longer be necessary to say anything else in this life. Somewhere there was an artist who had imagined this landscape. The depths, the sea stacks, the fog. And its impact on him had been so strong; it was like being hit by a gale-force wind. That was how he felt it. He was suddenly overcome by an urge to show it to her, just to see what would happen.

'Do you know anything about art?' he asked watching her. She yawned.

'Is there anything to know?' she said. 'You either like a picture, or you don't. Is there anything more to say?'

'There's a great deal more to say,' he replied.

'There is?' She staggered a bit and drank from the mug, greedily, the way a thirsty child gulps down a glass of milk.

'Come with me, I want to show you something!'

She followed him down the stairs to the ground floor. He went straight over to the wall and gestured towards the bridge with one grand, solemn gesture. She gazed at it attentively still holding the blue mug. She drank a few gulps, she took in the picture. Then she licked the corners of her mouth with the pink tip of her tongue.

'Right,' she said eventually. 'A bridge going nowhere. Amazing.'

'Yes, don't you think?' he said, pleased because he could see that the painting had moved her and it made him feel that there might be hope for her after all, that behind all this devastation there was a sentient human being.

'What's it called?' she asked with curiosity.

'*Broken*,' said Alvar dramatically.

She swallowed the rest of her coffee in one big gulp and handed him the mug.

'Nice title. Do you know, that's the only name it could have.'

He declared that he was in total agreement with her.

'I saw you on Bragernes Square a little while ago,' he said all of a sudden. He did not know why he said it, it just came out.

'Aha?' she replied.

'You were together with a man. A dark-haired man, older than you. Long hair. Perhaps it was your brother?'

She looked at him and then she burst out laughing.

'My brother? I don't have any brothers, or sisters for that matter.'

'How about parents then?' he wanted to know.

'No parents either,' she said sullenly and turned away from him. She started pacing in a circle on the stone floor. 'They've all gone.'

'Gone?' He did not understand.

'Gone away. Scattered by the four winds. That's all right. I'm not too bothered by it, family is just trouble. Folks you have to see just because you're related to them. Do you have any family?' she asked.

Alvar had to tell her the honest truth, which was that he was all alone in the world.

'No kids? No wife?' she said.

'No,' he said. It sounded lame. He felt interrogated, but on the other hand he had been the one to start it all off.

'And why not?' she said looking at him. Her blue eyes dissected him.

'It's just never happened,' he said. 'I can offer you no other explanation. I'm fine with it,' he added, looking back at her.

'You ought to get a haircut,' she said suddenly. 'Comb-overs are out.'

'Comb-over?' He touched his scalp. 'I'd better look after the little I've got left.'

'You'd look much better without it,' she stated.

She really is very cheeky, he thought, so very cheeky. I have never seen the like.

89

'Thank you for the coffee,' she said. 'I've got to go.'

'Have you?' he said and felt pleased about that. At the same time something happened inside him. He could not fully explain what it was, but it was becoming too much for him, this girl, the painting. Seventy thousand kroner. I need time to think, he told himself, I need to sleep on it. I want to have another look in the morning. If it has the same strong effect tomorrow, then I will buy it.

'I'm thinking of buying that picture,' he said, pointing once more to the bridge.

'How much is it,' she asked swiftly.

'Seventy thousand kroner.'

She rolled her eyes wildly. 'You have that much money?'

'I've got a bit put away,' he said proudly. 'I've been saving up for years.'

For one moment he thought he saw a flicker of light in her eyes.

'I see,' she said. 'You want the damaged bridge. That's all right. Bloody great picture,' she smiled. Her ravaged face cracked up and softened. He had a feeling that she was secretly laughing at him. He liked her and yet he did not like her, he was confused.

'Got to run,' she said firmly.

She staggered off on her high heels. She leaned against the oak door, forcing it open. Then she was gone. This time he didn't watch her from the window. In a sudden moment of despair because he had exposed himself in a way which was uncharacteristic for him, he carefully touched the top of his head. The lock of hair was still in its place.

When he left the gallery he took the route via Bragernes Square. He crossed into the pedestrian area, and as he passed Magasinet something strange happened. He felt driven by a sudden impulse and as he came to Saxen, a hairdressing salon, he went straight in. He had just ended up there, the urge had surprised him. It felt like floating. He looked down at his shoes, checking that he was still in contact with the floor. A young woman was busy cutting the hair of a small, long-haired boy. She looked up at him and smiled. Studied his old-fashioned hairstyle with a look of professional determination.

'Would you have time to cut my hair?' he asked. He instantly stroked his head, terrified. It had never occurred to him to have what little hair he had left cut off. He would be bald. All he'd have left would be a modest semicircle of hair at the back of his head.

'Yes,' she smiled, still watching him, 'if you can wait ten minutes. Have a seat please, I won't be long.'

He thought that she looked remarkably young, as if she ought to be in school. Her hair was cut short, it stuck out wildly and was dyed in several different shades. Her ears were heavily decorated with rings and studs and at the back of her head she had a small tattoo of a unicorn.

Alvar took a magazine, which he leafed through while he waited. He had to sit on a pouffe, it was horribly soft, he had no back support. Thus he sat, almost slumped, like a man with bad posture. On the pouffe next to him sat a woman, probably the boy's mother. She looked awfully pleased whenever the boy's hair landed softly on the floor. Alvar's pulse was rising. It was too late to leave now, after all he had sat down, and it would not do to storm out of the door at this point, even though this was precisely what he felt like doing. What had he started? A casual remark from a stranger had pushed him over the edge and now he would look like an idiot if he were to leave. If he walked off like some feeble-minded, gutless coward. He kept leafing through the magazine, but managed only to look at the pictures. The boy in the chair had now acquired a short haircut; finally his neck was brushed and he was allowed to get down. His mother paid with a note and they both left. Alvar let the magazine fall to the floor. He was told to sit down by the sink. He did so, resting his head on the neck support. This position, with his throat exposed, made him think of lying on the scaffold. The hairdresser tested the temperature of the water and started washing his hair; he liked the feel of her fingers massaging his scalp, they were strong and soft at the same time, she moved her hands in circles across his head.

He enjoyed it as best he could while he tried to convince himself that he had made the right decision. All the same he was shocked. How could he allow himself to be controlled by a young, blonde drug addict? A woman he did not even know. Because he knew that it was her comment about comb-overs being old-fashioned which had caused him to end up in this chair. He knew no other women. He was not used to people commenting on his appearance. And what would happen if she turned up at the gallery again and noticed that he had in fact done what she had said? Perhaps she would collapse in a heap of wild, uncontrollable giggling, slap her pointy knees and poke fun at him?

'Shall we get rid of the bit on the top?' the hairdresser asked diplomatically.

Alvar was seated in front of the mirror. He nodded. He sat looking miserable in his chair and watched the long tuft of hair fall to the floor. His scalp appeared, shiny like a mirror. He instantly looked older. It might very well be more modern, more contemporary, but it definitely aged him. But then again at least he would be spared the constant trips to the mirror to check that the tuft of hair was still in place. Now there was not a single hair on his head long enough to move or sway in the wind. He had enjoyed having his scalp touched. She smelled good, something sweet and mild. His regular barber kept his distance, he was formal, talked about the weather. But this young woman chatted away in a soft, feline voice. Alvar replied with brief sentences, but he did not feel threatened by her. Now she was using the hair trimmer at the back of his neck.

'There you are,' she said, brushing away any loose hairs. 'Nice and tidy.'

Alvar had to agree. When he thought about it, he did feel good after all. He was not pretending to have more hair than he really did. His baldness was plain for all to see, no more pretending. He straightened his shoulders, thanked her and paid, went outside on the freezing cold day. Hair or no hair, even young men shaved their heads, it was fashionable. It was masculine. And there was nothing wrong with the shape of his head. In fact, the back of his head was nicely rounded, a head he could be proud of. Perhaps this was an appropriate day to treat himself to something extra special for dinner? A fillet of beef, perhaps, or a piece of salmon? Again he went to the Cash and Carry, where he took a number as always at the deli counter. When it was finally his turn, he decided on an elk steak, and on the condiment shelf he found a jar of mountain cranberries. That's the thing, he thought, and headed homeward with this small exclusive meal in a carrier bag.

He let himself into his flat and went straight into the bathroom. He hesitated as he walked over to the mirror. He saw his bald head and was startled. Because this was his own mirror and the man looking back at him was him. The man he had seen in the mirror at the hairdresser's had not been him; we only see ourselves as we really are in our own mirrors, he thought, and this is the honest truth. Alvar Eide with no hair. Alvar Eide aged forty-two, with a modest band of hair at the back of his neck. It will take me a year to grow out my hair again, he thought, and this period, before his hair was long enough to be combed all the way over to the right side, would be an awful time. He tried to laugh at himself and went out into the kitchen. Unwrapped the elk steak and wiped it with a piece of kitchen towel so that the meat would be completely dry when it hit the browning butter in the frying pan. He found salt and pepper. He went into his living room and turned on the radio. He saw that Green from next door was coming home from work. When the meat was frying he stood there inhaling the wonderful smell. He even hummed a tune the name of which he could not remember, but it was played incessantly on the radio and he could not get it out of his head. Like a buzzing, persistent insect he could not be bothered to chase away.

He set the table in the living room. He sat down and ate while his eyes wandered around the room. Where would he hang the severed bridge? Above the fireplace, of course. Oh, how it would tower over the room almost like a monument, he thought. Seventy thousand kroner. Every single krone he had saved up. It was quite extravagant. Why did he have such a desire to own this painting? After all he could see it every day in the gallery. The picture might even hang there for months, and perhaps he might get sick of it after a while and want a different one. He knew that was not true. This was Alvar being sensible, practical, prudent Alvar. The part of him that kept him in check, the part of him that had kept him on the right course his entire life. On his own, but taking care of himself. But then there was another voice, a strong seductive voice. It pushed common sense aside and made him weak. The painting is meant for you, the voice said, it illustrates your very soul, this severed bridge in the mute darkness. The picture will complement your flat, the picture will soothe the unrest you sometimes feel at night, because all your fears have finally been articulated by an unknown painter. A soulmate. Someone who knows exactly how you feel. Thus the painting will become your most treasured possession. Everyone who enters this room will see it and wonder. At its audacity, the elegance of the construction, while they simultaneously shiver at the drama because it disappears into a silent, dark fog. They will see that you have taste, that you are a real connoisseur. But no one ever comes here, he suddenly thought. Salespeople only come as far as the hall, and my neighbour has never been in here, no one but me will ever get to see it. But surely you're buying the painting for yourself, the voice replied. And even if the painting is not of very high quality, it is nevertheless a good investment, isn't it? Yes, but I've never really been very interested in investments. I've always believed that when it comes to art you have to go with your gut instinct. True, but is it not your gut instinct talking to you now? Buy it, Alvar, buy it! Get up now and go to the telephone, call Ole Krantz. Tell him you're buying the painting. Then it's done, once and for all. I have to sleep on it, he thought then, it's not like it's going to go anywhere overnight. Unless a burglar turns up and swipes it from under my very nose. But they had never had any break-ins at Gallery Krantz. Touch wood, he thought, tapping the table. What is going on with me? I'm behaving like a little child. Of course I should buy that painting. I'm all over the place and there is a reason for that. You have to take these things seriously. You should always listen to your intuition; it too has its own inner voice. The body needs sustenance, food, drink and sleep. However, the soul needs nourishment too. He finished eating and went over to the fireplace. Above it hung three unassuming lithographs, now he took them down and carried them out into the hall. Then he went back into the living room and stood there looking at the empty wall. Yes, it would fit there. It would not only fit, the painting would also be beautifully lit by the windows in the middle facing it. It would look as if it had always hung there. When he closed his eyes he could visualise it clearly. But as he had already told himself, he ought to sleep on it. And tomorrow he would go to the gallery and see how he would feel then. Perhaps nothing would happen, perhaps it would be an anticlimax. It had happened to him before. The painting would cry out to him at first sight only to lose its impact later. It was a strange mechanism, but he preferred pictures that grew on him over time. Seventy thousand kroner. He forced himself to move away from the bare wall and carried his plate and cutlery out into the kitchen. Rinsed off the leftover gravy and cranberries, then sat down in his chair in front of the television. Touched his scalp and felt dizzy. None of the terrestrial channels were showing anything worth watching, so he picked up the newspaper and checked the satellite listings. Perhaps there would be something on National Geographic. '9 p.m.,' he read, '*When Expeditions Go Wrong*. 10 p.m., *Deadly Heat*. 11 p.m., *Seconds From Death: The Bhopal Tragedy*. 11.30 p.m., *The Eruption of Mount St Helens*. 12 a.m., *Trapped Undersea*.' This list of disasters made him feel anxious. Perhaps the severed bridge was a warning.

CHAPTER 10

'There was something I wanted to talk to you about,' Alvar says as he softly crosses my floor. 'And I don't mean to be rude, it's not in my nature, not in any way. But this is completely inappropriate!'

I look over my shoulder at him. His voice is falsetto.

'I'm not in the habit of chatting to people like that, volunteering personal information, I don't think it's appropriate and I certainly don't want total strangers to know. And I have never been dissatisfied with my appearance, that visit to the hairdresser's was entirely out of character. I've ended up looking like a fifty-year-old.'

He is genuinely upset. His newly shaven cheeks are flushed.

I tilt my head and look at him.

'Calm down. You look good. Trust me.'

He runs his hand over his naked scalp.

'Why did you reintroduce her?' he asks. 'I had almost forgotten about her, I was waiting for something else to happen.'

'It's not easy to change track once I've made a decision,' I reply. 'Let's wait and see where it takes us. There's no point in worrying about something that hasn't happened yet.'

'But,' he objects, 'so much is happening at the same time. You've created a longing in me that I never knew existed. That severed bridge won't leave me alone, I can't relax. If I buy the painting I spend all of my savings. That in itself is a huge risk and I never splash out. If I don't buy the painting I have to live with the loss of it. That awful feeling when the painting goes to another.'

'In other words, you're being forced to make a decision,' I reply drily. 'And you have to make it quickly.'

He collapses uninvited into a chair and folds his hands.

'Why are you putting all this pressure on me? Does it all have to happen so quickly? It unsettles me.'

I look at him across the desk.

'Well, that's how it's turning out. This is a short narrative, I don't have many pages at my disposal.'

'Not many pages? But why not? Surely that's up to you. Whether you want to write a hundred and fifty pages or six hundred?'

'No, it's not up to me. And I realised that as soon as I began. You're a modest man, this will be a modest tale.'

The thought of this depresses him.

'I am, in other words, not terribly important?'

I sigh heavily. 'Of course you're important. And surely you're not saying that a short life is less important than a long one? The real question is: does anyone see us while we are here on earth? I see you clearly. I'm showing you to others. But it would seem that you're still not satisfied?'

He blushes once again. Strokes his forehead with a trembling hand. 'I'm sorry, but I'm still worried. People will be able to judge me. My actions and my values. It's a frightening thought. Dear God, what will they think, what will they say?'

'Some might take you to their hearts,' I reply, 'others will pass by unmoved. That's how life is. The point is that you have to give them a chance. If you want to be seen, you have to put yourself out there, it's that simple.'

'But why does it have to be through a drug addict?'

I light a cigarette, I inhale. Get up and let the cat in, he has been scratching at the back door.

'That's just how it's turning out.'

He shakes his head. 'Your replies confuse me. It's as if you have no will of your own. You could have chosen someone different. You must have had a reason. Consciously or subconsciously. Can't you outline the plot so that I can relax?'

'No, not really,' I reply frankly. 'However, I needed a conflict. Your relationship with Ole Krantz is clear, there is nothing for me to explore. I needed a contrast. Someone who lives their life in a completely different way from you. The door to the gallery opened and there she was. I could see her very clearly. For the time being I am watching you from a distance waiting to see what will happen. And to be honest, I like being surprised. Perhaps I'll end up in a different place from where I originally intended. Perhaps you'll do better than I fear at the moment. You've had your hair cut,' I say to him, 'and I see how much you fret about this one spontaneous act. But changing your hairstyle does not make for very interesting reading. Anyway, it really suits you. More manly, somehow. And exchanging a few words with a stranger shouldn't exactly knock you sideways. Most people are well intentioned towards you. Let yourself go a little, Alvar, and see what happens.'

'So you're saying I should buy the painting?'

'That's not what I'm saying, I've merely offered you the chance. Now don't force me to analyse it too deeply, I need to be flying free in order to write.'

'There are times,' he objects feebly, 'when I wish I had called on someone else. On a writer with a better overview, more control.'

'Well, we've already discussed that,' I say. 'But as it happens you're here with me.'

He relaxes his shoulders. Gives me a sidelong glance.

'I guess I'm a complete nuisance,' he says. 'I suppose I ought to be pleased about what you've done so far rather than throw a spanner in the works. That was never my intention. That really was not what I meant. That was not what I meant at all.'

'You're not a spanner in the works. We're a team now, you and I, it's called letting things happen. You have no experience of that and that's why you're feeling afraid. So am I, I live with it every day. But my heart is still beating, as is my pulse, the minutes pass one by one. The sun will come up tomorrow, I'm absolutely certain of that. I really do pity mankind,' I say, 'we don't have the ability to live in the moment. Soon other things will happen, difficult things, they will happen tonight or next week. And even though we're not there yet, our thoughts race ahead like horses through an open gate. In other words, only genuine contemplation can stop this clock inside us ticking and ticking towards our death. A painting, a piece of music, an engrossing book, a chat to a good friend. Bad things will always happen, but they are not going to happen today. Because today the sun is shining and we get out of bed. We put our feet on the floor and breathe. There is actually a good deal of courage in you, Alvar, I'm absolutely convinced of that. But, of course, I'm worried that you've chosen to isolate yourself. If something goes wrong, you've got no one to turn to. Do you ever think about that? Do you understand what that means?'

His eyes become distant, they seek out the window.

'I've been thinking a great deal about dying,' he admits. 'Who will arrange my funeral, will anyone mourn me? Who'll clear out my flat, what will happen to my furniture and all my other belongings? But then again I'm only forty-two. And all sorts of things might happen before I grow old. I hope that time will take care of it for me.'

'It won't,' I say gravely. 'If you want things to change, you have to change them yourself. I'm with you all the way, but I rely on you grabbing the opportunities I give you. Otherwise we're never going to get anywhere. Do you understand what I'm saying to you?'

He gets up and goes over to the window. He stares out across the Lier Valley.

'You authors are a funny lot,' he says with his back to me.

'No, we're like most people. We work hard, we have a profession. We have office hours, we toil.'

'I can see all the way to Fjell,' he says over by the window.

'Yes, you can.'

'And all the greenhouses. They glow like gold bullion in the dark.'

'It's pretty, don't you think?'

'Does all this beauty inspire you?'

'No.'

He turns round. 'Really?'

'I would have preferred a cell in a basement.'

'You're not serious?'

'Yes. A single solitary source of light. No windows. A spartan room. Where no external influences can penetrate my mind. In spring, living as I do here, it's unbearable, with the pretty valley in front of the house and the woods right behind it.'

'What's wrong with the woods?'

'The birds just won't shut up! Doves cooing, cuckoos singing, and the woodpeckers, they drive me crazy. But I do like the cows when they start to low at five in the morning. You know, Alvar,' I explain, 'for human beings to be in balance, their external landscape must match their internal one. That's why I like fog. Darkness and storms. Northern lights, a full moon. Shooting stars. Heavy, persistent rain, leaves falling.'

'If that's your attitude then I worry that you're about to tell quite a dark story,' he says anxiously.

'Yes, it's in my nature.'

He comes back and finds his seat on the sofa.

'There's something I have to ask you,' he says. 'Do you like your work?'

'I love it. It's a passion.'

'But you're all alone. In front of your screen. Year in, year out.'

'That's correct. But I never think about it. There's no room for second thoughts once I've started. Then time stands still, it's like being on the crest of a wave. And then, when that day's work is done I'm spat out into reality where everything is equally intense. Then I find out that there's a war on in Iraq, that a vast number of people on this planet continue to starve, that there's still unrest in the Middle East. And that what I spent my time on has no importance whatsoever.'

'But surely as a writer you must feel that you matter somehow?'

'Sadly, no. But I don't want you to think I'm going to treat you and your destiny lightly. I take this very seriously. But I should have been in Africa building wells.'

He smiles sadly.

'Have you put any worries in your box?' he asks softly.

'Obviously,' I say in a tired voice. 'They come to me in a steady stream; I'm a terribly anxious person. When my alarm goes off in the morning I am overwhelmed by everything that might go wrong. I can barely find the courage to put my feet on the floor; this world will never be a familiar place to me, every day I have to navigate it as a beginner. The fifteen steps downstairs, the walk to the computer. But once I see the blue light from the screen, the tension within me subsides and I am back on familiar ground. I honestly don't know how to handle the real world, I stagger through my day, my heart beats unsteadily and I struggle to breathe. If the telephone rings, my heart skips a beat. If I see an unknown car on my drive I hide behind my curtains while staring like crazy at the stranger heading for my door. I look for fixed points the whole afternoon and when night-time finally comes I'm utterly disorientated. Because I lasted a whole day, because the disaster never happened. I take nothing for granted. Not the rest of my life, not tomorrow. Or you. And when the disaster finally strikes,' I say, 'I know what I'll say.'

'And what will you say?' asks Alvar gently.

'I always knew this would happen.'

CHAPTER 11

The next day when he let himself into the gallery, his entire body was brimming with tremendous excitement. He practically walked sideways across the floor in an attempt not to look at the painting. What if the bridge had gone? What if Ole Krantz had let himself in after the gallery had closed and taken the painting home to keep for himself? But it was there, in exactly the same spot, leaning against the wall, monumental and overwhelming. Alvar slowly walked up to it. He instantly felt a sense of inner calm, the painting made him feel whole. The severed bridge was somewhere he could deposit all those feelings he would never be able to articulate. Oh, he enjoyed reading books, he liked seeing himself reflected in the characters in them. But this. This wordless art, the immediate impression, how it could have such an effect on him, it was inconceivable. And I'm not an emotional person, he thought, I'm a quiet man with my life under control. I sleep well, I'm content. On my own, admittedly, but I'm nevertheless a hard-working and valid member of society. Not terribly interested in politics, or social issues for that matter, but I take good care of myself and I do my duty. So why do I need this painting so badly? How can this artist know how I feel?

He forced himself to walk away from the painting and went upstairs to the kitchen to make coffee. As he opened the cupboard he spotted the blue mug. He chose a different one, settled down by the table and opened the newspaper, which had been delivered to his flat earlier that morning. Every now and then he would look up at the three monitors. It was impossible to enter Gallery Krantz without the doorbell ringing, but as a precaution he kept an eye on the rooms all the same. Seventy thousand kroner, he thought. After all it's only money, mere digits in a computer, I've never actually seen it. Why don't I just ring Krantz right now and tell him that I want to buy the painting? Perhaps he'll give me an employee discount? Perhaps I can pay for the painting by instalments so I don't have to part with all my money at once? Surely we'll find a way around it? Will it make me happy? he wondered. Wasn't it rather that the painting had created a desire in him that he never thought he would experience? A desire to connect with other people? It felt as though he had been willing it to happen, he had longed for such an experience. Finding this one crucial painting. And now it was here, sitting downstairs. Why could he not just accept that and buy it? He drank his coffee slowly while he waited for the first customer of the day. He kept running his hand across his naked scalp, he could not get used to his bald head.

The first customers of the day turned out to be a young couple. Alvar put them somewhere in their twenties and they were clearly very much in love. He noted such things with great composure. It never made him feel embarrassed or insecure, or shy. Anyway, a young couple arrived. A slender, dark-haired woman and a tall blond man. They entered the gallery and as he sat there watching them on the left monitor, he realised that they rarely visited galleries. The way they moved around the space was hesitant. Nor had they realised that the paintings had been hung so as to present themselves most favourably, the intention being that you would begin by the left-hand wall and then move clockwise until you reached the staircase. That would take you to the first floor, if you were interested in looking at prints. They meandered from one wall to another. He let them wander around for a few minutes before he went downstairs. The moment he appeared they became shy, but he gave them a reassuring smile and he immediately knew that this couple would never be mesmerised by the severed bridge. Besides, they were unlikely to be able to afford it; he was safe — for now.

'Just take your time,' Alvar said, 'there are two more floors. On the second floor you'll find mainly foreign art if you have an interest in that.'

They nodded and continued to wander around, holding hands all the while. Alvar rearranged some silk roses in a jar; he displayed some brochures on a table. The couple moved from painting to painting, they did not speak, but studied the pictures with genuine interest. Finally the young woman stopped and remained in front of a picture for a long time. A sketch. Alvar suppressed a smile, women invariably stopped in front of this picture. At first glance it was an insignificant image in pale shades. It depicted a bird's nest and in the nest lay four turquoise eggs. The young woman was utterly taken with it.

'You have to see this,' she said, looking at the man. A frown instantly appeared on his forehead.

'Well,' he said, trying not to hurt her feelings, he was a considerate man, 'it's very pretty, but you can barely make it out. I mean, if we're going to have a painting above the sofa it should be a bit bigger, shouldn't it?'

'Yes,' she agreed, but continued to gaze at the picture all the same. 'I just really like it.' However, she already knew that it was a lost cause. They wandered on. Alvar fetched a duster so that he could potter about and do some work in the knowledge that his presence would be unobtrusive and yet he would remain accessible. They had reached the merry-go-round. The young man stopped and squatted in front of it.

'Now there,' he said, 'just take a look at this one!'

The woman joined him. She stared carefully at the painting with the skeletons for a long time. Then she wrinkled her nose.

'I think it's a bit gross,' she said.

'Gross?' He glared down at her, he was at least a foot taller than her and now it was his turn to look surprised; he simply did not understand why she found the painting gross.

'They've got maggots crawling out of their eyes,' she shuddered. 'Look.' She pointed. He leaned towards the painting.

'But you can hardly see them,' he argued. 'Only close up.'

'We can't buy a painting that we only like as long as we don't look at it close up,' she countered. This logic silenced the man.

'Anyway, it would be far too expensive,' she said. 'It's an oil painting.'

'But that's what we're looking for,' he said. 'If we wanted to buy a print we might as well have gone to IKEA. That's why we've come here.'

They reached no consensus and walked on.

'*The Merry-go-round* costs seventeen thousand kroner,' Alvar informed them from the corner where he was wiping dust off a frame.

The woman rolled her eyes. The man looked put out. But Alvar did not want to sell them the merry-go-round. They deserved something else, something better, he felt.

'How about this?' he said, walking over to a painting on the furthest wall, which faced the car park. It was a drawing by Bendik Sjur. The couple followed him enthusiastically. They looked at the picture for a long time. A creature was seemingly crawling towards them on a dark wooden floor. A strange creature, skinny, and soft and thin, like something out of the underworld. It looked right into the eyes of the observer with a devil-may-care look. Alvar was a great admirer of Bendik Sjur.

'Christ,' the young man said, 'he looks like Gollum. Gollum from *Lord of the Rings*,' he explained and looked at Alvar. Once more they were silent as they watched the strange creature. It was drawn with a delicate, light touch, it had a soul and a distinctive character. It simultaneously exuded calm and tension. The young couple was lost, they gazed spellbound at the painting and squeezed each other's hands. But they moved on, they were not the type to be rushed into anything. So while they slowly and patiently walked through both the first and second floors, Alvar went back into the kitchen and drank another cup of coffee. When he saw that they had returned to the ground floor and had stopped in front of the drawing once more, he went downstairs.

'Yes, we're interested in this,' the young man said pointing at Sjur's drawing. 'We think it's really cool.'

Well, Alvar thought. A cool picture. He supposed that was one way of putting it. Yet they still seemed to be hesitating. Money was probably an issue.

'Four thousand,' Alvar said. The man instantly brightened up. That would do nicely. He looked at his beloved. She, too, liked the creature from the underworld, if that was where he came from, he defied definition in any way; he was half-human, half-beast or rather a type of insect with deranged eyes. They bought it. Alvar took it down from the wall, wrapped it and wrote them a receipt. The man carried the picture out. The couple had frowned when they had seen the severed bridge; they had never been a real threat. Yet Alvar felt his body tense up every time the doorbell rang. At any moment someone might walk in, stand there open-mouthed staring at it, just like he had done. Why don't I just buy it, he wondered, am I really that gutless? I who have always claimed that you should follow your heart and not your head when it comes to buying art.

He went back upstairs to the kitchen and unpacked his lunch. Three open sandwiches with pastrami ham and slivers of cucumber. He halved the slices and placed them on a plate; he ate quietly. At times he thought about the young woman who had visited the gallery twice. But she had not come back, even though it was starting to get colder now. Perhaps she's got herself some warmer clothes, he thought. Some more sensible footwear. He went to the toilet after finishing his lunch and was once again confronted by his naked head in the mirror. His hair was so short at the back of his head that it pricked his palm. Ah, well. Nothing to fret about, *sic transit gloria mundi*. And I don't look all that bad, he comforted himself, and once again he marvelled at how a total stranger could make one throwaway remark about his hair which caused him to rush off to have it cut. What about the rest of his appearance? He looked at his reflection in the mirror, with his checked shirt and the black tie. He had never had much fashion sense and had never aspired to. He liked not standing out. In the autumn he wore a grey trench coat and in the winter a woollen coat, which at the time had been a great expense, but a good investment because it was a very fine quality and warm. In addition he wore smart, pressed trousers and black shoes. Brown leather gloves on his hands. A thin woollen scarf around his neck. He never took his car to work, he needed the exercise, so he always dressed warmly. As he came out from the lavatory he heard the bell ring. Ole Krantz came up the stairs with a picture tucked under his arm. He put it down in the kitchen and looked at Alvar. At the same time he planted his feet firmly on the floor and put his hands on his hips. He was a tall, broad man, masculine and ruddy.

'Good heavens,' he said, 'you've had a summer haircut in November.'

Alvar thought he detected a quick smile flash across his face, so he stared down at the floor while he ran his hand across his head in an apologetic fashion.

'I thought it was a good idea,' he said.

'Absolutely,' Krantz said assuredly.

And that was all that was ever said on the matter. He went to the cupboard to fetch a mug and poured himself some coffee.

'So what else is new?' he wanted to know. He knew the gallery was in the best of hands.

'I've sold a Bendik Sjur,' he said.

'Well done,' Krantz said as he sat down by the kitchen table. 'Who bought it?'

'A young couple.'

'I thought so.'

In the silence that followed Alvar thought about the bridge. He decided to make his move.

'That painting,' he hesitated, 'the severed bridge. I've been thinking about it.'

'Aha?' Krantz said and waited for him to continue.

'I've been wondering if I should buy it.'

Krantz raised his eyebrows. 'Really?' he said, surprised. 'It's expensive,' he added.

'I know,' Alvar said. 'But I have some money put aside.'

'Really?' Krantz said once again.

'It was just something I've been thinking about,' Alvar said, wanting to retract. It was very expensive. It would clear him out, it would put him in a financially vulnerable position that he had not been in for years. Where an unexpected dental bill would have the power to throw his monthly budget. Was it really worth it? Yes, it was worth it, it meant so much, this work of art was worth the price which Krantz and the artist together had assigned to it.

'I need a few days to make up my mind,' Alvar said, experiencing a sudden burst of initiative.

'I'm sure it'll be here for a while,' Krantz said, 'so there's no need for you to rush. We'll sell it sooner or later, it's a unique painting.'

As if Alvar did not already know. But he did not want to share his feelings for the picture with Krantz, he felt it was too intimate. So he spoke in the appropriate language for an art dealer.

'A rare picture,' he declared drinking his coffee. 'They are few and far between. Just consider the concept. What do you think inspired the picture? I mean, is there actually such a severed bridge?'

'Perhaps in a war zone somewhere,' Krantz suggested. 'They're always blowing up bridges. I don't know an awful lot about Lindström, he's the quiet type. But he travels extensively, that I do know. The picture needs plenty of light, but I'm sure you've thought of that.'

'Of course,' Alvar said.

'And it's gathered plenty of dust,' Krantz continued. 'Buy a fresh loaf of bread and make a ball from the crumbs. Work your way across the whole painting in circular movements. Best way to clean an oil painting. Bread absorbs well and you return a little fat to the painting's surface.'

'Fresh bread,' Alvar said. 'I'll bear that in mind.

That evening he poured himself a sherry.

The painting was never out of his thoughts. The bare wall above the fireplace was ready and waiting for the most breathtaking work of art. Am I ever going to take a single risk in my life, he wondered, follow my instinct for once? I never have. I wander around the town and I look at displays in shops. I look at beautiful furniture and rugs. But there's nothing wrong with what I already have. There's nothing wrong with it, I tell myself, it's too good to be replaced, it will last me years. I can't in all clear conscience buy a new armchair because there's nothing wrong with the one I have. Besides, I like this chair. He patted one of the armrests as if to reinforce his argument. He drank more sherry and thought further. But there's only one painting. No painting has ever captivated me like this, I've never been captivated by anything else. A Weidemann or an Ekeland has never had such an effect on me. It might never happen again, I'm past forty, this is my chance.

The sherry warmed his stomach and he sensed that he was moving towards a final decision. He poured himself another sherry, a large one. Of course, he could pay for the painting in instalments, thus avoiding having to part with all his money at once. On the other hand he had never liked the idea of paying by instalments, so he dismissed the idea as quickly as it had emerged. He would buy the painting and pay cash or he would not buy it at all. I'm going to buy it, he told himself, I'm going to buy it tomorrow. I'll go to the gallery and put a red sticker on the painting, then I'll go to the bank and transfer the money. Ole Krantz will give me a hand transporting the painting home. I want it. If I don't buy it, I'll regret it till the day I die. Regret it keenly and bitterly. Why does it have to be so hard? What a coward I am. And the sherry is starting to cloud my judgement. You should never make any important decisions when you're drunk, never ever. I need to sleep on it.

He cleaned his teeth and went to bed after having folded his clothes neatly. He closed his eyes and fell asleep. That night he had a strange dream. He dreamed that he went to the bank. He took out all his savings and put them in a bag. A brown bag, with a press stud at the top. He left the bank and made his way towards the gallery.

Suddenly he tripped on the pavement and fell. The bag split open and the notes flew off in all directions, seized by an unexpected and violent gust of wind. He got back on his feet and started chasing them, he found a note here another there, he clawed them back feverishly. His heart pounded fast as he scrambled for the notes. But they were impossible to catch. They surged in the wind, they were carried far, far away and he was left with just a few crumpled notes in his hand. The bag was empty. At that point he woke up, fraught and distressed. Then he had to laugh. What a ridiculous dream, he thought. But afterwards he began analysing what the dream might actually have meant. Perhaps it was telling him that he should not buy the painting. That he was literally throwing money away. That he ought to spend his money on something else. But what? There was nothing else he wanted. Irritably he tried to go back to sleep. When he woke up later he could still recall the dream and it continued to disturb him.

He was in two minds as he made his way to the gallery that morning. I'll leave it to fate, he thought eventually; he was rapidly losing patience with the whole business. Why was this painting, which he had fallen in love with at first sight, starting to become a problem for him? Presumably the only solution was to buy it. Could it be that simple? He passed the courthouse and realised that he was cold. Then he remembered that he had forgotten his woollen scarf. He pulled his coat tighter at the throat and walked faster to warm up. He decided to turn up the radiators in the gallery, it was important that people got a pleasant feeling of warmth when they stepped inside, when they put their feet on the stone floor. He let himself in, looked at the bridge with a mixture of reverence and misgiving and ran upstairs to the kitchen.

CHAPTER 12

I put the cat on my lap and force his jaws apart.

He instantly starts to scratch and kick me, his razor-sharp claws dig into the delicate skin on my arms and make my eyes water. I grit my teeth and endure it. How can a four-kilo cat have this much strength? I wonder. It's incredible, he's fighting for his life. Even though I'm doing this for his sake. I take the tiny pill from the table, drop it down his throat and force his jaws shut. I massage his neck and throat with my other hand until the cat swallows the pill. Alvar is watching me, petrified.

'What are you doing?' he croaks.

'Something entirely necessary. I'm worming him,' I reply. 'He's lost a bit of weight recently, he might have worms.'

'Oh,' he says, taking a step back. I seize the moment to let the cat go, he jumps down on to the floor and races to the garden door, he wants to get out. I open the door for him and watch him disappear into the bushes.

'So how are you?' I ask Alvar. 'Why don't you sit down?'

He perches on the very edge of the sofa, picking at his nails.

'I need an honest answer,' he says fixing me with his eyes. 'Am I miserly?'

I sit down again, dig out a cigarette from the packet on the table.

'I don't think so. No, you're not miserly. But you're wondering why you can't make a decision about the painting, aren't you? The severed bridge you so desperately want?'

He nods in agreement. 'Yes. I think there has been enough procrastination. In fact, I'm genuinely disappointed with myself because I can't act. Other people buy things they want whereas I've still got all my old furniture, most of which I've inherited from my mother. And I have enough money.'

'In other words,' I say, lighting the cigarette, 'you have everything you need in order to buy the painting. And now you don't understand what's holding you back?'

He hitches up his trousers before crossing his legs; he flexes his feet in the shiny shoes.

'I keep asking myself,' he says pensively, 'whether the money might be intended for something else.'

'What would that be?' I say, feigning innocence. I am no longer able to meet his eyes.

'Well, if only I knew. I can't think what it might be, but something is holding me back. Something vague and intangible. What do you think?' he says, looking at me. His gaze is terribly direct.

'Deep down you have an inkling,' I say. 'You know that something is bound to happen further into the story and subconsciously you're thinking that the money will come in useful later. That's why you haven't got the courage to spend it. You're waiting. You feel restless. If you buy the painting you will have achieved precisely what you wanted and everything will grind to a halt. And we're only about one hundred pages into your story. You want more space, so you let the painting stay in the gallery. While you're waiting for something else to happen.'

He watches me suspiciously; there is a deep furrow between his brows.

'True, a hundred pages isn't much to get excited about,' he concedes. 'So perhaps you're being brutal enough to show me the painting, yet you won't let me own it. I think that's hard for me to deal with because it's an important painting.'

'I understand,' I console him. 'But you'll just have to learn how. I once desperately wanted a painting by Knut Rose. I found it many years ago and it's called *The Helper*. I never came to own it, but it no longer drives me crazy. Let me put it this way: it's a mild grief.'

'A mild grief,' he echoes. 'Which you think I ought to tackle without whining?'

'Exactly.'

'But I'm not very good at dealing with emotions,' he says.

I flick the ash from my cigarette. 'Do they frighten you?'

'Yes. I don't want too many of them and I don't want them to be very strong. I prefer it when everything is slow and steady.'

'What about happiness?' I smile. 'That's an emotion too. Don't you want that?'

He shrugs shyly. He is actually a well-built man, but he never straightens up, never lets anyone see his broad shoulders.

'I suppose so. If it should come my way.'

'Come your way? Happiness is not some bird, Alvar, which suddenly lands on your shoulder, though poets like to put it that way. You need to set something in motion to achieve the good things in life. You have to act.'

He finds a speck of dust on his trousers and brushes it off.

'But you'll help me, won't you? That's why I came here. Do you see any happiness in my future?'

I close my eyes and concentrate. A host of images appears on my retina.

'Perhaps.'

He blinks. 'What do you mean, perhaps? That doesn't sound terribly reassuring.'

'A half-finished story is a delicate thing,' I explain. 'Never anticipate events, it's dangerous. Everything can burst like a bubble. Besides, I don't want to give you false hopes, or make promises I can't keep.'

'Can you give me anything at all?' he pleads.

I consider this. 'Yes, I can actually. There is one thing that has been on my mind a long time. But I don't know if it'll make you feel better, perhaps it'll only cause you more anxiety. It's a small, but well-intentioned gesture. Something which might turn out to be useful.'

He looks at me with anticipation. I get up from my chair and walk over to my desk. Scribble something on a yellow Post-it note, return and hand it to him. He grabs it hungrily.

'A telephone number?' he says, baffled.

I nod. 'Put this note by your phone and make sure you don't lose it.'

He folds the paper and puts it in his jacket pocket.

'A telephone number,' he repeats pensively. 'That's not a lot, is it?'

I protest fiercely. 'You're wrong. This number will lead you to another human being who will answer when you call. Someone who can think and act. A compassionate person. This number can save your life, Alvar.'

He is startled. He looks scared and his eyes widen.

'Are you going to test me?' he whispers.

'Alvar my dear,' I reply patiently, 'you're worse than a child. And I know that you're in a tricky place right now. It's like you're half finished. You're dangling, literally, in thin air. But if it's any comfort, Alvar, I'm dangling too. I'm halfway through my story, I'm still in the deep end. I'm struggling to sustain my faith in my own project. Doubt creeps up on me like an invisible gas, it goes to my head and it fills me with fear. Now what's this? I ask myself. Who would want to read this? Can I expect to demand my readers' time and attention with this story? Have I drawn you so clearly that they can see you as well as I can, that they will come to care about you? Have I found the right words?'

'But you love your work, too, you said so the other day.'

'I'm a very inconsistent person,' I declare. 'Yes, I love it, I hate it, I struggle. When it's at its best it sends shivers of delight down my spine, at its worst I'm tearing my hair out. I get up in the morning and I go over to the mirror. I look at my weary face and I tell myself that I can't do it, that it's too hard.'

He frowns. He looks sulky, he is pouting.

'So you don't think I'm worth it?'

'It might be the case that you're only important to me. And perhaps that's enough.'

'I know that I'm not important or amazing or exciting. But there's only one Alvar Eide,' he says, a little hurt.

'That's true. And I've always been of the opinion that every single one of us has a whole novel inside. Every single person you meet has their own life-and-death drama. Just take a look at people, Alvar, as you wander through the town. Look at their eyes, at how they bow their heads; their brisk, but also slightly hesitant, walk. Their anxieties. Their secrets. Oh, I want to stop every single one of them, lift up their chins and look them in the eyes. What do you carry, what do you hide, what do you dream about, please would you tell me so I can write it down, please let me show you to the world?'

'And then you can only pick a few,' he nods. 'What you can manage in your own lifetime. Now I'm starting to feel honoured because you chose me.'

'May I remind you that you anticipated events and made your own way into my house,' I say.

'True, but I was second in the queue anyway. My time would have come regardless.'

'Probably. So, is it time for us to move on? We have to go out into the cold, Alvar, it's the middle of winter.'

He gets up from the sofa. Takes a few steps towards the door.

'I really value our conversations.'

'So do I,' I reply, 'but I might end up deleting them.'

'What?'

He looks shocked.

'They might turn out to be superfluous. You might manage just fine with your own story and your own drama.'

He opens the door, turns one final time.

'It's freezing cold,' he says and shivers. 'Can you feel it?'

He walks down the steps and pauses on the drive for a while. The porch light shines on his bald head.

'I've felt so cold ever since I had my hair cut,' he says.

CHAPTER 13

It was the middle of January and still very cold.

The town was bathed in pale sunlight, white, glazed and shiny. She arrived at half past four in the afternoon just as Alvar was getting ready to close up. This time she was looking ravaged, pale and purple with cold. She looked at him with her kohl-black eyes, they were watering from exhaustion and the frost. She wore no gloves. Her thin neck was bare, a weak stem with thin, blue veins. Alvar rushed off to get her a cup of coffee, it didn't occur to him not to, but he felt a deep sense of unease, it was like sliding towards something unknown, something unmanageable. She took the mug with stiff fingers and went over to the staircase, where she sat down on the second step.

'You ought to get yourself some gloves,' he said, 'and a scarf.'

'I know,' she said indifferently, slurping her coffee. 'But I can't be bothered.'

'Can't be bothered?' he said, surprised because he did not think putting on a scarf was a major challenge. For a while he pondered. Then he decided that he wanted to do something nice for her, something more than just getting her a cup of coffee. After all, she had decided to come back, so events would have to run their course. He made up his mind to act on this whim, even though it was not in his nature. He went up to the kitchen where his outdoor clothes hung and returned with his thin woollen scarf. She accepted it reluctantly. Then she pressed it against her nose and inhaled it for a long time.

'It smells good,' she said, 'it smells of aftershave.'

He nodded. 'It's long,' he said, 'you can wrap it around your neck several times.'

She did so. It looked good on her. The scarf was camel-coloured wool and it suited her. It contrasted beautifully with her pale skin and her ice-blue eyes.

'My gloves are too big for you,' he said, 'so I'll keep them for myself.'

She nodded and drank her coffee, drank it quickly and greedily until she had emptied the mug. Then she put the mug on the step and began staggering around the gallery on thin, unsteady legs. Alvar watched her. He did not mind her being there, she was not making any trouble. She looked somewhat haggard, but she could pass for an ordinary customer if you didn't look at her too carefully. But up close you could tell. The fine veins in her temples, her lips drained of colour. Her ankle boots clicking against the stone floor. She had reached the bridge.

'You said you were going to buy it,' she challenged him.

He shrugged.

'I'm still thinking about it,' he said truthfully.

'And you can't make up your mind?'

'Well, it's expensive,' he said, 'that's why. It's a lot of money to spend in one go.'

'But you can afford it,' she said, 'you said you'd been saving.'

'Yes,' he said, 'I have been saving up. I've been saving for a rainy day. If I buy the painting, I have nothing to fall back on.'

She tasted the words 'fall back on'.

'Is that important?' she smiled. Mockingly, he thought.

'I've nothing to fall back on,' she admitted, 'I live from hand to mouth.'

He gave her a puzzled look. 'So how do you survive? Do you work?'

She laughed out loud. 'God, no,' she hiccuped, 'I can't be bothered with that. People work because they think they have to. I'd rather claim benefits.'

'That can't be very lucrative,' Alvar declared, 'when you can't even afford to buy yourself a scarf and a pair of gloves in the winter.'

'Of course I can afford to buy clothes,' she said, 'but I prefer to spend money on other things. It's all about your priorities.'

'Really?' He looked at her once more. At her incredibly thin legs and the pointy high-heeled boots. Perhaps she was one of those women who sold themselves when their benefit money ran out. He did not like the thought of it, so he instantly pushed it from his mind. But that was how they got money for drugs, he had read about it in the papers. It was truly awful. She was a lovely young woman, with a doll-like face and a tiny pale mouth. She was practically a child, he thought. Could she really be one of those women who got in and out of cars? At night, down on Bragernes Square, where they all congregated? He did not want to judge her. She might have been driven to it by some terrible event. Perhaps she had had an awful childhood, perhaps her father had hit her, or something worse, he didn't know what it could be, but his imagination was starting to run away with him. He didn't think of her as second-rate. But it upset him that she lived in such wretched circumstances when in all likelihood she was just as bright as he was in every possible way. She should have been living another life. But she did not seem to think so. She just drifted from one day to the next without purpose or meaning, without hopes or dreams. And perhaps this was enough for her, as long as she got her drugs, as long as she found relief. Her body was slowly breaking down, but it didn't seem to trouble her. True, it was not as if he knew her well and understood everything, but she did not seem doomed like so many of the others.

'I need to go,' she said suddenly. She handed him the mug and thanked him. She had to step to the side to regain her balance. He watched her disappear.

Later that day, while he was eating a simple meal at the table in the living room, he started thinking about her again. He wondered what her name was, where she lived, things like that. She had said she lived all over the place. There was something ephemeral about her, something transient. He wondered why she kept returning to the gallery. Was it really just to get a cup of coffee? Perhaps that was all there was to it. And he had welcomed her, even though he could have told her to get out. He was just about to leave the table when the doorbell rang. This did not happen often, and when it did it was his neighbour asking to borrow something, or a salesman. He composed himself and went out into the hall. He opened the door and gasped. She was standing outside, in her grey coat with his old woollen scarf around her neck. Alvar was speechless. He stood in the doorway staring at her as if he was hypnotised. She laughed when she saw his surprise, tilted her head and cackled, and he saw her teeth clearly, they were tiny and sharp.

'Hi,' she said cheerfully. 'I thought you might be in.'

Alvar had lost the power to speak. He rocked backwards and forwards on the threshold as he clung to the door frame with one hand.

'You're *here*?' he eventually managed to stammer. A dart of unease pierced his chest. A myriad bewildering thoughts rushed through his mind.

'Yes,' she said simply, letting her hands drop. It looked as though she was expecting to be invited in. Alvar did not want to let her in. He would never have believed that this could happen. Her coming to the gallery was one thing. It was open to everyone and he had been unable to make himself throw her out. But here. In his flat, his home, his castle. He hesitated. She stood there rubbing her cold hands, impatiently, in the doorway.

'How did you know I lived here?' he asked, baffled. He didn't mean to be rude, but he didn't have a clue what was going on.

'I followed you,' she said. 'A few days ago. I saw you go into this flat. And you didn't notice,' she added, 'you don't notice anything.'

She looked at him with her ice-blue eyes. 'Your name is Alvar Eide,' she stated.

'Yes,' he stuttered. He was still clinging to the door frame. His brain was throbbing violently, trying to find a solution.

'Can I come in, please?' she asked directly. And he thought, no, no you can't come in, this is my flat, my boundary is this threshold, I don't want you to intrude. But he did not have the strength to say it to her face. A skinny, fragile young woman was standing at his door wanting to come in. And he was not a cruel man, and he didn't look down on women like her. Nor did he think that she was out to cause him any trouble either, it didn't seem to be her intention. Perhaps she just wanted another cup of coffee. Or to warm up. He opened the door fully and she entered the hall. She gave no indication of wanting to take off her coat. Alvar liked that. That suggested that she would only be staying a little while.

He went into the living room, still marvelling at her presence, and she followed him and sat down on his sofa without waiting to be asked. She sat down as if it was the most natural thing in the world and inspected the room. Alvar collapsed in an armchair. Then he leaned forwards and started tidying away the newspapers, he didn't know what else to do. She followed him with her eyes. He grew nervous. He started to think she was laughing at him. Suddenly she put her feet on his coffee table. He looked directly at the narrow, spiky heels of her ankle boots. Alvar had never put his feet on the coffee table, he thought it was a nasty habit, and besides, she was wearing boots. But he said nothing, he just sat there waiting for something to happen. Perhaps there was a reason for her visit? Was there something specific she wanted? He decided that maybe he ought to make some coffee, as you do when you have guests. But he did not, he stayed in his armchair with a strong feeling of apprehension coursing through his body. He felt invaded in his own home, yes, indeed he did. She was calmly sitting there staring at him as if he were an exhibit in a museum. When she had finished staring at him, she started looking around the room. She looked at his furniture and his possessions with an open, curious gaze.

'So this is where your painting will go?' she asked out of the blue. She pointed at the vacant space above the fireplace.

'Yes,' he said, turning in his armchair. 'That's what I had in mind. But I need a few days to think it through properly.'

'You'd better hurry up,' she suggested. 'Or it'll be sold.'

I know that, he said to himself, but he did not want to appear argumentative. Instead he decided to ask her a few questions. He felt he had a right, given that she had come all the way into his living room in this brazen manner.

'What's your name?' he asked as he folded his hands in his lap.

'Lindys,' she replied.

'Lindys,' he repeated. He had never heard of such a name.

'Or Merete,' she said. 'Or Elsa. It depends.'

He was confused. 'Depends on what?'

'Well,' she said, flexing the pointy toes of her boots, 'it depends what I feel like that day.'

He lowered his head slowly. He was not feeling very well.

'I see,' he said and could clearly hear that his voice sounded tart. 'So what do you prefer today?'

She thought about it briefly. 'Helle,' she said.

'Very well,' he said. 'Helle. That's settled then.'

'So your name's always the same?' she asked and smiled playfully. She revealed her sharp teeth again.

'Of course,' he said earnestly. 'People usually keep the same name their entire life. And I know you're only joking.'

She laughed once more. Suddenly she took her feet off the coffee table. He experienced an instant sense of relief.

'You got any sweets?' she asked.

Alvar was taken aback. Sweets? Was she being serious?

He hesitated again. 'Sweets?'

'Yes. Sweets, fruit gums, chocolate,' she explained. A little perplexed because he was being so dim.

'No, no, I don't have any sweets,' he replied, shaking his head.

'None at all?' she pressed.

He felt his irritation rise again as he carefully tried to recall the contents of his kitchen cupboards.

'I might have a packet of raisins,' he remembered.

'Raisins?' She mimed munching them. 'Yeah, all right. Can I have them? I need sugar and I need it now.'

He sat there gawping at her. She was demanding that he fetched her some raisins. He did not begrudge her the raisins, but he was not entirely sure where she was going with this. He went out into the kitchen and found the packet. It was one of those snack boxes you put in children's packed lunches. He returned and handed it to her and she opened it immediately. She dug her greedy fingers into the contents.

'Chocolate is better,' she said, 'but raisins will have to do.'

Yes, they certainly will, Alvar thought. He sat watching her as she ate the raisins. She ate all of them and tossed the empty packet onto the coffee table. Again he felt a surge of irritation. She was so careless. She was his guest, but she was acting as if she owned the place. She certainly made herself at home. I guess I'm just being petty, he thought, I'm not used to having guests. I scarcely know how guests would behave. At the same time a chill passed through him. He was always alone and he was always in control and now he was being overpowered by a skinny girl and he did not have the guts to stand up to her. He decided to ask her where she lived. Even though he had asked her before and she had replied, 'Oh, all over the place.' All the same, he was sure that she lived somewhere, she was just unwilling to tell him. He felt very awkward in her presence. Surely his knees were too sharp and his arms too long?

He changed his mind and instead he asked her, 'How old are you?'

'How old? Well, how old do you think?'

Having to guess made him feel uncomfortable. Then he thought, I don't have to guess, I can tell her that I've no idea. But then he looked at her again and estimated her to be twenty.

'Eighteen,' she replied.

Alvar nodded. Perhaps she was lying about this too, like she lied about her name. She was still smiling and he noticed that she had bits of raisins stuck between her teeth. It didn't look attractive, but he couldn't tell her that. He was restless. He wondered how long she intended to sit there lounging on his sofa.

'You're over forty, aren't you?' she said, watching him.

'Forty-two,' he replied truthfully.

'Isn't it about time you got married and started a family?'

He squirmed in his armchair. He was not enjoying this conversation and he refused to expose himself.

'Don't do it,' she said the next moment. 'Family equals trouble. Responsibilities. No money. Endless guilt and a life of drudgery.'

'Does it?'

She ran her fingers through her hair, which was sticking out like a bristle brush.

'I prefer brief acquaintances,' she said. 'Same as you, I can tell from looking at you.'

'Can you?'

She looked around his flat, her ice-blue eyes scanned his possessions and his furniture. 'Christ, you're tidy. Potted plants and embroidered cushions, would you believe it.'

Alvar was feeling increasingly uncomfortable. It was weird that she was sitting there; she had flown right through his door like some strange bird. Even though he wanted to chase her away there was a big knot of resistance inside him which stopped him.

She had walked over to the window. She stared down at the lightbulb factory.

'The Mazda parked down behind the house, is that yours?'

'Yes.'

He squeezed his hands in his lap and tried to be patient.

'I don't have a car,' she said. 'Too much hassle. Who lives downstairs? Do you ever talk to them?'

'The Greens,' he explained. 'We exchange a few words every now and then.'

'Making polite conversation,' she said, 'how awful.'

He nodded in agreement.

'You're really wound up because I'm here, aren't you?'

He was shocked. His instinctive reaction was to protest, but he could not manage it.

'You're one of those loners who keep everyone else at arm's length. That's quite all right, I'm the same.'

'You just took me by surprise,' he said cautiously. 'I don't get many visitors,' he added.

'None,' she said, looking at him. 'No one ever comes here, not a living soul. Am I right?'

Alvar blushed. She was so direct and so forward that she took his breath away.

'You don't need to make excuses,' she went on. 'People come in all shapes and sizes, and I'm the pot calling the kettle black. But most of the time I feel sorry for people. They make it so hard for themselves to be who they really are.'

'And you don't?' he asked before he could stop himself.

She walked over and sat down on the sofa again. 'My life isn't easy,' she said, 'but it is really straightforward. I live one hour at a time. Right now I'm in your cosy living room and I'm enjoying it. I've no idea where I'll be spending the night. But I'm not worried about it. Whereas you,' she said watching him, 'you're already thinking about tomorrow. You're making plans and you'll stick to them. Rather than living in the moment. Am I right? I know I'm right.'

Alvar bowed his head. He could not see how there was anything wrong with making plans. But her presence was really getting on his nerves now and he was desperate for a way to end the conversation.

'No,' he said abruptly and patted the armrests on his chair, 'and anyway, I've got things to do.'

He could not look her in the eyes as he said it, but he got up from his armchair to signal that her visit was over. She just looked at him with wide eyes.

'Really?' she said, puzzled. She did not get up. 'What is it you need to do?'

'Well,' he hesitated. 'Some paperwork.'

She considered this. To his immense relief Alvar saw that she was getting up. He thought, she'll be gone soon and I'll be on my own again and if she rings the doorbell another time, I won't let her in. I won't open the door because I'm in charge here. Then he realised that he would not be able to see who was outside. He did not have a spyhole in his door. Never mind. He decided not to open his door to anyone. No one ever turned up anyway, and if someone did ring the doorbell in the next few days it would probably be this Lindys. Or Elsa. Or Helle. Whatever her name was. She went out in the hall and he followed her. Suddenly she stopped, turned and fixed her eyes on him.

'Could you lend me a grand?'

Alvar gasped for air. Was she out of her mind? Were there no limits to her importunity?

'I don't think I have that much cash on me,' he blurted out. He made an apologetic gesture. She kept looking at him.

'Can't you check?' she asked. 'I'm totally skint and I need a fix.'

Alvar started shaking. His wallet was in his coat pocket, it hung in the hall less than a metre from where they were standing. And he did not understand why he acted as he did. At that moment all he could think of was getting her out of his flat at any cost. He stuck his hand in the inside pocket and pulled out his wallet. She watched it hungrily. He opened the note section and quickly counted the contents. Seven hundred and fifty kroner plus a bit of loose change in the coin compartment. He pulled out the notes. She stared at them. And before he had time to blink she had snatched them from him. He was left startled and empty-handed. Go, he was screaming inside, just go. Please, please go!

She placed her hand on the door handle and opened the door.

'You're all right, Alvar,' she said softly. Her voice was suddenly tender and almost feline.

Alvar melted instantly. It had been a very long time since anyone had last paid him a compliment. Had anyone ever done so? He was not feeling very well. Yet at the same time he was moved.

Then she was gone. She practically darted around the corner of the house like a squirrel. He remained in the hall for a while to calm himself down. I'll never see that money again, he thought. He was well aware of it. Yet he worried all the same. She would spend it on drugs. Yes, of course she would, he thought, in which case I haven't done a good deed after all, I'm contributing to her ruin, that's what I'm doing. He went into his living room and walked over to the window. Leaned against the windowsill and gasped for air. He watched her disappear down the hill. He followed her with his eyes. He could not shake off the feeling that he had done something very stupid. That's it, he thought, you'll never get rid of her now. You let her into your warm home. You go looking in the cupboard for raisins, you lend her money. You can't let her in ever again or you'll be trapped. At the same time it was a rare experience for him that someone actively sought his company. Although it was not his company she was interested in. She wanted his money. He collapsed back into his chair and ran his hand over his bare scalp. She had not commented on his new hairstyle and for that he was deeply grateful.

CHAPTER 14

Another icy morning.

A day when the earth was a frozen shell, impenetrable. He snatched the newspaper from his letter box and set off down the hill towards Engene. He was wearing his winter coat, it was warm, but he missed his scarf. The chill gripped his neck tightly like a claw. He marched on and gradually his body began to warm up. Yesterday's discomfort was beginning to lift, but he was still feeling uneasy. There's no point in worrying about what might happen, he reasoned with himself, because it probably never will, I worked that one out long ago. However, this argument did not make him feel much better. I'm on thin ice, he thought, I have to tread carefully, not lose my head. Stay in control, maintain a firm grip. Thirty minutes later he let himself into the gallery. He was still feeling unsettled, as if he was expecting Lindys, or Elsa, or Helle to turn up at any moment. Something inside him was waiting for her. He did not want her to come, she was a disruption in his life, something unpredictable. But here, in the gallery, he could not refuse to open the door; she could open it herself and walk right in. Having allowed her in the first time it would be difficult to refuse her now. How stupid he had been, how naive.

He went into the workshop to find something to occupy himself with, he needed to be distracted. He cut glass and cardboard, he polished and glued and tagged. He tried to enjoy this tinkering, but he wasn't able to. Weidemann's painting with his own thumbprint had dried ages ago and now it hung out in the gallery next to the bridge. He kept peeking furtively outside. First she would appear like a shadow outside the window, then the bell would ring. But he saw no one. The hours passed. Perhaps I was worrying about nothing, he thought. Perhaps she was just in a tight spot, but she'll stay away from now on. She won't be coming here any more. She is far too unstable to form a bond with anyone. This logic comforted him. Other customers came and went, he made polite conversation with them, maintaining his usual defensive stance. You should never underestimate a customer, he thought, the most unassuming individual might turn out to possess an impressive knowledge of Norwegian art. His approach was always cautious, a kind of tentative dance. He did not initiate a conversation with a customer until they had exchanged a few pleasantries.

The customers started to thin out and he seized the opportunity to eat his packed lunch. He spent the afternoon replacing a number of light bulbs, there was a spotlight positioned above every single painting. He felt terribly pleased at the end of the day because she hadn't showed up. The painting of the bridge had begun to take second place in his mind; it seemed as if Lindys was taking up all the space, as if she was standing inside his head shouting in a manner that was impossible to ignore. As he was about to leave he paused a metre from the painting. The pillars and a stump jutting out above the void, a dense, mystical fog. Faint contours of rocks and the mainland, but no horizon, no divide between sky and sea. The painting consumed him once more; it seemed to re-establish his inner balance.

He avoided Bragernes Square on his way home. He thought she might be drifting around there together with the dark-haired man who was not her brother. Have I really let a prostitute into my life? he thought as he walked home. No, I haven't let her in, she won't be coming back, I'm certain of this, those people are so restless. That day he shopped in Rimi. He bought fish fingers, which he would eat with potatoes and tartar sauce. Cheap and good for you, Alvar thought. He put his shopping in a bag and went back out into the street and started walking up the steep hill to his flat. At the letter box he met Green, his neighbour, who nodded to him briefly; Alvar nodded briefly back. Had he seen Lindys the previous day when she came to his door? Seen her slumped there in all her wretchedness? What must he have thought? She looked like a mere child, but the life she was living had so obviously left its mark on her. The Greens were probably gossiping at long length about her over dinner. He shuddered at the thought. He loathed the idea that other people might be discussing him, might be thinking about him, because it was beyond his control. For a moment he felt unwell, he felt disjointed and awkward, it was like falling apart. Then he pulled himself together and let himself in.

As he entered the flat he was suddenly filled with a sense of purpose, it rose within him like mercury in a thermometer. He went straight to the telephone and called his bank to find out the balance of his savings account.

'The available balance is: seventy thousand three hundred and sixty-seven kroner and thirty øre,' the voice announced. Alvar was delighted. Tomorrow morning he would go straight to his bank and transfer the money to Gallery Krantz. He would do it before he went to work. He would call his boss and ask him to drive the painting over to his flat, he would hang it on the wall. He would pull his armchair over to the fireplace, pour himself a sherry and sit down to look at the painting for the whole evening. Drown in it, lose himself in it, possess it. The thought filled him with joy. Then he thought of Lindys again. From now on whenever he saw a blonde head in the street, he knew he would jump. He was certain her name was Lindys. Alvar possessed a little insight into other people. The first name she had given him was her real name. The others were just to wind him up. Banter. She was like that. He decided to think of her as Lindys. When he thought of her. Because he was thinking of her and he did not understand that either. He was unaccustomed to another human being occupying his consciousness, someone just appearing and destroying his protracted and meticulous way of thinking. Again his thoughts were drawn to the painting. An extravagance, it struck him, the greatest in my life. A turning point. What will it be like to have the painting in my home? Perhaps it will drive me crazy? Now while it's hanging in the gallery I pine for it. But once it's on my own wall perhaps it will be different. Once it's here all the time, every time I lift my eyes and look above the fireplace. When I come into the living room in the morning and in the evening. Always this severed bridge. This dark, mysterious bridge, which ends abruptly in nothingness. Will it make me happy? Yes, a voice inside him said, it will make me happy.

CHAPTER 15

'Now I understand it all,' Alvar says, 'I'm no longer confused. She's my challenge, this Lindys.'

He assumes a dramatic mien. Contrary to all his good habits, he stuffs his hands into the pockets of his newly pressed trousers.

I look up from my newspaper. I nod.

'It certainly looks that way,' I say. 'Are you disappointed?'

He pulls his hands out of his pockets.

'I'm nervous. I'd been expecting something else. We don't speak the same language, she and I, and she makes me feel incredibly inept.'

I cannot help but smile.

'You *are* inept,' I say. 'But you can learn how to interact with other people. God knows you need the practice. I gave you a young, damaged woman because I needed a contrast. I needed something that might turn nasty.'

'Is she nasty?' he asks swiftly. His grey eyes darken.

'Not at all,' I assure him. 'But she lives in a rough world and she has been hardened by that. I would advise you to proceed with caution, Alvar. She probably knows a lot of people you wouldn't be able to handle.'

'Will there be more of them?' he asks.

'I'm not sure yet. I'm still thinking about it.'

His eyes look haunted. He takes a seat on the sofa, brushes the knees of his trousers. He is immaculately dressed as always, his shirt is white and freshly ironed.

'I suppose it's for the best if I break off all contact with her immediately,' he says after a pause. 'That I toughen myself up. That

I don't let her in, especially not into my flat. Do you know something? She puts her feet on my coffee table. It's a flame birch table from 1920. My mother would turn in her grave.'

I give him a wistful smile. 'Do you really think you can manage that? You don't have it in you, Alvar, you're not able to turn anyone away. Especially not a fragile young woman. Did you know,' I continue, 'at the start I contemplated sending you a child? A chubby, cheeky child.'

He looks up.

'A child? That wouldn't have worked very well,' he declares. 'I'm not good with children, I don't know how to behave in front of them. They always stare at you, it's like they're spying on you, and then they drool.'

'Yes, they do, don't they?'

He leans forward across the table and rests his hands on his thighs.

'In that case I'm really pleased that you changed your mind,' he says, relieved. 'I'll just have to manage as best I can. One day at a time. But am I allowed to make a wish?'

I hesitate. I fold my newspaper.

'As long as you don't wish for a happy ending,' I say eventually.

He runs his hand across his head. Still somewhat surprised at his baldness.

'No, I'm not asking for anything specific. A pleasant interlude, perhaps. A moment, an experience. Anything.'

'It won't be easy,' I reply, 'you're not terribly spontaneous, Alvar, and consequently not much happens in your carefully organised life.'

'But what if I make an effort?'

I nod. 'Let's go for it, let's see what happens. I'll offer you some bait and we'll see if you take it.'

'There was one other thing,' he remembers. 'I don't mean to be pushy, but when do you think we'll finish?'

I shrug. I mull it over. 'We're talking about a year probably. But this assumes I'm allowed to get on with my work without too many interruptions.'

'You think I'm pushy, don't you?'

I nod. 'You're pushy in a very disarming way,' I reply. 'I'll make an exception this time, but I've no intention of making it a habit. You spotted an opening, Alvar, and caught me off guard. Now I want to let events unfold, and I hope we both make it to the end. And please forgive me for saying this, but I never intended for you to be an ambitious project.'

He frowns and his face droops.

'So what was I meant to be?' he asks feebly.

'Well,' I venture, 'a lesser work. Something charming, unpretentious. A fleeting joy, a pleasant acquaintance. A minor literary game.'

'In other words,' he says, 'not a masterpiece?'

I am taken aback. 'That's asking for too much. Now you're making me nervous.'

'Allow me to add,' he says quickly, 'that I'm quite happy so far, I really am. I would hate to complain. But I suppose I had a faint hope that I might be heroic. In some way.'

'You are,' I tell him, 'in your everyday life. The question is what you'll do when you're tested.'

He looks at me closely.

'What does your gut instinct tell you?' he asks.

Again I cannot help but laugh. It is liberating, I laugh till the tears roll down my cheeks. 'You're unbelievable, you really are,' I hiccup. 'I've never experienced such pestering, you're worse than a spoiled child. Now please be patient, Alvar, I have a good feeling about you, I'll admit that much, and that's a good sign. All the same,' I add, 'based on my past records I can be quite brutal. Besides, I need to resolve something within myself along the way. Your weakness, this tendency to keep your distance from everyone and everything, your inability to act, your bashfulness, your modesty, your meticulousness, how do I honestly feel about that? Where do I place you in terms of morality, what do I think about the way you live your life? Are you a coward, are you arrogant, are you socially maladjusted or are you an attractive man with a pure heart? You have a fair amount of resources and talents, but you've isolated yourself and you're terrified of going off the rails.'

'So you want to derail me? You want me to crash?'

'I'm afraid you're right,' I reply.

Alvar turns pale. He takes a handkerchief out of his shirt pocket and wipes his forehead.

'But that doesn't mean that you won't recover,' I add. 'Perhaps you'll get back on another, an even better track. What do you say to that?'

'I'm not very fond of changes,' he admits.

'Me neither,' I say honestly. 'I know how you feel, Alvar, I empathise. But sometimes I get frustrated. You stay within the confines of your safe existence and as your audience I get fed up with it. Just let yourself go a little, I urge you; swear out loud, tell a customer to clear off, start slamming some doors.'

'That wasn't the done thing when I was growing up,' he says quickly.

'But you're a grown man now,' I retort.

He folds the handkerchief neatly and returns it to his shirt pocket.

'I'm no good at confrontation,' he says quietly. 'I like it here with you,' he adds, 'you never lash out.'

'I'm afraid to,' I say. 'Like you, I'm simply too scared.'

'Why, what do you think would happen?' he asks.

'There are times when I just want to scream, but I'm afraid to because I think the windows would shatter.'

'Why?' he insists.

'Because the scream would be so loud.'

He goes silent again, he looks distant.

'Do you want me to leave?'

'Yes, I do actually. If that's all right with you. I want to do another hour of work or two.'

He gets up from the sofa.

'Like I said,' he emphasises, 'we all have free will and I have chosen an ordered life with fixed routines. You're saying you want to derail me, but you'll have to expect that I will protest.'

'Really?'

'You'll just have to wait to see if I can take care of myself, if I can scope out the territory and watch my own back.'

CHAPTER 16

February came and took the edge off the worst of the cold.

Ole Krantz had finally hung the painting of the severed bridge on the wall and angled a spotlight to illuminate it properly. Alvar was still debating whether or not to buy it. The decision had to come from somewhere deep inside him; he oscillated between hope and fear. Hope that one day he would own it. Fear that someone would snap it up before his very eyes. He obviously wanted to buy it and possess it, he just had to get into the right frame of mind, it was a huge and important purchase. It was one thing to buy a print by Jarle Rosseland, people did that without a second thought. However the painting *Broken* was something else, so overwhelming, enormous and dramatic. At seven minutes past five he left the gallery and made his way as usual to the Cash and Carry. He headed straight to the delicatessen and bought the home-made meatballs with pickled gherkins and paprika. Then he continued around the big store and picked up some coffee, a packet of sandwich biscuits and a newspaper. He paid and was just about to leave when he spotted the large noticeboard on the wall by the exit. On the spur of the moment he decided to read the notices, as if an awareness of other people's lives had suddenly flickered in his consciousness. He put down his bag and started going through them.

Childminder in Bragernes available. Non-smoker. Good with kids of all ages.
For sale: two-seater sofa in brown leather, slightly worn, bargain buy.

Yoga course starting now. Beginners and Intermediates.
Have you seen Pilate? Green parrot missing since January.

Alvar kept on reading. The noticeboard was completely covered with scraps of paper and he realised that he would be unable to tear himself away until he had read every single one of them.

Home-made griddle cakes and marzipan horns made from traditional recipes. We bake to order.
Bric-a-brac needed for charity sale on the 20th.
Fancy singing in a choir?

Alvar took a step back. No, he did not fancy singing in a choir, absolutely not, he had no talent for singing. The thought of mingling with so many people was also quite impossible for him to entertain. Then he stepped forward again and read another note.

Free kittens. Four females and one male, house-trained and ready for collection.

And then a photo of them, five tiny fluff balls in a basket. Alvar felt his heart beat tenderly. A cat, he thought, I've always wanted a cat. But I have never done anything about it, it's embarrassing. A cat could look after itself and it would offer him silent companionship, precisely what he was looking for. True, a cat was a commitment, but he had only himself to look after and he had plenty of spare time. It was also true that he had absolutely no clue how to care for an animal, but he would learn by doing. And there was a veterinary surgery only ten minutes' walk from his house where he could get all the help and guidance he needed; in case the cat fell ill or required injections. A cat, soft and warm. A cat slinking around his flat, a cat lying on his sofa purring. A cat sleeping at the foot of his bed at night.

Maybe. He kept looking at the photo. He liked the grey one the best, but he was adamant that he wanted a tom. If the grey one turned out to be the tom, he would get it. If they had not already found new homes for them; there was no date on the note, it could have been up there a long time. There was both an address and a telephone number. Haugestad Farm in Frydenlund. It was ten minutes in the Mazda. There's no harm in looking at them, he thought, I can go there to see them and then give myself a few days to make up my mind. But to have a cat. Someone to chat to, someone waiting for me, when I come home from work. And if I worm it then I'll avoid those disgusting regurgitations that I was so repulsed by as a child. He stood for a while looking at the small fur balls. They would probably need a few bits and pieces, it occurred to him. A basket to sleep in, toys. Vitamins. He pondered this for a long time. Then he snapped himself out of his trance and started walking home.

He let himself in and put his shopping on the kitchen counter, then he went over to wash his hands. That was when his doubts resurfaced. A pet ties you down, after all. If he wanted to go to Copenhagen for a weekend, for example, he would not be able to do that. Not that he had ever spent a weekend in Copenhagen, but if he wanted to one day, then the cat would have to be left on its own. But of course there was always Green downstairs. True, they never really spoke, but it was surely acceptable to ask his neighbour to please put some cat food in a bowl and top up the water over the weekend. Green's teenage children would do it for him, he was convinced of that. A cat, he thought, that would be bouncing around happily, it would be a joy every day.

He took the meatballs out of the bag, placed them on a plate. He put the plate in the oven. Now the seed had been planted it gave him no peace at all. To top it all the cat was free, so it could not be deemed an extravagance. He was so excited he ate his food in record time, carried his plate to the kitchen, rinsed everything off and went to the bathroom. There he washed his hands and combed the small semicircle of hair with a fine-toothed comb. He took his car keys from a hook in the hallway and left. He wondered if the Mazda would even start, he did not drive it very often. Sometimes he started it and let the engine run for fifteen minutes so it would not stop working altogether.

He got in and turned the key. Heard the engine splutter to life. He was ready to go. He pressed the accelerator, but it was not enough. He turned the key again, revving the engine harder, and finally the engine started to hum. He sat in his seat for a while waiting for the engine to warm up. He had no complaints about his car. The Mazda had never let him down. Then he drove out through the gate and onto the road. A cat. If they still had any left. Perhaps he should have phoned in advance, it occurred to him, but there was always someone around on a farm. He turned left at the light-bulb factory, found the right lane and kept an eye on the traffic behind him in his rear-view mirror. He considered himself to be a good driver. He always drove slightly below the speed limit just to be on the safe side, and he always drove defensively. He had the fjord on his right, it was blue grey in colour and there were ripples in the water caused by the evening breeze. His heart was racing. If they had no more kittens left, he would be terribly disappointed. Because now, halfway through his life, he was finally ready for this event. He had no trouble locating the farm and swung onto the driveway. Stayed in his car and looked around. A dog came padding towards him, it looked like a setter. A woman appeared in the doorway; she waved. Then she leaned against the door frame expectantly. Alvar stepped out of his car. He started walking towards the whitewashed farmhouse.

'I'm here about the cats,' he said, 'I saw the picture of them in the Cash and Carry. But perhaps they've all gone?'

She smiled broadly and gestured to him.

'No, don't worry, I've still got some left. Do come in. Come on, in you come!' she said warmly and opened the door wide. Alvar walked slowly up the steps. They shook hands and he was ushered into a warm farmhouse kitchen with a long table, a fireplace and curtains with colourful pelmets.

'I've got three left,' the woman said, 'they're all over the place; you see, they're already nine weeks old. But why don't we go into the living room and see if we can find them?'

He followed her. Noticed an adult cat on a chair. Curled up next to her were the kittens. Dear Lord, Alvar thought, how tiny they are. How fragile.

She picked up a black kitten with a white chest. Alvar remained standing, fiddling with his fingers, not even sure that he had the courage to hold it. He could see himself dropping it on the floor out of sheer fright. The woman put the kitten on the table and it staggered around. Its tail was short and stuck right out, and its eyes were blue.

'And then we've got the grey one,' she said, lifting up another one. Alvar recognised it from the photo. 'It's a tom,' she said, 'the only one in the litter. Which do you prefer?'

'The tom,' he said swiftly. 'I can't risk it having kittens, I know nothing of such things.'

'Then that's the one for you,' she said happily, 'and when it's eight months old you take it to the vet's and have him neutered, then he won't stray. And he'll fight less with other cats. There you are,' she said, holding out the kitten, 'do you want to hold him?'

Alvar held out his hands. She placed the kitten in them. It sent shivers down his spine. It was so soft. It was so light and warm. He felt a faint vibration in the palm of his hand.

'He's purring,' the woman said excitedly, 'he's taken to you already. The kids call him Bugs Bunny.'

'Bugs Bunny?' Alvar shook his head baffled. 'Why?'

'Because he's grey and white,' she explained. 'But you can decide on a name yourself, he's your cat. That's right, isn't it? He's your cat now?'

Alvar nodded. He was in awe. My cat, he thought, is most certainly not going to be called Bugs Bunny.

'I'll get you a box,' the woman said. 'With a lid. And some holes for ventilation. Place it next to you in the car and drive carefully on your way back.'

'Does he need injections right away?' he asked solemnly.

'Injections?' she chuckled. 'Here on the farm we don't worry too much about injections. If they're going to make it, they'll make it, after all we've got plenty of them. But if you want to do it properly then just call a vet and they'll tell you all you need to know.'

'What kind of food does he eat?' he enquired.

'Buy pellets. And buy the cheapest brand. I know the vets say it's old, pulped IKEA furniture, but the cats seem to love it.'

'IKEA furniture?' Alvar gave her a horrified look.

'Well, vets too have their contacts which they have to keep sweet, don't they?' she laughed. 'No, give him what you like, for God's sake. Leftovers, slices of bread with liver paste. But always make sure he has plenty of fresh water. And if I were you I'd buy a tray with cat litter. Yes, it's a bit messy, but soon the cat will claw at the door when he wants to go outside. He's practically house-trained already.'

She walked briskly back to the kitchen. Alvar followed her. Holding the cat firmly all the time. She lifted the seat of a bench and pulled out a grey box. Then she grabbed a roll of kitchen towel, tore of a few sheet and lined the box with them. 'In case he pees on the way back,' she explained. Alvar put the kitten in the box. Immediately he started squeaking like a mouse. The lid had three large holes, he could see the kitten's head in the semi-darkness.

'Just give me a call if you've got any questions,' she said cheerfully.

'Well, I'm sure I'll be fine,' he said, holding the box carefully against his chest. 'Where would I get cat litter?'

'From the pet shop in Bragernes. You'll find everything you need there. And you don't have to worry about bad smells, because the cat litter they make these days is very good.'

He nodded. Held out his hand and thanked her. She escorted him to his car and watched him as he placed the small box on the seat beside him.

'Go easy over the speed bumps,' she ordered him.

Alvar nodded. 'I will.'

Then he started the car and turned out into the road. The woman stood on the steps watching him.

Alvar drove.

He could hear how the kitten clawed frantically inside his box.

The poor thing was sitting in there in the dark, brutally torn away from his mother. How merciless, Alvar thought, but that's what human beings do. And he will soon get used to me. Perhaps he will sleep on the rug by my bed, that would be cosy. The box was rocking, he noticed, the little creature was trying to escape and he realised that he was beginning to feel stressed. What if the kitten got sick? Or run over? Or some other dreadful thing happened to it? He drove into the town centre and left the kitten in the car while he bought a tray, some cat litter and some dry food.

'I want a good quality cat food,' Alvar stated firmly. 'None of that pulped IKEA rubbish, if you don't mind.'

The girl behind the desk laughed at him. 'Then you'll want this one,' she said. 'Royal Canin. The very best. But it's pricey.'

'Never mind. Can't be helped,' he said and paid without blinking. He was remarkably flash with his money, nothing but the best for his cat. He carried everything out into his car and packed it in the boot. Shortly afterwards he pulled in to his own backyard. First he carried his purchases upstairs, then he got the kitten. He pressed the box carefully to his chest. At this point his neighbour appeared. He stared at him. There was something about the grey box which aroused his curiosity.

'Got yourself a hamster?' he chuckled.

Alvar shook his head fiercely. 'Oh, no. It's a kitten.'

'Really? A kitten?' Green sighed. 'That's it, I'll never hear the end of it now, the kids have been pestering me for years to get a cat. Really?' he said again. 'How much did you have to pay for it?'

'Nothing at all,' Alvar said. 'But I had to get some equipment, you know, trays and whatnot. And that was fairly expensive.'

His neighbour came over to him. Very carefully Alvar lifted the lid and they both looked down at the terrified animal.

'What a gorgeous little thing,' his neighbour said.

Alvar agreed. He made as if to leave but his neighbour remembered something.

'There was someone at your door today.'

'Oh?'

'A young girl. Or a woman, I should say. I'm not quite sure. Skinny and blonde. She rang the bell for a long time.'

Alvar felt his stomach lurch. His neighbour scrutinised him as though waiting for further explanation.

'That doesn't sound like anyone I know,' he lied and headed for his own front door.

'Are you sure? I could swear that I've seen her before,' his neighbour persisted. 'In fact, I recognise her from Bragernes Square,' he added.

Alvar's cheeks burned. He tucked the box under one arm and unlocked the door with his other hand.

'Of course,' his neighbour said eventually, 'it's none of my business, but you can't give those people an inch. They'll just take a mile.'

Alvar felt an icy chill down his spine. 'I'll bear that in mind,' he said, averting his eyes. Then he went into the hallway. He put the box with the kitten on the kitchen table and lifted the lid. Lifted the little bundle out. It stood up on trembling legs looking confused. He thought the kitten was absolutely perfect. It had a white chest, but was otherwise grey with a tiny pink nose. Tiny, tiny paws. Bright blue eyes that soon would turn yellow or green, he guessed. Then he remembered that it might be thirsty. He put the kitten on the floor and found a bowl in his kitchen cupboard, which he filled with water. The kitten came over straight away to drink. This was a momentous occasion for Alvar. He was responsible for this tiny animal, he had to look after it, take care of it, feed it, and these were things he had hardly ever done for another living creature. He sat down on the floor and watched it as it drank. And you need a name, too, he thought. And given that art is my passion, I'll name you after a painter.

How about Rembrandt? he thought. No, it was too big and cumbersome. Picasso was out of the question; da Vinci? No, that was conceited. How about the Norwegian painters? he wondered. Kittelsen, how funny would that be? Or Heiberg, perhaps. He instantly dismissed it as ridiculous. He stood up again and thought on. Started preparing a litter tray for the kitten. It would have to go in a corner of the kitchen for the time being. Suddenly he felt deeply moved by everything that had happened. And how quickly it had all come about. From the minute he had gone over to the noticeboard up to this moment when he was standing in his own kitchen with his very own kitten. It was really so unlike him to let himself go like this. He spread out the sand so it lay evenly in the tray and then he pushed it up against the wall. The kitten grew curious, it soon climbed into the tray and did its business. Alvar sank down onto a kitchen chair, cupped his chin in his hands and admired the little bundle. I'm going to treat myself to a sherry tonight, he decided, as the cat bounced around. In his mind he was flicking through great sections of art history. Finally he decided to name the kitten Goya.

At this very moment someone rang the doorbell hard.

Alvar jumped in his chair, he grabbed the kitten and he ran into the living room. His heart was pounding. Was it her again, Lindys? Or a salesperson, perhaps, or his neighbour? He stood petrified, clutching the kitten to his chest. If he just kept totally still whoever it was would eventually go away; right now he did not want to be disturbed. The bell rang again, sharply this time. His heart leapt to his throat. Why had she come to his flat, what did she want? What had he done wrong? Why did she have to blight his peaceful existence? The bell rang for the third time. Whoever it was, was leaning on the bell, the sound cut through the flat. His cheeks were hot with despair. Then it struck him how ridiculous it all was; him standing there shaking with fright just because someone was ringing his doorbell, and how pathetic he had become. It was a simple case of refusing to open the door, she would give up eventually. Because now he was quite certain that it was Lindys on the other side of the door. The bell rang for the fourth time. Or, he thought, I'll open the door and I'll ask her to go away once and for all. He rehearsed the words in his head. Go away once and for all. Suddenly everything went quiet, he thought he heard voices. Had his neighbour gone out? He went over to his kitchen window and looked out. Then the bell started ringing again. He could not bear it any longer; he clutched the kitten and went to open the door.

'Christ,' she said, putting her hands on her hips, 'what took you so long? You were here the whole time!'

Then she spotted the kitten. She melted instantly.

'Oh, but just look at you,' she said taking the kitten from him. She simply snatched it from his hands and pressed it confidently to her pale cheek.

'So when did you get this one? What's his name? Is it a boy? How old is it?'

Alvar struggled to deal with four questions simultaneously.

He cleared his throat nervously. 'I got him today. He's nine weeks old. His name is Goya.'

'Goya,' she repeated dubiously. 'Why?'

'Because,' he said, 'I named him after the Spanish painter. Francisco de Goya.'

'Right.' She still did not quite follow. 'Can I come in?' she asked then.

'I was just about to go out,' he spluttered. He reached out for his kitten, but she refused to give him back.

'I just need a few minutes,' she said, and before he knew it, she had stepped past him and into the hall. Alvar bit his lip.

'He's got blue eyes,' she said joyously.

He looked at her kohl-black eyes. She did not seem to be high and she was not slurring her words, that was always something.

'They'll turn green eventually,' he explained. She sat down on the sofa and put her feet on the coffee table. Alvar remained standing, clenching and unclenching his fists in frustration. She had clearly never been taught manners of any sort and her ankle boots were far from clean.

'You're lovely, you are,' she said, kissing the kitten on his pink nose. Alvar stood in the middle of the floor watching them. The kitten dangled like a toy in her hands.

'Don't squeeze him too hard,' he warned her. He couldn't bear it that she had taken the kitten from him.

'Oh, cats can cope with anything,' she said. 'They've got nine lives, didn't you know?'

'I have to correct you there,' Alvar said, 'they only have one, actually. And this kitten is my responsibility.'

She laughed at him. She stroked the head of the kitten with her fingers.

'So you're going out?' she said then. 'Where are you going? Are you taking the car?'

He nodded. 'I've got some business to attend to. In Oslo,' he lied.

'Cool!' she burst out. 'Can I come with you?'

He took a step back as he inwardly cursed himself and he started babbling. 'Yes, no,' he gibbered, 'I'm not leaving right now. I'm not altogether sure when, I need to go into town first, I've got some shopping to do there.'

She fixed him with her ice-blue eyes. 'Good God, you're a busy man,' she said. Then she laughed again, her laughter was shrill and loud.

'Well, I've got several things to do,' Alvar said again, 'in several different places. You'll just be bored waiting for me here, there and everywhere. It would be better if you took the bus,' he said rapidly. 'Or the train.'

She put the cat down on the table. Alvar leapt forward and grabbed it immediately.

'I didn't think you'd be so dull,' she said then.

Dull? Am I dull? Alvar thought. No, I certainly am not. But I'm floundering, how am I going to get this person out of my house?

'Do you have any more raisins?' she asked.

He shook his head firmly. 'No raisins. No chocolate. Nothing at all.'

Suddenly she started patting the pocket of her grey coat.

'One fag, that's all I need, I'm not staying long. You can get ready in the meantime. Do you leave the cat on his own when you go out? Then always remember to put the toilet seat down when you've been to the loo. I had a cat once and one day I found it drowned in the loo.'

Alvar was shocked. 'So,' he said when he had recovered, 'it only had eight lives left then?'

She made a face at him. Stuck a cigarette in her mouth, fished out a lighter advertising a convenience store.

'I was trying to give you a piece of advice,' she said, 'but if you're not interested then that's no skin off my nose.' She blew a column of smoke out into the room. Alvar hated it, he was not used to the smell of smoke, he did not even own an ashtray, so he went into the kitchen and found a bowl. Put it in front of her on the coffee table. She immediately flicked the ash off her cigarette.

'Don't you have something you should be getting on with?' she said. He sat down in his armchair. He felt he ought to make conversation, but at the same time he wanted her to leave.

'What have you done with the scarf?'

'The scarf?' She gave him a perplexed look.

'Yes,' he said, 'the scarf I gave you. The Mulberry scarf. It's a very fine scarf.'

She shrugged. 'Not a clue,' she said. 'It's not so cold any more, just as well.'

Alvar felt deeply depressed. It was an expensive scarf, and she had discarded it carelessly and he had been taught a lesson. His neighbour had been right, you could not trust those people.

'Why haven't you bought the painting?' she asked, nodding towards the blank wall above the fireplace.

'Ahem, I haven't got round to it,' he replied.

'Got round to it?' She laughed again. 'The painting is hanging in your workplace. All you have to do is unhook it. You're not very quick off the mark, are you?' she stated. 'You really wanted it. Are you that indecisive, Alvar?'

He could feel his cheeks burning again. He certainly was not indecisive, on the contrary he was controlled and organised. Yes, he was going to buy the painting, but not because she was pushing him. It would happen of its own accord, he would know when the time was right, when he was ready to act.

'My mum could never make a decision,' she said suddenly.

'Oh?' Alvar enquired.

'Yes. She had a phobia. And this phobia was so great that it paralysed her. All she could do was sit in her chair all day. She couldn't manage any decisions, she never ate. She couldn't leave her room, she never left the house.'

'What was she scared of?' Alvar asked.

'Dying,' she said. 'She was so scared of dying that she wasn't able to live life like other people. She ended up killing herself with some pills the doctor had given her.'

'She was so scared of dying that she killed herself?'

Alvar was perplexed. He could see no logic in this.

'Weird, don't you think?' she said, inhaling. 'People can be so strange.'

Alvar's living room was now dense with cigarette smoke. He detested it. The stress was building up in him and he was certain that she was aware of it, but she pretended not to notice.

'Do you have any spare cash?' she asked, stubbing out her cigarette in the bowl.

Alvar jerked. 'No,' he said brusquely. 'Absolutely not. I have no cash.' He got up and stood next to his chair.

'But you've got a cashpoint card?' she said in a commanding voice. Her eyes had lit up in a way that scared him.

'A card? Yes, of course I've got a card.'

'Good, since you're going to Oslo anyway you can give me a lift to the Cash and Carry, where there's a cash machine. You can get some money out. You'll probably need to get some for yourself as well,' she declared.

Alvar paled. Were there no limits to her impudence? He put the kitten down on the chair and inhaled deeply as he got up.

'Don't get your knickers in a twist,' she said, 'I was just asking you a question. I'll meet you downstairs. I'll be waiting by your car.'

His head was turbulent with chaos. On top of everything it seemed impossible to abandon the kitten, which had only just arrived. The kitten was running around confused in a strange house. Overwhelmed by concern he lifted up the little bundle, carried him out into the kitchen, put him in the box and replaced the lid. Then he went outside. She was hanging around by the car.

'It's open,' he coughed. She went round and got in. He got in behind the wheel. I can't believe this is happening to me, he thought, I can't believe I'm doing what she tells me to do. He started the engine and pulled out into the road. Changed gears and drove down the hill.

'Well,' she said, looking around the car, 'it's not exactly a Jaguar, is it?'

Alvar did not reply. He had nothing more to say, he just wanted her to leave and he would never, ever open his door the next time someone rang the bell. He drove right up to the cashpoint. Got out, found the card in his wallet.

'I need a thousand!' she called from the car. Alvar's fingers trembled, she was watching him like a hawk. He inserted the card and entered his PIN number, glancing quickly over his shoulder to see if she was getting out. She was. Her boots clicked businesslike against the tarmac. The machine ticked and whirred. Then his card came out and shortly afterwards his money. He held it in his hand for a moment as if frozen solid. She snatched it from him and stuffed it in her pocket.

'You're a dear,' she exclaimed joyfully. Suddenly she leaned forward and kissed his cheek, a big sloppy kiss. Then she walked across the road and was gone.

CHAPTER 17

Lindys has entered my life.

This was what Alvar was thinking as he opened the gallery at five to ten on a Monday morning in late February. She has entered my life and I need to make a decision. Whether I want her there or not. If I want her in my life I need to have a strategy in place for dealing with her. If I don't want her there, I need to get rid of her. And I have to devise a strategy in order for that to happen. In other words, I need to make a choice. Does she need me? he asked himself. Maybe. But he could not know for certain. She had kissed him on his cheek, but surely that was just an affectionate gesture, he thought, and not an expression of love or devotion. That was how the young behaved these days; they would kiss anyone and not be the least bit embarrassed about it. The cynical part of him was utterly convinced that she was only interested in him for his money, but he did not like to be so cynical. Rather, he decided, she was looking for several things. Companionship and warmth, and money for drugs. She had even opened up to him, she had told him that her mother had killed herself because of her phobia. Her confiding in him had genuinely moved him. But he also felt disturbed. She was so unpredictable, she only showed up when she wanted to. She never cared if it was convenient for him. Alvar decided that if they made a proper date, if for example she said, 'I'll be back again on Friday around six o'clock in the evening,' then he would be prepared and everything would be easier. Of course he could also ask her, he could mention it in passing, are you thinking of dropping by one of these days? But that sounded like an invitation and he certainly did not want to invite her. Then it might spiral into something he would have no control over whatsoever and the very thought made him cold with fear.

The trip to the cashpoint had left him feeling very tense because he was finding it hard to accept that he had acted the way he had. He had walked like a servant to his car, driven by a vague sense of duty, quite simply because the word 'no' was so difficult to articulate. No. I don't want to, you won't make me, we can't do this, it's out of the question, are you out of your mind? He had all these words in his head, but they were too deep inside. In addition he found it terribly hard to get angry. He was not used to people wanting something from him and even less used to them asking for what they wanted in such a direct manner. What would happen if he gave in? And how could people around him make themselves so accessible? They gave out their telephone numbers without a moment's hesitation, they gave out their email address and their home address, they travelled abroad and met foreigners whom they invited to Norway, why not? If you're ever in this part of the world, do drop by. Had they no idea of the risks they were running? And when it came to Lindys she was a damaged person on top of everything else and the circles she moved in were even worse. For all he knew she might be a thief, a prostitute, a liar. She might have been to prison, she might have been a drug dealer and that was a criminal offence. Of all the people he could have run into in this world, it had turned out to be someone like her. Was this significant? At the same time it was also an opportunity. All of his deepest feelings and values were tested. Others would have handled this in a far more straightforward manner, it struck him, others would have turned their back and cut the tie with a machete. Ole Krantz would have lifted her up and carried her out into the cold, dumped her in a gutter outside perhaps, and he would not have thought twice about it. But I'm not Ole Krantz, he thought, I'm Alvar Eide. I might lack something that other people possess. What could it be? A sense of entitlement? Do other people have rights which I don't award myself? And if this is the case, why is it so?

He struggled with these thoughts as he walked around the gallery. Stood in front of the severed bridge and stared at it. Out of the darkness and the fog he saw the construction rise, soar, beautiful and brutally severed, just as his ties to other people had been cut. Can such damage be mended? he asked himself. Can you regrow the stumps, can you become whole again? Once more the bridge had this healing effect on him, he was transfixed. Was there communication between people which could bypass distance, time and culture? He had never met this painter, Lindstrøm. And the bridge was in every way a direct message to him personally. He was aware though that other people might be equally mesmerised by the painting, even though it had not happened yet. Then the doorbell rang and he spun round. Ole Krantz came striding in with a frame tucked under his arm.

'Look at you standing there drooling,' he smiled. 'Like a kid in a sweet shop. So, what's it gonna be?'

Alvar hesitated. 'Well,' he said reluctantly, 'of course, I'll have to buy it. If I don't I'll regret it for the rest of my life.'

Krantz squatted down. He was wearing green wellies and he had rolled down their tops.

'This painting is a good investment, I can promise you that.'

He wiped a drop of moisture from under his nose with the back of his hand, got up and planted his hands firmly on his hips. So stands a man who owns his own world, Alvar thought. He did not mention that he was not at all interested in the investment aspect.

'I can drive the painting over to your place today,' Krantz said, 'then you can hang it and keep it for a couple of weeks. That way you'll get a sense of how it affects you. If you then decide to hold on to the painting, you'll pay me, let me see, we'll knock a bit off, let's say sixty thousand. If you don't like it as much as you thought you would, I'll just come and pick it up.'

Alvar hesitated. This was one of Ole Krantz's standard sales pitches and he used it frequently. Initially it sounded reasonable, but when push came to shove most people found it hard to hand back a painting which had found a space in their living room. A painting they had fallen for for some reason. Hardly anyone returned their paintings, they did not like the emptiness that followed when the painting was taken down. But these customers never became regulars. They felt tricked and went to another gallery in future.

'No, thank you,' he said after a pause. 'I'd rather give myself a deadline. Let me see, I'll make up my mind before Friday.'

'So what will you do if a buyer turns up on Thursday?' Krantz wanted to know. He tilted his head and smiled a proper salesman smile.

Alvar thought long and hard about that. 'In that case I'll have to take my punishment,' he said presumptuously.

Krantz shook his head. He had little faith that Alvar Eide was the kind of man who could take his punishment.

The familiar sound of the doorbell startled him again. Up until now he had always enjoyed this sound and would enjoy going down the stairs to be of service. Now he hesitated and stared nervously at the monitor. It might be Lindys and now it had become utterly impossible to get rid of her. No, this was a taller person, it was the outline of a man. He was tall and broad and solid. A relieved Alvar left the kitchen. The man was standing in front of the bridge and when Alvar appeared on the stairs he bowed to him in an old-fashioned way.

'Lindstrøm?' he said, pointing at the painting.

'Yes. Yes, exactly,' Alvar stuttered because here was a customer who was familiar with the name of an artist Alvar had only just heard of.

'I've seen his work before,' the man stated. 'If I remember rightly, he's very popular in the States.'

Alvar gawped. Was he perhaps standing in front of another Nerdrum? An artist who was unappreciated at home, but celebrated abroad?

'Lindstrøm's style's somewhat dramatic,' the man went on. 'He shouts rather than speaks, if you know what I'm saying.'

'Indeed,' Alvar whispered. He was growing anxious. 'However, I don't think that he takes it too far, nor does he merely paint for effect either, not the way I look at it.'

He dug his fingers into his palms behind his back. He watched the customer furtively.

'Perhaps,' the man hesitated, 'he borders on shouting too loud. I mean, here we have a bloody deep canyon and a massive severed bridge. And all of it clouded in some sort of medieval mist. A bit over the top, don't you think?'

Alvar could feel how his cheeks were starting to get hot. It felt like the customer was analysing his own love affair with the painting, but then he realised that he was merely overreacting.

'True, he's good,' the man went on, 'there's no doubt about it. I have a good feeling about this painting, I really do. But as to hanging it on my living-room wall,' he paused and a frown appeared on his forehead as he considered it. 'I'm not sure I'd go that far. But it would look impressive in the hall. There is no furniture and the ceiling is high. This bridge needs to be kept far away from curtains and floral cushions. This painting is a monument.'

Alvar cleared his throat. 'Well, we're all different,' he said, managing a weak smile. 'Floral motifs always sell well. Or Norwegian mountain landscapes. And most people think it's important to have a nude, in their bedroom perhaps. But I agree, this is a very powerful painting. There needs to be a certain order in the room where it will hang.'

The man walked right up to the canvas, studied a few details before stepping back again.

'A painting like this can almost darken your mood,' he suggested. 'One thing that does occur to me when I look at it is that some enormous and irreparable damage has been done here.'

'Really?'

Alvar's cheeks paled. He had never viewed it in this way, he had regarded the bridge as an image of his deepest self. Irreparable damage? he thought uneasily. Am I irreparably damaged?

'I've discussed it briefly with Ole Krantz,' Alvar said. 'Do you think his inspiration might have come from some war-torn country?'

The man shook his head. 'I doubt it,' he said. 'This is wholly symbolic. And this Lindstrøm, he has a few problems of his own, I know something about that.'

Alvar's eyes widened as he listened.

'He satisfies all the requirements for the struggling artist. They say he's in his studio working up to twenty hours without a break. He forgets to eat, he forgets to sleep. At times he has collapsed on the floor from exhaustion only to get up and continue painting. And he drinks too much. He won't live to be an old man. I'm passionately interested in art,' he said, smiling broadly, 'but I've never understood why it's necessary to live on the edge, like Lindstrøm does. Anyway, let's hope he succeeds in painting several good pictures before he finally kills himself.'

Alvar was shocked. 'Might he do that?'

'Absolutely,' the man assured him. 'He lives a hard life. And the fact that he's fairly successful abroad doesn't make it any easier, he can't handle it. He's like a wild animal in a cave. He only comes out to fight.'

'Life's not easy,' Alvar said, gesticulating clumsily.

'No, indeed it isn't.'

The man looked at the painting again. 'It's terribly good, of course. Imposing even. But dark, really very dark. It beckons you and scares you at the same time. How much is it?'

Alvar shuddered, suddenly consumed by fear. 'Seventy thousand.'

'I see. Seventy thousand? Fancy that. Who would have thought it? Seventy thousand for a Lindstrøm, that's nothing. In New York this painting would have sold for two hundred thousand.'

'Is that possible?' stammered Alvar.

'In five years he'll command the same prices at home, I'm

convinced of it. I really ought to buy it, purely because it's such a good investment.'

Alvar held his breath. Was it about to happen, right before his eyes? A man with better knowledge of Lindstrøm than him was calmly considering the painting, with a pensive look on his face. A man who furthermore did not value the painting for the right reason; he was nowhere near as mesmerised as Alvar. He was impressed. Though he thought the painting was average, he believed buying it would be a sound investment. Alvar exhaled. Should such a man be blessed with that which he himself so desperately desired?

'Do you know what, I'll give it some thought,' the man said. 'I'll take a couple of days. I'll pop by, I want to view it a few more times.'

Alvar nodded and gulped.

'Like I said, it would look good in the hall. Anyone who comes into my house will have a very dramatic entrance, you can't deny that.'

'No, precisely,' Alvar mumbled.

'In terms of colour it will match the ivory walls and the grey stone floor.'

'Undoubtedly,' Alvar said quietly.

'And then I'll have a touch of red as well, preferably near the painting. In the form of red candles in tall candlesticks or a bouquet of roses. That would be the finishing touch.'

'It sounds great,' stuttered Alvar.

'And as far as the frame is concerned,' he continued, 'I was thinking of charcoal grey. Not too dark, just a shade darker than the painting. You frame paintings here as well, don't you?'

'We do,' said Alvar restlessly.

'Well, well.' He took a few steps backwards and started studying the other paintings in the room. Alvar dragged himself towards the staircase. He disappeared into the kitchen and sat down at the table. He followed the man on the monitor. Was this how it was going to turn out? Would he end up in the workshop cutting lists, tagging and gluing them, framing the painting for another person purely because he lacked the fundamental ability to make a decision?

CHAPTER 18

It was three days before she reappeared.

Alvar was sitting in front of his fireplace staring at the naked wall where the bridge was going to hang if only he could make up his mind. The kitten was lying in his lap, curled up into a fur ball, he could feel it warming his thighs. It was nine in the evening when the doorbell broke the silence. His heart leapt to his throat, then he lifted the kitten carefully and put him on the floor. He thought, it's Lindys, I guess. I don't have to open the door. What will the neighbours be thinking of her coming and going? How was he going to stop it? By refusing to open the door, he told himself firmly. The doorbell rang again, longer this time, she was holding the button down. It hurt his ears. Finally he buckled and went out into the hall to open the door. She was standing outside with a swollen black eye and make-up running down her face.

'For God's sake,' she exclaimed, 'what took you so long? I know you're in!'

'Have you hurt yourself?' he stuttered in a frightened voice.

She marched past him and into the living room without waiting to be asked. Peeled off her grey jacket and left it in a heap on the floor.

'I got beaten up,' she muttered, touching her eye.

He closed the door and followed her, alarmed.

'Beaten up? By whom?'

She turned round and looked at him. She was as white as chalk and her eye really looked very nasty, she could barely see out of it. It had swollen up into a purple ball and he thought it might burst at any moment.

'By a bad-tempered creditor,' she said. 'I owe him some money.'

Alvar felt his heart sink.

'You've got to go to A&E,' he told her.

'Nope,' she said, shaking her head. 'There's no way I'm going to A&E. They don't want us, anyway, so I'm bloody well not going to bother them.'

He ignored her swearing and watched as she made herself comfortable on his sofa. She put her feet on the coffee table straight away.

'Could I stay the night?' she asked him.

Alvar gasped for breath. Had he heard her correctly? Stay the night, here in his flat? A woman, a total stranger?

'I'm not really sure,' he began, squirming like a worm on a hotplate. He was still standing with his hands folded across his stomach. He thought the room was starting to sway.

'On your sofa,' she said, watching him with her undamaged ice-blue eye.

'But,' he stammered, 'don't you have your own place?'

'Yes,' she said, putting her hand over her swollen eye. 'But he'll find me there and he's very upset. I need to keep out of his way until he's calmed down. Sod it, I tried to outrun him, but it's no good running in these boots.'

'Who's after you?' Alvar asked.

'Rikard. A dealer. I owe him twenty grand.'

Alvar gave her a horrified look. 'How much did you say?'

'I've no hope of ever finding that kind of money,' she groaned. 'And if I can't get it, he's going to beat the crap out of me.'

Alvar bit his lip. 'But you've got to find some sort of solution,' he said feebly.

'You think I don't know that?' she replied sarcastically. Then she sighed deeply and sincerely and dug a packet of cigarettes out of her pocket. Alvar instantly went to the kitchen to find a bowl for the ash. Eventually he managed to sit down. He watched her as she lit her cigarette, watched her damaged face in horror.

'Can you see out of that eye?' he asked quietly.

'Are you thick or something?' she replied simply.

'Does it hurt?'

'I can handle it, I'm no sissy.'

'So what are you going to do?' he asked.

She shrugged. 'No idea. But I'm probably going to hell eventually and I've always known that. Bloody stupid idea to buy drugs on credit, but I had no choice. And then the tosser has added a ton of interest. I guess he'll break my nose next time. Or my front teeth. His right hook is like a piston.'

She looked at him again. 'Can I stay the night?'

Alvar felt that he had crossed a line and a vast void was opening up. Now he was clinging to the edge and he clenched his fists so hard his knuckles ached. The word 'no' was ringing in his ears, filling his mouth, but it was refusing to come out.

'Well,' he said in a little voice, 'I can probably find a blanket somewhere. One night wouldn't hurt, I suppose.'

He stressed the word 'one'. At the same time he was horrified at this development. She is devouring me, he thought, where will it end?

'You're one of the good guys,' she said suddenly.

Her smile reached up to her healthy eye.

Alvar felt warm all over.

'Others would have said no,' she said, as if this surprised her.

'Well,' he said modestly, 'it's no big deal to let you have the sofa just for the one night.'

Again he stressed the word 'one'.

'By the way, sleeping on that sofa is not a bad idea, I sometimes have an afternoon nap on it,' he confessed, 'and I never end up with a bad back or anything like that.'

She began laughing. She puffed blue smoke out into the air looking quite comical with her swollen eye.

'You're really quite all right,' she said.

Her voice was both teasing and affectionate.

'All right how?' he wanted to know.

'You know. A bit different. Like an old woman.'

Alvar tightened his lips. What sort of description is that? he thought. I'm not effeminate, I never have been, I'm one metre eighty-seven tall and fairly broad-shouldered.

'Are you hurt?' she smiled.

'Certainly not,' he lied, crossing one leg over the other and brushing away a speck of dust.

Suddenly she put her feet on the floor and got up from the sofa. She had spotted the kitten. Now she went over to pick him up and take him back with her to the sofa.

'He's such a sweetie,' she said, stroking the kitten's head. 'When I was a little girl I always wanted to have a kitten, but I never got one. Those people gave me nothing.' Her voice was angry, bitter. 'But I can pretend that he's mine. Hello, kitty,' she chirped, 'I'm going to visit you lots and lots and you will be mine. I'll fuss over you and take care of you for ever and ever.'

Her words sent a chill down Alvar's spine. Had she not just declared that she would keep coming back, to his flat, to his kitten? What had he started?

She leaned her head back and closed her eyes. The kitten settled on her lap and started purring.

'Do you know what I fancy right now?' she said, looking at him. Alvar was tormented by her bruised eye. He shook his head nervously.

'Hot chocolate,' she said softly. 'Hot chocolate with lots of sugar. Please would you make me some, please, please, please?'

Alvar was not sure if he had any cocoa as he preferred tea or coffee. But there might be something in a packet somewhere, probably well out of date. He got up to check, driven by her needs in a way he resented. Again he felt like a servant. And this confused him, because he was in charge of his own life. Now with her simple request she had switched their roles. He opened the cupboard and had a look inside. Searched among bags of flour and spaghetti and rice for the brown cocoa packet. And there in the furthest corner he discovered some Kakao Express. Well, why not? he thought. It'll warm her up and she probably needs that. And they had to do something to pass this long evening. He found some milk in the fridge and poured it into a saucepan. Put it on the stove. Found a mug and a teaspoon and a bowl of sugar. From where he was standing he could see into the living room. Help, he thought, there's a stranger in my flat and she'll be here right until tomorrow morning. I can't find the words, I won't be able to talk to her, she has taken all my power from me and I'm helpless. He added cocoa powder to the milk and stirred with a wooden spoon; steam quickly started to rise. We're in a labyrinth, Lindys and I, and now we've run into each other on one of the many crooked paths, and we can't get past each other, everything has ground to a halt. My breathing, my heart, what am I going to do, move to a hotel for two weeks, so she'll think I've sold the flat? He instantly realised how ludicrous this idea was, as he struggled to find a solution. The milk was starting to boil, so he took the saucepan off the hob and poured the milk into a mug. Added a few extra spoonfuls of sugar and brought her the drink.

She let go of the kitten and grasped the hot drink eagerly.

'Christ, it's hot,' she burst out and licked the corners of her mouth with her pointy, pink tongue. 'But it's delicious, Alvar, it really is.'

He sat down again, touched by hearing the sound of his own name. He rarely heard his name spoken by others and he was filled with conflicting thoughts. Now she was stroking the kitten with her left hand and holding the mug in her right.

'You're probably thinking that I've made a right mess of my life,' she said in between gulps of cocoa.

He could not think of anything to say in reply, so he raised his eyebrows instead, as a sign that she could go on.

'On drugs, shooting heroin. Unemployed, battered and miserable. You probably think I'm the lowest of the low. A pathetic, broken creature who doesn't deserve to live in a welfare state.'

Alvar gave her a startled look. 'No,' he practically cried out, 'I've never ever thought that!'

'You haven't?' She looked at him sharply and narrowed her healthy eye.

'I don't know much about these things,' he said reluctantly, 'but you probably haven't had an easy life.'

His reply caused her to look serious.

'No,' she said in a tired voice, 'I haven't had an easy life. My mum was always ill, she spent most of her time in bed and my dad travelled the world selling ankle socks which don't cut off your blood supply when you wear them.'

Alvar, who had been studying his hands, looked up.

'So you were on your own a lot of the time,' he said softly.

'Practically all the time,' she said. 'And whenever she did get out of bed she would sit in a chair shaking like a rag doll because of her phobia. Have you ever seen phobia close up? It looks like someone's being electrocuted. She took a lot of pills, not that they seemed to do her any good. The curtains in our house were always drawn because she was scared of the light. She was scared whenever someone rang our doorbell, she was afraid of the telephone. We never had any visitors, she was scared of people. I could never bring any friends round.'

'But,' said Alvar, shaken to his core, 'when your father came home, what happened then?'

'Then he would drink,' she said simply. 'Binge drinking two to three weeks at a time. He would turn into someone I couldn't recognise. I had to cook my own meals, no one ever helped me with my homework. When my mum took an overdose, my dad got so scared he left the country. And I was taken into care.'

Alvar leaned forward a little to show his sympathy.

'What was it like there? Were they nice to you?'

She smiled an acid smile.

'Sometimes,' she said and suddenly became indifferent.

Alvar did not understand.

'Either they were nice to you or they weren't.'

'It was too late,' she said, 'I was fifteen years old by then. The damage had already been done.'

Damaged, Alvar thought, broken like the severed bridge. A strange feeling of solidarity filled his heart. Here he was talking to a total stranger, and yes, they were having a real conversation. He suddenly thought he was observing the scene in his own living room from a distance. A skinny girl with a mug of cocoa and a kitten on her lap. He in an armchair, the adult, being supportive. Peace and mutual understanding. Snow melting outside.

'But,' he said, suddenly feeling very reckless, 'surely you could get help somewhere? Couldn't you ask to go into rehab?'

She looked at him with mild reproach.

'And lose the only thing that gets me through the day? I wouldn't dream of it. It might sound crazy to you, but this is how I want it, I don't want to be on this merry-go-round any more. It's riddled with ghosts.'

Alvar recalled the painting and nodded.

'But,' he said, raising his voice because he was beginning to engage deeply, 'you're so young. You might get a job one day, and a flat and a kitten. Wouldn't that be something?'

At that she smiled broadly. 'But I've already got that,' she said, nodding down at the kitten. Alvar started to feel dizzy. He got up from his chair, he felt in urgent need of a large sherry. Did she want to join him?

She shook her head adamantly.

'Growing up with a drunk teaches you to stay clear of alcohol, if nothing else,' she said, sipping her cocoa demonstratively.

This made complete sense, Alvar thought, even though her argument seemed somewhat flawed given that she had substituted alcohol with heroin. But he said nothing. He fetched the bottle from the cupboard and poured himself a large glass. Fell back into his armchair and tasted the golden liquid.

'You're very tidy,' she said, watching him.

He clutched his glass.

'Yes,' he conceded after a long pause, 'I like to know where everything is.'

'Or you'll start to fret?' she teased him, scrutinising him from head to toe.

He shrugged and put the glass on the table.

'That's who I am,' he said simply. 'I can't stand mess. It makes it impossible to find anything.'

She laughed and threw back her head. 'So what are you looking for then?' she said, her voice filled with laughter. 'We're all set on the same path, the one that leads to death. Just in case you didn't know that.'

That irked him. He did not like that she was talking about death, nor did he feel that he was on the same path as her.

'I'm just talking rubbish,' she consoled him. 'My life's chaotic. Getting high, getting beaten up, desperation and strange disgusting men, that's all I have. I bet you have a lot that I'll never have. A well-paid job. Family and friends.'

Alvar looked down. He had none of those things.

'Is it all right if I take a shower?' she asked.

Alvar jumped again. 'I suppose so,' he said.

'I feel so filthy and grimy,' she explained, 'and it's not often I get the chance because I don't have a shower in my room.'

He nodded again. Once more he felt that she was devouring him, but, having given her cocoa, offered her sherry and a bed for the night, it felt impossible to deny her a shower. She leapt out of the sofa and placed the kitten on his lap.

'I know where it is,' she called out and made a beeline for the bathroom. Again he sat there with his heart in his throat. He could feel his cheeks burning. A woman would be standing behind a thin wall with no clothes on. The water would wash over her. The same room where he carefully washed and got himself ready every morning and evening. Her smell, her hair in the plughole. He gulped down more sherry, he could think of no other solution.

At eleven he switched on the TV to watch the late-night news. Lindys was lying on the sofa, her hair was damp. The kitten had snuggled up to her chest and had fallen asleep. She was not interested in the news, she lay calmly with her eyes closed. Her swollen eye worried him, but it did not seem to bother her. Alvar was halfway through his second sherry. Human beings can cope with far more than we think, he decided, as a mild level of intoxication reached his head. There's a woman lying on my sofa and I haven't panicked. I'm taking it all in my stride, I'm a self-assured man. After a while he could see that she was asleep. She had neither a pillow nor a blanket, so he got up and went to a cupboard in the hallway where he kept a pure wool Berger blanket. He returned to the sofa. Stood there for a moment watching her. Her blonde, almost white hair had fallen over her cheek where the skin was stretched tightly over her cheekbones. The swollen eye looked truly nasty. He could not understand how anyone could have the heart to hurt such a defenceless girl. His initial thought had been to spread the blanket over her, but it seemed such an intimate gesture that he did not dare. Instead he laid the blanket over her feet. Perhaps she might wake up during the night and pull it all the way up. What would tomorrow bring? he wondered. What might she get up to while he slept? Could he trust her? No, Ole Krantz would have said, you can't trust people like that. Get rid of them, Alvar, get rid of them! He switched off the light, turned off the TV and went to the bathroom. He remembered that he had forgotten to provide her with a clean towel, so she had used his. He noticed black stains from her eye make-up, too. He took a clean towel from the linen cupboard, brushed his teeth and washed his hands. Left the bathroom light on and the door ajar, so she could find her way in the dark in case she woke up during the night. Then he quickly went out into the hall to retrieve his wallet from his coat pocket. He brought it into his bedroom and placed it in the drawer of his bedside table, and this small precaution felt like a nasty sting.

When he woke up she was standing by his bedside.

He yanked his duvet up under his chin. Her eye looked even worse, he thought, and what time was it anyway?

'Like I said,' she spoke firmly, 'I need twenty grand. If I go back into town without that money, he'll kill me.'

Alvar sat up in his bed. He could not believe his own ears.

'As long as I owe him that money, I'm fair game. I can't even return to my room.'

She stuck her chin out and planted her hands on her hips.

Alvar ran his hand across his bare head. He had been ambushed, it felt unbearable.

'But,' he moaned, 'you'll never be able to pay that back.'

'Oh, sure,' she said confidently, 'I can sell some drugs. Spring's coming, that means I can start working the streets again. I always make a lot of money this time of year.'

Alvar rubbed his eyes.

'I've made coffee,' she said proudly. 'And then we're going to the cashpoint.'

He looked at her in disbelief. Hugged his duvet tightly.

'I don't even have that much money in my account,' he tried in a desperate attempt to escape the humiliation she was subjecting him to.

'But you've got seventy thousand,' she said. 'You've been saving, you told me all about it.'

'It's for the painting,' he objected feebly.

'But you haven't bought it. That wall in there,' she nodded towards the living room, 'is still bloody empty!'

He wanted to get out of bed, but he could not bear the thought that she might see him in his underwear, even though his boxer shorts were perfectly acceptable.

'It's in another account,' he said, 'a savings account. I don't have a card for that.'

She rolled her blue eyes. 'Then we'll go to your bank,' she said lightly. 'They open at nine.'

She went back into the living room.

'I let the cat out,' she called to him over her shoulder.

Alvar forgot all about his embarrassment and jumped out of bed. 'What did you just say? You let him out?'

She came back in, stopped in the doorway.

'Yes, of course I did. Don't tell me you're keeping that poor little creature cooped up in here all day.'

Alvar reached for his neatly folded clothes on the back of the chair near his bed.

'But what if he can't find his way home?' he said miserably. At this she burst into a fit of laughter.

'What are you on about? I've never heard anything like it. Of course he'll find his way home. And he's not as helpless as you think. When you come home from work today, he'll be waiting on your doorstep, he's not stupid either, he knows who feeds him. Now get a move on, the bank opens in thirty minutes.'

He got dressed. He went to the bathroom. He stared at his terrified reflection in the mirror. If he did not give her the money, she would get another beating. If he gave her the money she would become indebted to him and then she would have to walk the streets to pay him back. Both options were unthinkable. If he swore at her and told her to get the hell out of his flat, he would not be able to live with himself; after all, he was a good person. He went through his usual morning ritual; he lingered and dawdled as much as he could. There was music coming from the living room, she had turned on the radio. Finally he came out. She was sitting on the sofa with a cup of coffee and she had put out a cup for him too. They drank their coffee in silence.

'I'm not going to come with you inside when we get to the bank,' she said after a long pause. 'I'll wait outside. I'll sign an IOU,' she added, 'if you want me to.'

He shook his head. 'No, what would be the point of that?' he said dully. There was no way she was ever going to pay him back. Now she had become something he had been lumbered with. He looked

169

at her, he looked at his coffee cup, which she was holding in her hands as if it was the most natural thing in the world. And the kitten outside now on his own, he might get run over. Alvar moaned inwardly.

'Don't be scared,' she said all of a sudden.

'What do you mean?' he asked.

'You're always so scared, you don't have to be. You see, there's nothing to be scared of.'

He bowed his head again. He could no longer see a way out. He could barely imagine this day ending. From now on everything was up in the air and he could not handle it. Days needed to follow like pearls on a string, even, round and smooth. Safe, measured days that he had complete control of. Now he could only see as far as the bank.

She got up. 'Come on,' she said, 'we're going.'

He got up too. Went out into the hall and put on his coat. She slipped out before him. They'll see us, he thought, my downstairs neighbours, they'll see us walk down the road together, and they'll talk.

God help me.

There were no other customers in the bank.

The cashier looked up at him with a welcoming smile. He asked to withdraw twenty thousand and even though it was his own money and even though he was going to give it away he felt greedy. He folded the notes and put them in his pocket. Signed for them and left. She was waiting outside. When he gave her the notes she crumpled. It was like watching butter melt in the sun.

'Thank you,' she said and burst into tears. 'Thank you, thank you, thank you! You've taken such a load off my mind. Oh, you're so nice, so nice!'

Again she gave him a big wet kiss on his cheek. Alvar felt her soft lips on his skin. He was so overcome by emotions that he had to look away. She stuffed the notes into the pocket of her grey jacket and started walking towards Bragernes Square. He followed her tiny figure with his eyes. Then it dawned on him that he no longer had enough money to buy the severed bridge. He also realised he might never see her again. That this was what she had been building towards the whole time. Settle her debt so she would be left in peace. He stood there for a while, wondering about himself and life's twists and turns. The strange direction his life had taken. A feeling of anxiety made his chest ache.

CHAPTER 19

He drags himself across my floor with heavy footsteps.

'So,' I say, 'there you are.'

'Yes,' he says, 'here I am. And you might get angry with me now. Because I keep interrupting you, but I can't help it.'

He glances at the table. 'You're relaxing with a glass of wine, I see. Rather a large glass, I must say. It's practically a bowl.'

He looks fraught. 'I'm up to my neck in problems. I've tried to escape, but it's gone too far.'

I point towards the sofa, ask him to sit down.

'You sound as if it's the end of the world,' I say. 'You've found yourself in unfamiliar territory and it frightens the living daylights out of you.'

He rubs his tired face.

'That's not to say there are no solutions,' I say, 'but you need to act. When you're in a situation involving another person, you need to take a stand. There's nothing wrong with listening, supporting and encouraging. But don't lose sight of your own interests. You've been swallowed up by her needs and her greed. She is walking all over you. You need to start asserting yourself. That doesn't mean you can't help her, but in my opinion you're entitled to make certain demands.'

'Like what?' he asks quickly.

'I think you should demand one hundred per cent honesty, for example.'

He looks at me suspiciously. Raises his eyebrows.

'Where are you going with this?'

I look at him gravely. 'She's told you her life story. Illness. Neglect, alcoholism, foster homes and violent drug dealers.'

'Yes. It's just awful,' he says.

'Indeed it is. If it's true.'

He is startled. 'Is she lying?'

'I don't know. What do you think? It strikes me that you take everything at face value. That she's a victim, that she never had a chance to become anything other than a heroin addict. You've had little experience of dealing with other people,' I continue. 'God knows you don't know much about human nature. If you did you might have questioned her in more detail and perhaps found out that she may not be who you think she is.'

He braces himself as if hit by an icy wind.

'What you're saying now doesn't exactly make me feel any better,' he says.

'I understand that completely. But you've come to me with your questions and you have to accept what you're given. That was the deal we made, wasn't it?'

He contemplates this for a long time. He rests his chin in the palm of his hand.

'It all began so promisingly, I did everything right. She entered the gallery and she was freezing, I decided to do a good deed. In my heart of hearts I didn't think I had the right to throw her out into the cold. So I gave her a mug of coffee. And that coffee,' he agonises, 'was probably my first mistake.'

He hugs himself. 'What kind of a world is this? Where good leads to bad? How are we meant to behave when there are no consequences, no logic or justice? And not only that. Imagine if I had indeed sent her packing the very first time I met her, then she would simply have gone somewhere else and another person would have made the same mistake. There is no solution to this, none at all. And what will this experience do to me? It'll mean that the little goodwill I still possess will just dissolve and evaporate. In the end, I'll just think of her the same way she already thinks of herself. A crooked human being, who's a pain and a burden to everyone.'

I have to smile in response to his reasoning.

'Do you think she's a crooked human being?'

'No,' he says, 'are you mad? I don't think of people like that, never. But I'm having to deal with her and I'm getting really irritated. But only with myself, because I can't find a way out. Do I have to be lumbered with her now, I wonder, is there no way out of this mess?'

'Alvar,' I say watching him, 'you won't find a way out of this mess until you open your ears and eyes.'

'You mean I haven't?'

I raise my glass and drink. 'No, you haven't. You're actually quite self-obsessed when you're with other people. You spend all your energy fretting about how you behave and how you come across, how important it is that you remain polite, and correct and nice. And that's why you miss what's really going on.'

'You've lost me,' he whimpers. 'I've no idea what you're talking about.'

I light a cigarette and blow the smoke towards the ceiling; I follow the blue column with my eyes, the smoke spirals under the lamp.

'She stayed the night in your flat.'

'Yes,' he nods. 'But only on my sofa. With a blanket.'

'Did you check if anything was missing from your flat when you got up this morning?'

Alvar looks sick.

'Did she steal something? That's not possible, she's not like that, I'm certain of it. She wanted money and that's bad enough, but I've no cash lying around the place, only some change in a bowl in the kitchen. And let me add, given that you've brought up my boundless naivety, that I hid my wallet in my bedroom when I went to bed. I have no other valuables.'

'We'll see,' I say. 'But I'll continue to argue that you're naive, even if you don't like it.'

'That doesn't surprise me,' he says. 'But it's better than being a cynic. I've been standing outside your house for years, I've seen people go through a great deal.'

I burst into a hearty laugh. 'I care about everyone who comes to my house,' I say, 'you all grip me in different ways. If I was indifferent to you there would be no story. And I certainly don't feel indifferent towards you, Alvar, I think about you night and day. I hope you'll cope, that you'll do the right things. I may not be able to promise you happiness, but I can promise you hope. Besides, you need to understand that once I've written the last page then you're on your own. With the tools I've given you.'

'Tools?' he says, baffled. 'What tools have you given me?'

'Of course I've given you tools. I'm trying to open your eyes, I'm trying to force you out into the real world, which you've never been a part of. You've been given a name, a job, a voice and I've placed you on a well-lit stage. If we're lucky you'll have an audience too and they will judge you mercilessly. But some might recognise themselves in you and be touched. Others might smile at your defensive and very cautious nature, some might get up and leave halfway through the show. But you've been given something that many people will never have. The chance to show yourself and be seen.'

'But I don't want an audience,' he protests.

'Oh, of course you do. Even if you're not aware of it; you think of yourself as modest, and you can't even bear to entertain the idea. But we need other people, we need to mirror ourselves in them. Naturally there's a risk that we might run into individuals we don't want to meet, but that's part of the price we have to pay.'

'Yes,' he says despondently, 'I'm paying, literally. Twenty thousand kroner, to be precise, left my account today.'

'Because you were incapable of saying no.'

'I didn't think I had the right.'

'Who took that right away from you?'

'I've never had it.'

'Why were you never given it?'

'I don't know. Who hands it out?'

'Your parents,' I say. 'And after them your brothers and sisters and your friends.'

'My parents were very stingy,' he says, 'and I've never had any friends to speak of.'

'In other words,' I say, 'you need to get yourself some friends. They'll give you what you need.'

He gives me a defeated look. 'If you've intervened in order to help me establish a friendship with someone, why have you sent me a heroin addict who's spending all my money?'

'I can understand that you feel used. This isn't what you wanted, you don't need this kind of person.'

'Correct. I don't.'

'But she needs you.'

His grey eyes blink.

'I need to look after the interests of everyone in the book,' I explain. 'You're only concerned with your own part. I'm responsible for the whole story, for everyone involved.'

'But you're on my side, surely?' he asks anxiously.

'That goes without saying,' I reply.

He ponders this for a while, he narrows his eyes.

'You're saying something has gone missing from my flat. That she's taken something. Are you going to tell me what it is?'

I take another sip of my red wine, which is just the right temperature.

'There's a time and a place for everything, Alvar. Think of this book as an equation. It all needs to add up in the end, that's the idea.'

'And if it doesn't add up, what then?'

'Then there'll be no story.'

'But what about me and what you've started?'

'I'll put you on ice. I put many ideas on ice. Four years ago full of enthusiasm I started a new book. It was about three inmates who absconded from Ila security prison. They escape in a van and drive to Finn forest, where they hide out in an old cabin.'

'And then what happens?'

'They're still there. I never managed to move them on.'

He looks disgusted at this thought.

'I'm leaving now,' he announces, 'so that you can finish your work!'

He leaps up from the sofa and goes to the door. 'I just have one small favour to ask you,' he pleads. 'Please forgive me for mentioning this, I don't mean to interfere in your business, but I can't stop myself.'

'No, you can't, can you?' I say. 'What is it?'

'You need to get up early tomorrow morning; you've got work to do. So don't drink so much that you make yourself sick.'

CHAPTER 20

Ten long days passed before Lindys reappeared.

At that point Alvar had started to relax and become his old self again. His shoulders were no longer hunched, his nerves had calmed down. What a fool he had been. He had been thinking this invasion would be permanent. Him, Alvar Eide. The loner. The oddball. Ultimately he was not a very interesting person, so she had probably found someone else to attach herself to, someone else she could fleece. He walked through the town with a spring in his step. He had finished work for the day. His life was once again his own, order and control ruled supreme. The snow melted, it trickled everywhere, people unbuttoned their coats and enjoyed the sun. He quickly popped into the Cash and Carry for some food before making his way up the hill to his flat. Outside he met Green who was emptying his letter box. Alvar nodded briefly, he didn't feel like talking. Green didn't say anything either, but he gave Alvar an odd look. Green's hand appeared holding a pile of junk mail whereupon he went to his own front door and vanished into his flat. Alvar felt a dart of something. What did that look signify? It was such a condescending look, as if his value as a human being had suddenly tumbled. He felt an instant, inexplicable sense of discomfort. He fumbled for the key in his pocket and stuck it in the lock. He tried turning it clockwise, but the key refused to budge. Now what was this? Had the lock caught? He tried again, this time with more force, but was at the same time scared of twisting the metal. Out of sheer frustration he turned the key anticlockwise. He heard a sharp click. What's this? he gasped. He turned the key clockwise again and there was another click. He turned the door handle and the door opened. The explanation revealed itself to him in its full horror. He had left his flat without locking his front door. He went into the hall with a strong sense of unease. He stopped and listened.

'Hiya!' It came from the living room. He froze instantly.

'I let the cat in,' he then heard. 'And afterwards I took a shower. You don't mind, do you?'

Several seconds of silence followed. 'You don't mind, do you, Alvar?'

He wanted to take a step forward, but he was paralysed. Finally he forced himself to move. She was lying on his sofa under a blanket. She propped herself up on her elbow, supporting her head in her hand.

'You can stop staring at me,' she said, 'I'm not a ghost.'

'But,' he struggled to find the words. 'But,' he said again and could manage nothing else.

She sat up on the sofa and arranged the blanket across her lap.

'I just needed some time out,' she explained. She reached for a mug on the coffee table. The kitten was asleep in an armchair. Alvar was speechless.

'I've made myself a cup of tea,' she went on, drinking from the mug. She slurped the tea. 'Well, go on, sit down. I don't bite.'

'But,' he said for the third time. He looked out into the kitchen, he stared out of the window, he did not understand a word of it.

'You can relax,' she said drily, 'there's no one else, only me.'

'Did I leave the door open?' he croaked.

'No, why would you think that? You're not absent-minded, Alvar. I've got a key.'

She picked up something from the coffee table. The metal gleamed in the light.

He took a step closer to the sofa. He was indignant now because he could not understand how that had happened, he could think of no explanation.

'But how did you get hold of that?' he finally managed to ask.

'From the key cupboard in the hall,' she said lightly. 'Most people have more than one set. I took it the last time I was here. I thought I could let myself in and out. You don't mind, do you?'

She peeked up at him with her ice-blue eyes.

He finally collapsed into a chair. The kitten was purring. Lindys drank her tea. Alvar sat like a log, trying to compose himself. Her eye had healed, he noticed. The grey jacket she always wore lay in a heap under the coffee table. He closed his eyes. Unable to take in what had happened.

'For Christ's sake,' she said suddenly, 'you don't need to make such a drama out of it, I'll leave soon, I promise.'

'But the key,' he whispered. 'You can't just help yourself to things like that, people just don't do that.'

'Yes,' she said. 'I do. I help myself. Whereas you never do.' She smiled, showing her sharp teeth.

'I've been thinking of moving,' he said abruptly. It just burst out of him.

She laughed out loud.

'Oh, you're so naive, matey!'

He bowed his head.

'Now take off your coat. Do you want me to make you a cup of tea?'

He shook his head. No, he was screaming on the inside, no, no, no!

'You're nervous,' she said more mildly this time. 'I can tell. But surely you can see that I'm not high?' She spread out her hands and beamed at him.

No, she was not high. And she was more brazen than ever, he thought.

'But you know,' she carried on, 'that's not something that can continue for very long.' She smoothed the blanket a little. 'I need a grand.'

He shook his head, terrified. She narrowed her eyes.

'You know what will happen if you say no,' she said, suddenly sounding vulnerable. 'I'll go cold turkey, and that's not a pretty sight.'

He bit his lip. Gave her a doubting look, wrung his hands in his lap.

'But don't you worry about that, I can always turn tricks. I would have to, anyway, in order to pay back what I owe you. You're thinking you won't ever see that money again, you think I'm robbing you blind and that I'll never repay you. You don't think very much of people like me.'

Her lower lip protruded, she was sulking.

'I'm not really sure,' he began.

'Exactly. You're like all the others. With your fine flat and your job and your cat and your savings while the rest of us are on the street living hand to mouth.'

He shook his head again.

'I don't want to be mean,' he said then. It felt as if he was falling down a pit. He fumbled for his wallet in the inside pocket of his coat, opened it and looked into the notes compartment.

The painting, he despaired. If this goes on, I'll never be able to afford it. It's like the bridge is sliding away from me and another person with a more forceful character will snatch it right before my eyes. A staunch, resolute man. A man who makes decisions without even blinking.

'I've only got five hundred in cash,' he whispered.

She turned her head angrily. 'Bloody plastic,' she said fiercely. 'I've got friends begging on the streets of Oslo and that's all they ever hear. *I don't carry cash.* I'm gonna get one of those little Visa terminals,' she said, 'and I'll swipe their bloody cards until they light up like a Christmas tree.'

He put the notes on the table for her, his hand was limp. She snatched them greedily.

'Just finishing my tea,' she said.

Has she stopped saying thank you? he wondered. Are we where I thought we would end up? Suddenly he felt exhausted. He rested his head in his hands and closed his eyes.

She immediately slammed her mug on the table with a bang. 'Why are you looking so tormented? You look like you're on your deathbed and you're clearly not.'

'I'm just a little tired,' he explained. He looked at the kitten. He wanted to lift him up and stroke his back, but he could not do it while she was looking, as if stroking the kitten was something terribly intimate.

'What have you got to be tired about?' she demanded.

He merely gave her a deep sigh in return.

'Oh, I get it, the picture,' she said, leaping up from the sofa. 'Anyway, it was nice to have a shower. I'm going to go now so you can get some peace. You don't need to get so stressed out just because you come home and find someone in your flat. Most people can handle that,' she claimed.

She retrieved her jacket from under the coffee table and put it on. Stood unsteadily on the high-heeled ankle boots. She went out into the hall. Alvar sat as before, immovable, with his head in his hands.

'See ya,' she called from the hall. He heard the door slam. Nevertheless he remained on his chair. And then a new wave of despair rolled over him. He had not got his key back.

Eventually he snapped out of his trance.

He fetched his shopping bag, which he had abandoned in the hall and went out into the kitchen with heavy steps. There he stopped and stared aimlessly at the worktop. Parts of him were still paralysed, he was unable to lift his hands. She had got him now. She had him in a vice, she was spending his money and using his bathroom, she was drinking his tea. She had the key to his flat in her pocket. She could have ten copies made of it and hand it out on Bragernes Square, it was only a matter of time before they would all be going to his flat and he risked coming home from work to find them there, perhaps a whole gang of them with their feet on the coffee table. And her with the kitten on her lap. He shuddered. This prospect almost brought him to his knees.

He lifted the shopping bag onto the worktop and unpacked the food. For weeks, he thought, for months, for years she would burden him, what am I going to do? These thoughts distressed him deeply. They circled places he did not want to go to. How do you get rid of someone you do not want? What would his neighbour think? Would he end up drifting around the town himself, too scared to go back to a flat filled with strangers, would he end up being forced out of his own home? No! a voice inside him screamed. Fate can't be that cruel. I don't deserve this. Though he did not believe in justice. Misfortune could strike anyone, he realised, and now it's my turn. Or I've got it the wrong way round, she's the unfortunate one. She needs heroin; she walks the streets in thin clothes. He clasped his head with both hands while he stared at a coil of Cumberland sausage. Suddenly he had an idea. The solution was so obvious, so brilliant in all its simplicity, and in addition totally achievable; he just had not thought of it until now. When my mind is darkened my thoughts go around in circles. I'll replace the lock, he exclaimed joyously, I'll do it right away. And get new keys. Then she won't be able to let herself in. And I'll never open the door when the bell rings!

The plan energised him and he hurried into the living room where he snatched the Yellow Pages from the shelf. Looked up a locksmith. Ran to the telephone to punch in the number. He lifted the handset cautiously and heard the dialling tone. It took a lot out of him to make the call. Asking for anything was so terribly hard for him that he wavered. He inhaled deeply several times before dialling the number. He heard the ringing tone. At the same time he looked at his watch. They were obviously closed, it was almost six in the evening. He would have to wait until tomorrow. He left the Yellow Pages open on the floor and went back to the kitchen to prepare his dinner. While he cooked he visualised her face the next time she would be standing outside his door with a key that no longer fitted. He could imagine disbelief, disappointment and rage, he saw anguish and desperation. But sod it, he thought and was startled by his own language, even though he had not said it out loud. I need to take charge here, before everything goes completely off the rails.

He put butter in the frying pan and watched it melt. After a while it started to sizzle, then it turned golden and later nut brown and that was when he cut up the sausage and placed it in the pan. He opened a packet of sauerkraut and heated it in the microwave. He arranged the food attractively on his plate and carried it into the living room. He felt awfully pleased with himself. Something was stirring inside him now, a completely new sensation, and he would never have believed he could feel this good. He was angry, pure and simple. He was angry with Lindys, he was angry with himself, he was angry with drug dealers and he was angry at the injustice of the world. The food tasted delicious. Afterwards he lay on the sofa, filled with a deep sense of calm. He felt serene and determined. The kitten jumped up and settled by his feet.

At exactly nine o'clock the next morning he rang the locksmith. When he had finished the call he felt very proud of himself. He had carried out his plan in a firm voice, employing a polite and friendly tone, it had gone like clockwork. The locksmith would arrive at six in the evening with a new safety lock and two keys, the cost of which would be two thousand three hundred kroner including fitting the lock. Alvar's peace of mind returned and on his way to the gallery he felt the sun warm his face. Of course solutions could be found, of course he was a man of action. He clenched his fists out of sheer joy and punched the air because he felt so strong. He unbuttoned his coat and savoured the faint touch of spring in the air. He was even capable of looking at people he passed in the street, looking at them with an open and friendly face. He straightened his back, he lowered his shoulders, he strode on, imbued with energy. Then he remembered the severed bridge. Which he could no longer afford to buy. This thought depressed him. Then he tried to trivialise it. It had only been a fleeting infatuation, he told himself, and these things always pass. Perhaps he would fall for another painting sometime in the future. Human beings are so unpredictable, he thought, they change, they let you down. Take Lindys, for example, there was no way you could trust her. And when it came to Ole Krantz, well, he was a nice enough chap and he meant well, but when push came to shove he would inevitably look after number one. That's how it is, Alvar Eide thought, as he walked through the town. He reached the gallery at two minutes to ten. He disabled the alarm and went inside. He stopped in front of the painting of the severed bridge. Suddenly it struck him how sombre it was, how dark, almost brutal. On the other hand he had no eye for bright, colourful pictures of naked rocks, glittering lakes or pretty flowers. Beauty, he thought, is all well and good, but it's not what we base our lives on. He continued up the stairs and into the kitchen where he started making coffee. He opened his newspapers and bent over to read.

The locksmith was on time and went to work straight away. Alvar made himself comfortable in an armchair and listened to the drone of the drill. A new lock, he thought, delighted. From now on only I can get in, no one else can disturb my peaceful life. He switched on the television and watched the news. Pope John Paul II was dying. The locksmith worked on. Alvar's heart beat like a drum, he felt empowered in a new way. He was also very good at his job, even if he did think so himself. He could see only clear skies ahead. Everything will be fine from now on, he thought, because I've taken control. Then the locksmith finished and Alvar tried the new lock. He inserted the shiny new key and turned it. A sharp, precise click sounded.

'That's excellent,' he enthused. He thanked the locksmith profusely and settled his bill. The locksmith left. He decided to celebrate his newly discovered vigour with an early evening sherry. Now she could ring his doorbell for as long as she liked, he had shut her out once and for all. Then he turned and looked straight at Lindys.

She had come out from his bedroom, her hair all tangled and messy. Alvar could feel himself starting to sway, he had to steady himself by putting his hand on the wall.

'Christ Almighty,' she said, 'what a racket. What is going on here?'

She stared at him with wide-open eyes, her clothes were crumpled.

Alvar was struck dumb. He just stood there supporting himself against the wall, staring at her in disbelief. At the same time he also felt as if she had caught him with his hands in the till.

'Was that you drilling?' she asked.

He opened his mouth in an attempt to breathe.

'What's your problem?' she said in an exasperated voice. 'I told you I would be coming and going. I wanted to have a nap so I locked the door. That mattress of yours is rock hard, I don't know how you sleep on it.'

He was still incapable of uttering a single word.

'Now just calm down,' she told him, 'it's not like it's a crime to have a nap.'

He opened his mouth, not a sound came out.

'I could hear that you had visitors,' she said, 'and I didn't want to disturb you. What on earth were you doing?'

He was still leaning against the wall, while his heart pounded wildly. She took a few steps into the living room; she scanned it with sharp eyes. However, she found nothing unusual in the bright room. Then something occurred to her. She briskly walked into the hall. Alvar held his breath.

'Bloody hell,' he heard, 'you've replaced the lock! You've only gone and replaced the bloody lock!'

Alvar's knees turned to jelly and he blushed crimson from shame. She returned. Stopped in front of him and planted her hands on her hips and jutted out her chin.

'What's wrong with you?' she raged. 'Cat got your tongue? If you don't want me here you can just tell me to go to hell. Just tell me straight to my face, because that's what you really want to do, isn't it!'

Alvar inhaled. No, he did not want her to go to hell, he just wanted to be left in peace. But he could not find the words.

'Is that what you want?' she challenged him. 'You just want me to piss off because you can't bear the sight of me? Well, if that's the case, why don't you just tell me?'

He shook his head in despair. He tried to straighten up, but his knees threatened to give way. All his vigour deserted him. He was weak, he had shrivelled up and he felt mortified. His chest was hurting too, he realised, as if someone had jabbed a potato peeler into his heart and was now twisting it slowly.

'So we're cool?' she asked in a milder voice. 'I mean, surely we can sit down and be honest with each other. Can't we?'

'Yes, of course,' he said, still upset by everything that had happened.

'So, you're saying we're cool?' she repeated.

'Yes,' he whispered, 'we're cool.'

She was silent. For several long seconds. Then her voice sounded bright and cheerful again.

'That's all right then,' she said, relieved. 'So I'll just have a quick shower and I'll be off.'

She marched into the bathroom, slamming the door behind her. Alvar was still leaning against the wall. Then he tried to stagger over to his armchair. His knees continued to tremble, his heart was starting to calm down, but the pain in his chest still scared him. I'm going to cause a scene, he thought, perhaps I'll collapse and I'll be discovered by a drug addict, lying face down on the floor, no pulse, not breathing. He collapsed into his armchair and clung to the armrests; he could hear the shower running in the bathroom. Now he had really been pushed over the edge. What's your problem? she had asked him. Well, what was his problem, why did his own will evaporate like mist before the sun, whenever it was confronted with another person's determination? An eternity later he heard her turn off the water and then a few minutes of silence followed. She came back out again, bright and cheerful, smiling broadly.

'I feel much better now,' she said running her fingers through her hair, which ended up sticking out all the same. She looked at him and pursed her lips.

'Have you still not got your act together?'

Alvar was afraid to look her in the eyes. 'Of course,' he coughed, but his voice told a different story.

'I need to go out,' she said and headed for his bedroom where she had left the grey jacket she always wore.

'I need another shot,' she declared, 'I'm starting to crave it. In here.' She put her hand on her chest. 'You got any money for me?'

'No,' he said without thinking.

She froze. Then she gawped at him.

'Really? You don't have any money?'

'No,' he said for the second time. The word felt foreign, but also liberating.

'You're telling me that you have spent everything that you own? You're skint? Your bank account has been cleared out and your savings have gone?'

He pressed his lips together. Refused to reply.

'You're lying,' she said fiercely. 'Of course you've got money. But if you don't want to give it to me, then that's another matter, so why don't you just tell me? Didn't we promise each other that we would be honest?'

He lowered his head. He could not fight this creature and her logic; he could not find the words or the strength. Wearily he went out into the hall where his coat hung. He found his wallet, opened it and took out the notes.

'Six hundred,' he muttered and went back. She instantly snatched them from him.

'You're a star!' she declared and kissed his cheek. She went out into the hall. 'And I'll take one of the keys for the new lock. If that's all right with you.'

Alvar was gobsmacked. He could not believe his ears; she spoke these words so casually that it took his breath away.

He ran out into the hall; she already had her hand in the key cupboard.

'You can't just help yourself like that,' he stammered and yanked the key from her. In the confusion he accidentally scratched her hand. Her eyes bored into him. Her jaw dropped.

'This is my flat,' he continued, 'and I need to have some control over who comes and goes here.'

'But you never get any visitors,' she argued.

'All I'm saying,' he said feeling like a complete idiot, 'is that I would like to be in charge of my own home.'

'But you are, aren't you?' she objected with big, wide eyes. 'All I'm doing is sitting on the sofa while you get on with whatever you're doing.'

'Yes, but you know, a key,' he said, 'a key might get lost, I need to have a certain amount of control.'

Her head dropped to her chest, an ominous silence followed.

Alvar had to look down too while he struggled to find the words.

'It's nice that you pop in every now and again,' he said cautiously. 'But there needs to be some order. And you know, you don't give a key to just anyone. Only to close friends.'

That was when she lifted her head and looked him straight in the eyes.

'So I'm not a close friend?' she said pitifully. Her lower lip quivered. 'I'm an unwanted friend, is that what you're saying?'

'No, no,' he protested fiercely, 'but we don't know each other all that well. Not yet.'

She tilted her head as she considered this. 'So what you're saying is that after a while when we know each other better, then I can have a key?'

He was struggling to keep up with her, let alone be ahead.

'Yes,' he shrugged. 'Something like that.'

'How much time are we talking about?' she asked him directly.

Again he shook his head in confusion.

'So how long does it take before two people have become good friends?' she insisted.

'Well, that depends, I'm not really sure, I don't have a lot of experience,' he admitted.

'I think of you as a friend,' she said quietly. She lowered her head gain. 'But I was wrong.' She turned away from him, turned her back on him. 'I always end up getting rejected,' she whispered, hurt.

'But I'm not rejecting you,' he assured her, 'I'm just saying that I need more time!'

'That's easy for you to say. You're not going down the drain like me and I haven't got time. This might be the last time you ever see me!'

He took one step forward. He raised one hand and wanted to place it on her shoulder, but he was afraid.

'Now don't be like that,' he comforted her, 'I'm sure you'll be all right, you always are.'

'You might end up regretting saying those words,' she said. 'People like me drop dead all the time. You know that, we're at risk. You'll probably just breathe a sigh of relief, lock your door and lie down on your sofa and forget all about me.'

'Oh no,' he said quickly. 'Not at all, don't think like that. I'd be beside myself if anything happened to you, I really mean that.'

'So you do care about me a little?' she said softly.

'Of course,' he said firmly.

'But not enough?'

'What do you mean?'

'Not enough to give me a key?'

Alvar went totally quiet. It dawned on him that he had run out of words, that he would never win this battle. So he held out his hand and gave her the new key. She instantly closed her fingers and gripped it. A second later the front door slammed.

He stayed in his armchair for a very long time.

The television was droning on in the background, but he did not even notice it. She is like a pebble in my shoe, he thought, every single step I take hurts. She is like burdock, you cannot pull it off without hurting yourself, she is like an itch that gets worse and worse. She spreads likes a disease, she grows like a tumour, she makes me want to scream. His vicious thoughts frightened him. He was not a violent man, not at all. He was angry with her, but his anger instantly ricocheted back on himself. He felt faint when he thought about his own incompetence. He would never hit her, he did not know how to argue, he had never been taught how and he never felt the desire. And yet he could still feel pressure building up inside his chest. He listened carefully to it. Yes, it was a roar, there could be no doubt. He had never heard himself roar and he was terrified of letting it out. He imagined a wild animal in there baring its teeth, hurling itself against the bars of its cage, desperate to get out. Then he started to sob. It was a dry, pathetic sob and it made him crumple as he sat there in his armchair. Alvar Eide is sobbing, he thought, my life has become so dramatic that I have lost my self-control. He dried his tears, but he was unable to get up from his chair. A sherry, he thought, that's what I need to calm my nerves. He pulled himself together and made himself go into the kitchen to get the bottle. His hands were shaking, the tears were flowing. He felt like a nervous wreck. And all because of a girl of forty-odd kilos. He found a milk glass and filled it almost to the brim. Raised it to his mouth and drank. He leaned against the worktop gulping sherry, and suddenly he had to laugh. He observed himself through the eyes of another. A lonely man reduced to drinking sherry from a milk glass with tears streaming down his face, just because some girl had been to his home. The whole business was so demeaning it made him cringe. He continued to laugh, louder now, it began to resemble a kind of braying, sounds he did not know he was capable of making filled the whole kitchen. Every now and then he would pour himself another sherry, swigging it as if it were juice, followed by more outbursts of his braying laughter. With his free hand he gripped the worktop tightly.

This, he realised, is the end of the road for me.

CHAPTER 21

'I'm already beaten,' Alvar says.

It is hard for him to accept this realisation, and his back is bent. His eyes shine from too much sherry and his hands are shaking badly.

'Sit down,' I order him. 'Let's talk about it.'

'No one in my family ever had a drink problem,' he adds.

'Is that right?'

'I just wanted you to know that. It's not a path I wish to take and I don't usually knock back sherry like this.'

'I'll bear that in mind,' I reply. 'So let's say that you needed to let off some steam very badly, but that it's not going to become a habit.'

'Thank you.'

He lets himself fall onto my sofa. There are beads of sweat on his shiny forehead and hints of dark shadows under his eyes.

'There's something I've been meaning to ask you,' he says in a tired voice.

'Fire away.'

'Is she the strong one or am I?'

I consider his question. 'What do you think?'

He shakes his head. 'I don't know. But I need to take my share of the blame for the situation I've ended up in. At the same time she is so slippery, like an eel between my hands. I try to find a way out, but as things stand now, I can't see it. There are times when I just feel like giving up. Leave the responsibility for everything to you. Just drift along while you let things happen, whatever those things might be. It's not as if it can get any worse, can it? Can it get any worse?'

'What precisely are you scared of?' I ask.

He thinks about it. 'Well, many things, I guess. Perhaps I'm scared of losing my mind. Sometimes it feels like that might happen and I'm frightened that the fragile thread that I have with the outside world might snap. Though there is no history of mental illness in my family either, not as far as I know, anyway. And I'm also scared that I might act on impulse.'

'Why is that scary?'

'Surely that's obvious,' he exclaims. 'We can't allow ourselves to be controlled by impulses.'

'Which particular impulse did you have in mind?' I ask.

'The one that controls your temper,' he says darkly.

I lean forward across the table. I look him straight in the eye.

'Alvar. Dear Alvar. I know you, you wouldn't be able to hurt a fly.'

'I've always thought so too,' he says, somewhat relieved. 'I've always striven to behave as calmly as possible. But sometimes I get this gut feeling. It tightens and it spreads to my arms in a horrible way. And before I know it I clench my fists ready to fight. Because everything around me is exploding and because I can't find the words, so I lose my footing and I stumble over the edge. Are you turning a peaceful man into a thug, is that your plan?'

'No, Alvar, calm down. God knows you're a peaceful man,' I say, 'and I'm not going to tamper with this feature. Mankind's tragedy, however, is that too much peacefulness can sometimes lead to disaster. You ought to read Zapffe,' I suggest, 'he's your kind of philosopher. I've got his essays here on my bookshelf, if you want to borrow them.'

'Thank you.'

'Incidentally, I have always believed that you ought to judge people on the basis of their actions,' I continue, 'not on what they say, think or mean. There are plenty of people ready to shoot their mouths off.'

'But I'm not that type either,' he says quickly. 'I don't act and I don't judge. All I'm doing is pacing up and down this labyrinth looking for the exit. Like a lab rat. A repulsive, trained lab rat.'

'I think you're being very hard on yourself.'

'You're the one being hard, it's your book.'

'Our book,' I correct him. 'Don't underestimate your own part in this collaboration. I listen to you, I can be influenced. Especially at this point, when we're well into the book.'

'It's going to be dramatic, isn't it? That's what I'm picking up from you. We've peaked and now we're going to start running down the hill. And I can't even pray because you haven't given me a God.'

'Would you like a God?'

'I imagine all lost souls would. It's the loveliest fairy tale in the world,' he adds, looking sad. 'Reserved only for the few.'

'Try to believe in yourself,' I say, 'believe that you're worth something. That you can do something. That you possess great reserves which you can draw on in times of crisis.'

'You believe in me,' he said miserably. 'But I'm scared that I might end up letting you down. That I can't run the race you have entered me in.'

I look at him solemnly and say sincerely, 'It has never, ever happened that one of my characters has let me down.'

'There's always a first time.'

'With that sort of attitude you might well be right. It takes a lot out of me too, don't forget that. I'm worn out.'

He gets up from the sofa and takes a walk across the floor. His head is bowed, his hands are behind his back. Then he stops, he has remembered something.

'In some strange way I actually like Lindys,' he says, somewhat surprised by his own, stumbling admission.

'Tell me more.'

'She doesn't give a damn about anything. She doesn't follow any rules, she helps herself to whatever she wants. She doesn't care what people think of her. She never tries to please anyone and she doesn't care about consequences. Her attitude is devil-may-care and perhaps that's a kind of freedom. She's on heroin, she lives her life one hour at a time. Whereas I, on the other hand, am trapped inside myself. I have order and control and structure, but I can't get out.'

'And deep down that's what you want? To finally show yourself as you really are, warts and all?'

'I never used to think so,' he says, 'but now I can see that this is what it's all about. I'm fed up with being careful. Anonymous. Correct.'

'What do you think we would see if you finally escaped?'

He stops. He folds his arms across his chest.

'That's the problem, this is what truly worries me. Perhaps I have nothing to show, perhaps what you see in front of you standing here on the floor is all there is to see. Or, I might open up only to discover terrible things.'

'Such as?'

'Cowardice. Brutality. Panic.'

'But no great passion,' I smile, 'no bubbling joy, no heartache, no wild and uncontrollable laughter.'

He goes over to the window and stares out of it. His shoulders sag.

'I can see all the way into town.'

'Yes, it's beautiful.'

'All the lights,' he adds, 'street lights, lights from the houses, they glow.'

'Everything looks beautiful at a distance, doesn't it? Even when seen through shimmering, polluted air.'

'When will the battle commence?' he asks, abruptly turning round.

I shift slightly in my chair, 'Are you asking me for an actual date?'

'Why not? There's no escape for me anyway.'

'November,' I propose. 'The eighteenth.'

'Why November exactly?'

'I need rainstorms and fairly cool air. I need rotting leaves and muddy roads. The kind of shivering quality that characterises November. The grey, naked landscape stripped of everything that grows and comforts us, but not yet blessed with white, icing-sugar snow. A bleak time in many ways, a brutal time. It is as if everything surrenders in November and we huddle in corners and light candles. I love November.'

'But why?' he repeats.

'I was born in that month, on the sixth. It was a wild night, God-awful weather, when I saw the world for the first time. November is in my blood, a darkness, a melancholy. A permanent feeling of sadness. My hands are like bare branches, I have fog in my head and storm in my heart. You were born in September,' I tell him, 'and you are marked by that, the summer was drawing to a close when you were born. The holidays had ended, but the harvest had yet to come and Christmas was far away. No expectation,' I say, 'just an orderly, eventless time between bright sunshine and crisp frost. But I love all the months, each has its own tone, its own hue. Imagine this wheel. January, for example, bright blue and white and a trumpet with clear, sharp notes. February, almost identical, with the sun a little more yellow and I hear a cornet. March, grey and white, I hear a viola, there lies a faint hope in its deep note. April, yellow and white. Violins,' I say, 'with a hint of trapped despair. May, yellow and green. People dancing around a maypole. June, airy and sky blue, accordion. A big flaming bonfire, sparks flying off out into the night. July is a deep yellow, the colour of sand, the sound of a radio. August, the summer is fading, I hear a faint guitar. Then comes your month, September. It is the colour of earth and now I hear a cello. October,' I continue, 'rusty red and with a strong beat. Someone is playing an oboe. November, as I mentioned just now, bare. In November I hear kettledrums and a moaning trombone. Then we finally reach December, with candles and tinsel. And so the years pass, in an ever-recurring circle. If you live to be eighty, Alvar, you will have existed nearly thirty thousand days. Or, approximately seven hundred thousand hours, if you like.'

He pales. 'And how many minutes is that?'

'Forty-two million. It's almost three hundred million heartbeats.'

Alvar comes over and steadies himself against my chair.

'You mustn't say such things. Now I too can feel every single heartbeat.' He places his hand on his chest.

'It's fine,' I say, 'it's fine that you can feel your heart. I think we need to feel alive, I think we need to expose ourselves to pain. But in our society this is not acceptable. People have always used their shrewdness and imagination to relieve pain. Today everything must be easy and it mustn't take time. I hate disposable cutlery,' I confess, 'and ready meals. Parboiled rice. Powdered hot chocolate and instant coffee. Part-baked bread. Things like that. Living takes time. We need to give each other time.'

He finds his place on the sofa. 'November,' he says lamely. 'It's eight months away and from now on I'll be aware of every second. Lindys has knocked through my shell and left a gaping hole. I feel the cold differently now and nearly all sounds have become noises. I'm not used to such sensitivity.'

'It's about time your body found out what it means to be alive,' I say. 'And yes, it hurts. But that's also how you'll learn to let in a little joy.'

'I don't need very much of that,' he claims, 'I prefer security. And you have taken it away from me.'

'In order to give you something else,' I say. 'Experience.'

CHAPTER 22

The days passed, and the weeks.

Alvar carried out his job with the same diligence and pride as he always had done. He was friendly, correct and polite, and when he framed pictures in the workshop it was with great care and attention to detail. But in the late afternoon, when it was nearing closing time, he was consumed by a nagging anxiety. What if she was lying on his sofa, or even worse, in his bed? Perhaps she was having a shower in his bathroom now? Perhaps she had robbed him blind? Though he had no valuables to speak of. He had acquired another idiotic habit. He always stopped by the cashpoint outside the Cash and Carry on his way home. As long as he had money, she would take it and go, it was the only way he was able to get her out of the flat quickly. His savings dwindled slowly and steadily. One day there would be no more, he thought, one day I'll be as poor as a church mouse. What's she going to do then?

He left the gallery at five in the afternoon. The knot in his stomach grew as he walked through the streets to the Cash and Carry. He got to the cashpoint, he took out his wallet and found his card, which he stuck in the machine. The card was checked, please enter your PIN. He entered the code and all the time a voice inside was telling him that this was insane, but he was unable to stop himself. The money was his only weapon and with it he bought back his own freedom. He took out six hundred kroner, put the notes in his wallet and headed home. The cat was sitting on his doorstep and he experienced a brief moment of bliss. His front door was locked, but then she usually locked it from the inside, presumably so she could hear when he came back. He unlocked the door and went in. He spotted her immediately; she was lying on the sofa under the blanket without moving. He took a few more steps towards her. Then, to his horror, he saw something on the coffee table. A syringe, he realised, and a thin light grey rubber tube. He clasped his mouth in fear. He stared at her for a long, long time, but all he could see was a bit of her cheek and locks of her blonde hair falling over her forehead. Out of sheer desperation he coughed violently to see if she would react. She did. She turned her head and opened her eyes, her gaze was unfocused.

'You can't bring this back here,' he yelped, pointing at the table, at the syringe and the tube, which frightened the living daylights out of him. She grunted something incomprehensible and closed her eyes. He remained where he was while his brain was working overtime. He had put up with so much from her, but now he was overcome by an irresistible urge to put his foot down. To tell her that there were limits to what he was willing to tolerate.

'Lindys,' he said louder this time, 'you can't bring drugs in here!'

Again she opened her eyes and she gazed at him dully. 'Why are you calling me Lindys?' she slurred. 'My name's Rikke.'

He let out a soft groan. 'I'm not having it!' he said, still in a tone of voice bordering on falsetto. She sat halfway up, turned and lay down with her back to him. Alvar waved his hands in the air. It felt as if he was fighting a shadow, which kept slipping away so that he would never be able to punch it. He looked at the syringe on the coffee table and shuddered. Here, in his living room. A girl on heroin. Had his neighbours seen her arrive, and what might they be thinking? He spun on his heel abruptly and went out into the kitchen. Stood for a while leaning against the worktop while he thought furiously. I need to eat, he thought, I need to eat to get through this, I mustn't panic. I need to talk to her when she wakes up, properly. I need to be firm and decisive and resolute. Yes, he thought, I need to stop giving her money. I will make this a condition. She will not get another krone if she brings drugs into my living room. It's that simple.

Cheered by this resolution he opened the door to the fridge and found a box of eggs. An omelette was what he needed, he could grate some cheese and sprinkle it on top, have some bread with it. The cat appeared for a drink of water. There were no sounds coming from the living room. He tried to ignore the fact that she was in there. Then he cracked two eggs against the edge of a bowl. She'll be gone soon, he told himself, and perhaps I'll get several days without a visit. Again he had another flash of inspiration and an idea began to take shape in his head. She had taken his spare key, perhaps it was in the pocket of her grey jacket? He took a few steps and looked into the living room. Yes, it was in a pile on the floor. And Lindys was still sleeping. Or Rikke, or whatever her name was. What if he stole it back? What if he gave her a taste of her own medicine for once, used her own methods? This is what it means to be shrewd, he realised, and now there was a time and a place for it.

He tiptoed into the living room. His heart began to pound, but she was clearly on a different planet, he could not even hear her breathing. Then he got hold of the collar of her jacket and pulled it carefully towards him. First he tried the left pocket, but there was nothing but fluff. Then he eased his hand into the right pocket and there it was. His key. He snatched it and put it in his trouser pocket and he instantly felt like a thief. He replaced the jacket on the floor and went back to the kitchen. I had no idea I could be this devious, he thought, amazed. Soon she'll wake up and rub her eyes. Then she'll ask me for money and then she'll leave. Still thinking that the key is in the pocket of her jacket. Two to three days will pass and then she'll return, but she won't be able to let herself in. There'll be trouble, he thought anxiously, what am I going to do if she starts hammering on the front door with her fists, what will the neighbours say? He started to worry, unable to live with what he had done. Perhaps it was best if she had her own key anyway? Then he became massively irritated at his own indecisiveness, he was perfectly entitled to retrieve his key.

He whisked the eggs with a fork and added salt and pepper to the mixture. He poured the eggs into a frying pan, and they started to congeal instantly. He grated some cheese and sprinkled it onto the eggs, he sliced some bread and buttered it. When the meal was ready he carried it into the living room. Again he looked at the syringe and the tube. He felt ill at ease. Something like that was dangerous, he knew, the papers wrote all sorts of things about infection, and here he stood with his freshly cooked food which he was just about to eat. He rushed back out into the kitchen and found a pair of Marigold gloves, pulled them on and went over to the coffee table. Picked up the tube and the syringe, went over to the bin under the worktop and dropped them into it. Finally he could breathe more easily and he went over to eat. He switched on the television and still she did not stir. Where are you now? he wondered, and looked at her blonde hair. In some kind of paradise? A place free from hurt, worries and discomfort? A place with no concept of time, no pain? A place where you float? Perhaps it's like being in warm water, the light is low and the silence complete. Soon she would wake up and then what would happen? He ate quietly, taking care to breathe steadily and calmly the whole time; unless he focused on his breathing, he would whip himself into a state of frenzy within seconds. When he had finished he clinked his cutlery a little to see if she would react. She did. She rolled quietly onto her back and faced him. Her eyes were black.

'Hi,' she said softly.

He did not reply. He was not sure whether she was present in the same way he was, and if she wasn't then there would be no point in trying to have a conversation with her.

'Christ, I'm so thirsty,' she said, 'do you think you could get me a glass of water?'

She brushed her hair away from her face with a drawn look.

He looked at her, but still did not reply. He carried out his plate and cutlery, found a glass in the cupboard and got some water from the tap for her and carried it back. She sat up on the sofa, grabbed the glass and drank greedily; he could hear how the water glugged down her narrow throat.

'Your neighbour,' she said eventually, 'he's a very bad-tempered man.'

Alvar looked at her.

'He started asking questions when I was outside. As if it's any of his business what we get up to.'

Are we getting up to anything? Alvar wondered.

'He told me you were out,' she went on, 'and I told him I had my own key. You should have seen the look he gave me. As if I was a piece of rubbish someone had thrown on his lawn.'

'You can't bring your drugs in here,' Alvar said abruptly.

She looked up. Suddenly she looked sulky.

'No, I suppose you would prefer it if I sat in a doorway and shot up for everyone to see.'

He could think of no answer to that.

'But,' he objected, 'I don't want to get mixed up in anything like that.'

She drained her glass and slammed it down on the coffee table. 'You're not mixed up in anything,' she stated irritably. 'I don't row with you, I don't make you take drugs, do I?'

'No.'

'So what are you whingeing about?'

'Well,' he whimpered, 'I don't mean to whinge. But it makes me a little nervous.'

'That's because you're a sissy,' she declared.

'But, Rikke!' he moaned.

'Rikke?' She gave him a baffled look.

'I've got some cash for you,' he said before he could stop himself. 'Six hundred kroner. You can have it, but then you have to do this somewhere else. I make this a condition,' he said, his voice getting louder. He instantly felt his strength return.

Her jaw dropped.

'You're blackmailing me,' she said, hurt. 'You know I'm desperate and now you're putting pressure on me.' She buried her face in her hands. He thought he could hear her snivelling. Her slender shoulders jolted.

'But you have your room?' he said. 'Isn't that right?'

'I don't have a room,' she sobbed.

'But then where do you sleep?' he exclaimed.

'Here, there and everywhere,' she cried. 'Surely you can understand that people in my line of work don't have all the stuff that normal people have. A bed. Food. A regular pay cheque. I've got none of those.'

He scanned her face for tears, but found none.

'I don't think I'm asking for much,' she said, 'and I don't know what your politics are, but I thought you were a decent person.'

'Of course, I'm a decent person,' Alvar said. 'Look here.' He got out his wallet. 'Here's some money.'

She snatched it as swiftly as she always did and scrunched it up in her hand.

'If you cut me off then I'll have no one,' she said in tears. 'You know I'm going straight to hell and it would have been nice to have some company for the last bit of the journey.'

'You're not going to hell, are you?' he asked, perturbed.

'Don't be so bloody naive!' she screamed.

'Hush!' he said quickly. 'You mustn't shout, not in here!'

His heart had started pounding again. He found it unbearable when people shouted, his whole body shrank.

'I don't think you've got it in you,' she claimed, looking defiant. She got up from the sofa and ran her fingers through her hair. She stumbled then regained her balance.

'But I'm going to go now and leave you in peace. Pour yourself a sherry, Alvar, let yourself go a little, why don't you?'

She picked up her jacket from the floor; Alvar's heart skipped several beats. In the distance he thought he could hear the faint roll of drums slowly getting louder. She put on her jacket, buttoned it and quickly brushed herself down. Then she stuck her hands in her pockets and Alvar held his breath. She searched for a while, then her eyes widened.

'The key,' she said dully. For a moment she looked confused. Alvar froze.

'The key, it's gone.' She looked at him with disbelief and anger. Then she exploded.

'You've pinched it!' she shouted. 'You've pinched my bloody key!'

Alvar felt as if he was being melted down and poured away, his cheeks were burning hot.

'I see.' She folded her arms across her chest, her face hardened. 'So you've finally shown your true colours, it took you long enough. So this is what all your supposed goodness boils down to. You were just faking, you were just pretending to be a good person. You're the most deceitful person I've ever met. The most cowardly, the most devious!'

Alvar started to shake in his armchair.

'You're just as bad as all the others,' she went on, her voice jarring. 'You'll open your door to some sorry creature, but that's all. That's fine by me, I'll get out of your way once and for all and you'll never see me again. I'm going to get myself another hit, a big one, which will make me forget this bloody shithole which is all this world really is!'

'No. No!' Alvar screamed, getting up from his chair. 'Don't say things like that! Look, look, here is the key.' He pulled it out of his trouser pocket. 'I don't mind you coming here, I really don't; I'm not going to throw you out, that's not what I meant. Please don't get angry, it's just me, I get really anxious sometimes,' he stuttered.

She accepted the key. Studied the new, shiny metal and looked at him with narrow eyes.

'The problem is,' she said slowly, 'it's a bit difficult for me to believe what you're saying. Because now I don't know if you really mean it.'

'I mean it,' he pleaded, 'please, please forgive me, I'm such an idiot.'

'God knows,' she said, somewhat appeased now. 'Well, well. I'm counting on you then. I'm relying on the fact that you've finally made up your mind and that you'll keep your word.'

She went out into the hall. Alvar stared after her. She opened the door and turned one last time. Then she sent him a look that made him wince. I know who you are all right, the ice-blue eyes said. I know how to handle you and I'm much stronger than you. The door slammed shut.

CHAPTER 23

In April, May and June she came and went as she pleased.

Alvar went about his business with a knot in his stomach. He thought of the knot as a grey tumour and imagined how it would spread to the rest of his body. How it would devour him from the inside, wrap itself around his internal organs and strangle them. He was always overwhelmed by relief whenever the flat was empty. When it was not he mobilised all his remaining strength to deal with her. Keep some kind of conversation going, give her money and get her out of the door as quickly as possible. His savings were dwindling dangerously fast and at times he caught himself longing for the moment when he would withdraw his last krone. Then it would all be over and she would have to go elsewhere. At the same time he knew that as long as he gave her money then she would not have to walk the streets, something he could not bear to think about. She would not have to make her frail body available to complete strangers, in an alleyway, in the back of a car or in some disgusting room.

She had kept her part of their bargain and he had not once returned to find her syringe on the coffee table. But she was often high. Then her eyes were so distant that he knew she must be in another universe where he was unable to reach her. If she were, he would wait in his armchair until she came round and then they would chat about everyday stuff. Often he was appalled at how little she knew about what went on in the real world. Her existence was narrow and dark, and it was all about satisfying her violent addiction to heroin. Nothing else mattered. She disappeared on a few occasions. Once she was gone fourteen days and Alvar became strangely restless. He did not understand why. Perhaps she has gone to another town, he used to think, or she might simply be sick. Not that he downright missed her, but he could not handle the uncertainty of it.

His neighbour, Green, had stopped talking to him; whenever they met, he would merely nod and disappear into his flat. They were probably wondering what on earth was going on, but Alvar did not have the energy to worry about it, and he could not cope with arguments or conflicts, so he nodded politely in return and pretended that everything was just fine.

He had become very fond of his cat. The kitten had grown in record time and turned into a fine, handsome animal. Of course, he ought to have him neutered, but he could not find it in himself to call the veterinary surgery and have this brutal procedure carried out. He could not bear the thought of witnessing the operation. He just did not have the strength, it was that simple. As a result the cat often came back home with cuts and tears all over his body from fights with other cats in the neighbourhood. And he clearly had an inbuilt alarm clock because he always sat on the stairs waiting for Alvar when he came home from work. If he was not there it usually meant that Lindys or Rikke or whatever her name was had let herself into the flat and let the cat in at the same time.

As he walked up the drive he could not see the cat. He waited for him on the bottom step for a while; he called out a few times to see if he would turn up. And then something grey and white stirred in the bushes. And the cat came towards him. He unlocked the door and went inside; the cat followed him. There was no one on his sofa. So she was probably not going to turn up today either; that would make it six days since he saw her last. The cat walked around the floor, sniffing. He followed him with his eyes, but when he went to lift him up, he hissed furiously at him. He was shocked. The cat had never hissed at him before. Perhaps he was hurt. He checked him for cuts and bruises, but he looked unharmed and healthy. He went out into the kitchen with the shopping he had just bought. Some bacon, a leek, a litre of milk, a loaf of bread. The cat followed him and went over to his bowl straight away and started to eat his pellets. Alvar diced the bacon with a sharp knife. He chopped up the leek and fetched eggs from the fridge; he wanted to cook himself a really delicious omelette. The cat ate until he was sated, then he returned to the living room where he was in the habit of settling down in an armchair or on the corner of the sofa. But today he did not do that. He stopped in the middle of the floor and started miaowing plaintively. Alvar followed and looked at him. He had a strong feeling that something was wrong, but he couldn't pinpoint what it was.

'Why don't you want to go on the sofa, Goya?' he asked. The cat miaowed again. So he went back to finish his cooking. That was when he heard someone open and slam the front door shut. And there she was, dressed in a pink angora jumper and leggings so washed out they hardly had any colour. The same ankle boots with those ghastly heels.

'Hi. What are you making?'

He glanced at her sideways from the kitchen and nodded. She joined him immediately and asked for a glass of cold water.

'I'm thirsty all the time,' she explained, leaning her head back as she drank. He nodded a second time. He did not really understand addicts, but suddenly it was rather nice that she had turned up. And she never stayed for long, he had to give her that. Most of the time she was simply sleeping on his sofa while he got on with his business. Also, she was not high and her ice-blue eyes were completely clear. How bright they are, he thought, as hard as jewels. Yet again he was struck by her transparency, her green veins, her pale cheeks, her skin stretched tightly across her bones. She put down her glass on the worktop and went into the living room. She settled down on her regular spot on the sofa. She called the cat immediately; her voice was soft and enticing. Alvar whisked eggs. He put the diced bacon and the leeks into a frying pan. The smell of bacon and leek began to fill the kitchen. Did she want anything to eat? No, she never wanted anything to eat. He did not believe that she ever ate. He would estimate that she weighed around forty kilos, a frail skeleton stripped of muscles. He peeked into the living room. She had got up again, and she walked across the floor to get the cat. He hissed aggressively at her. She straightened up, folded her arms and looked at Alvar, who had poked his head round the door.

'So what have you gone and done now?' she asked.

He had no idea what she meant. He rushed back to the stove to turn the heat down.

'What have I done wrong now?' He gave her a baffled look.

'The cat,' she said, looking at him and shaking her head at the same time.

'Yes, he's a bit odd today,' Alvar said, watching the cat. He had jumped up onto the windowsill where he was trying to hide behind a potted plant.

'Odd?' she said, exasperated. 'Is he odd?'

'What I'm trying to say,' he replied, 'is that he's been behaving a little strangely today. I think he might have been in a fight. He won't let me pick him up.'

Suddenly she walked up to him with long striding steps.

'But dear God,' she said loudly, 'haven't you got eyes in your head?'

'Yes,' Alvar hesitated. 'Of course I have.'

'No, you bloody don't. Take a look at him, go on!'

She pointed towards the windowsill, her finger quivering. Then she began to laugh out loud.

'Just look at the cat!' she ordered him.

'But what about the food,' he whimpered.

She quickly moved the frying pan away from the heat and nudged him into the living room. Alvar felt confused. But he did as he was told; he went into the living room and over to the window where the cat was pressing itself against the pane. His eye teeth were bared, they were sharp as needles.

'Is he pregnant?' he asked sheepishly.

At that she threw back her head and laughed heartily.

'Pregnant? Are you out of your mind? It's a tom, for God's sake!'

'But, something's wrong,' he said perplexed, shaking his head, 'and I don't know what it is.'

'It's not your cat,' she laughed.

'Eh?'

He let his hands drop and he wriggled his fingers nervously.

'You've dragged someone else's cat into the flat.'

'No,' he said quickly.

'Yes! Surely you can see it's not Goya. Goya has a white chest and grey paws. This one has a grey chest and white paws. It's also smaller and it's frightened out of its wits because it doesn't know you. It wants to get out, but it can't find the way. Alvar, go and open the door. I bet you Goya is sitting out on the step wanting to get in.'

Alvar stared at the strange cat, his arms still hanging limply. He felt like a complete idiot. She was still laughing. A silvery, playful laughter tinged with superiority.

'You really are something else,' she hiccupped. Alvar wanted to laugh, but he could not manage it. He went out into the hall and opened the door. Goya shot in. The strange cat darted across the floor like an arrow and was gone in a flash. Alvar's cheeks flushed scarlet. That he could be so absent-minded, it was unbearable. Angrily he marched out into the kitchen and put the frying pan back on the heat; he heard the butter starting to sizzle again and added the eggs. He frantically began talking about other things. How much he needed a holiday and how he was thinking about maybe going away for a few days. He peered furtively at her to see how she would react.

'I can look after your flat for you,' she suggested enthusiastically. 'And water your plants. Can I stay overnight? It's so comfy. I won't bring anyone here, I promise.'

He didn't reply, but he thought about what she was saying.

'And I can clean the floors and collect your post.'

He folded the omelette and eased it out of the frying pan with a spatula.

'But do you think you could leave me some money before you go away?'

He sighed. Found cutlery and poured himself a glass of milk, placed everything on a tray and carried it into the living room. She followed him.

'And I can feed the cat. You can't just leave him, you know, he needs his food.'

'I could put him in a home,' he argued.

'Oh, but that's so expensive,' she replied.

'You won't lose the key, will you?' he asked. 'I'm scared that it might fall into the wrong hands.'

'I'll take good care of the key,' she said. 'Look. It's around my neck on a piece of string.'

She stuck her hand down the pink angora sweater and pulled out a blue string and there was the key.

'I won't let anyone else in, I won't talk to your neighbours and I won't tell anyone that you've gone away; I'm not stupid, Alvar.'

He believed her. In spite of everything there was a part of her that wanted to be honest.

'Where will you go?' she asked, flopping onto the sofa.

He pulled his chair closer to the dining table and started eating.

'Well, not far. Only a few days. A short break, to Copenhagen possibly. Or maybe Sweden, where they have all these hostels.' As he said it he realised that the idea of sharing accommodation with a group of total strangers did not appeal to him in the least. 'Or I might find a cheap hotel,' he said. 'I might drive around in the Mazda for a bit and see the countryside. Värmland, for example, is said to be very pretty, and a change is as good as a rest.'

'Yes, it is, isn't it?' she replied warmly. 'I fancy a change as well. I hate this town,' she went on, 'all those people staring at you, young guys fighting the whole time, I'm fed up with it. And it's so bloody cold in the winter, there's a wind from the river, it's like someone pinching your cheeks with icy fingers. Have you ever felt it, Alvar?'

Yes, he had. All the same one of his favourite things about the town was the river running through it. The bridge, the boats. The promenade where he liked to go for walks on Sundays.

'You're so good at managing on your own,' she said abruptly.

He looked up.

'You cook proper food. And it's always so neat and tidy in here, and so clean. Your plants thrive, all lovely and green.'

He shook his head, slightly embarrassed by her praise.

'I mean, single men are usually so messy.'

'Really?'

'I know a lot about that,' she said, 'I've visited a lot of them.'

I don't doubt that, Alvar thought, drinking his cold milk.

'Don't you have any vices at all?' she asked.

He considered this. 'I drink sherry,' he said, 'in moderate quantities.'

'Then it's not a vice,' she stated. 'Merely a harmless habit. It doesn't mean that you are genetically disposed towards dependency.'

'There is such a gene?' he asked.

'I swear on my life,' she said. 'In fact, addicts like me are innocent victims. You must realise that, Alvar.'

'I'm not judging anyone,' he said, hurt.

'I know,' she said softly. 'You're a sweetheart.'

Alvar choked on his milk and was overcome by a violent coughing fit.

'And you press your trousers,' she laughed. 'I don't know anyone else who does that.'

Alvar ate the rest of his omelette in silence. From time to time he glanced up at her, there was something he was dying to ask her. She lit a cigarette; he went into the kitchen as he always did to fetch her a saucer. He returned and placed it on the coffee table.

'What's your real name?' he asked, bending down.

She threw her head back and laughed. 'It's Ella,' she said, 'Ella Margrethe Riis.'

'And what will it be tomorrow?' he asked.

'Well, let me see, Linda, perhaps. Or Britt. You can call me what you like.'

'Heidi,' he suggested.

She snorted. 'What? That's just so naff.'

He pouted and pretended to look stern. 'You were the one who wanted to play name games so you'll just have to put up with it.'

'All right, all right then,' she conceded. 'My name's Philippa.'

'And I'm supposed to believe that?'

She shrugged. 'I'm supposed to believe that your name's Alvar. Even though I think it's a weird name. What were your parents thinking when they gave you that name?'

'How would I know?' he said. 'I imagine it's a family name of some sort,' he added. 'It might have been the name of my great-uncle or something, and I was named after him.'

She inhaled her cigarette.

'Do you have any family?' he wanted to know.

She was quiet for a long time. 'Perhaps. But I never see them.'

He frowned at her reply. 'Either you have family or you don't.'

'Of course. That's what I was just saying. I might have some family, but I don't know what they're doing.'

He sighed. 'You're not easy to get on with,' he said then.

'Is that what it's all about?' she asked. 'Being easy to get on with? I think you have turned being nice into a full-time job. I bet you're nice even when you're on your own.'

'Of course,' he said. 'Should I be nasty to myself?'

'Some people are,' she said. 'Some people are at their worst when they're alone. They get plastered, they overeat, they cut themselves, they bang their head against the wall, they play their stereo at full blast and blow their eardrums, they stand by the window and howl at the moon.'

'Do they?' he said, horrified. 'Why?'

'To relieve their despair, obviously. You know about despair, don't you?'

'No, not really. Not much,' he admitted. 'And surely raging against it won't make it any better?'

'Yes, it will. It gets the adrenaline flowing,' she said, 'and that's a great rush. You ought to try it sometime.'

'It's not in my nature,' he said.

'You're just scared,' she claimed, 'you're scared of what you'll find and where it will take you.' She looked around the tidy living room.

'If I were going to go mad in here, I would throw all those glass sports trophies at the wall. Oh, they would make a great sound and my ears would ring. Haven't you ever wanted to?'

He looked at the sports trophies on the mantelpiece. 'No. And please don't go mad in here,' he said, horrified.

She laughed again. 'No, no. Nothing will happen as long as you do what I say. That's my basic technique. It works on almost everyone.'

'But not on Rikard?'

She looked at him quickly. 'Who's Rikard?'

'The man who sells you the drugs?'

'Oh. You mean Roger. No, it doesn't work on him. Nothing works on him, he's a nasty piece of work.' She got up suddenly and lifted the cat onto her lap. She caressed his head.

'Oh, you gorgeous Goya munchkin,' she said softly. 'You have no worries. If I get to live my life all over again I hope I'll come back as a beautiful cat. Who can curl up on someone's lap. Have you felt his heart?' she asked. 'It beats so swiftly and so lightly. His nose is cold, is it meant to be cold? And his paws, they're all pink. And so lovely to touch. Tiny, tiny strawberry-flavoured chewy sweets. I wish I had a cat.'

Alvar sat still listening to her. Her bright, light voice filled his ears. Now, when she was sitting with the cat on her lap she reminded him mostly of a lost little girl. Impossible to handle, but very sweet in the pink sweater with the puffy sleeves.

CHAPTER 24

He saw less of her in July and August.

The thought had crossed his mind that everything would feel strange and empty if she vanished altogether. He was slowly beginning to enjoy her chatting to him from the sofa. The way she stroked the cat, her laughter, so silvery and bright. He also liked it when she lay quietly sleeping. Then he would sit down in his armchair with his newspaper or a good book. Or he would treat himself to an evening sherry, which he would enjoy slowly. Then he would watch her and be filled with a kind of serenity. The cat would often lie at her feet, a grey, curled-up fur ball. The two of them, he thought, are all I have in the world. But it's enough, it's more than enough. Yet a new worry had entered his life. There was hardly any money left in his savings account. It had trickled away in a steady stream and the inevitable moment was approaching. The day he would have to say, I don't have any more money, it's over, we've spent it all. Her eyes, her ice-blue eyes, would darken and fill with hatred. Some nights he could hardly sleep. In dreams he lived this moment over and over, her disbelief, her rage, his despair. Then he would awaken with a gasp. He kept pushing the reality aside. The severed bridge still hung in the gallery. How naive he had been to think that he would ever own it. It puzzled him that no one else had bought it, that no one else had fallen for the drama of the great painting. Now it served as a reminder of his own weakness, his capricious nature, and he could no longer bear to admire it, delight in it or pine for it. He scowled at it, like at forbidden fruit.

She turned up again in the middle of September and from then on her visits became more frequent. She was sometimes gentle and chatty, but more often she was silent and grumpy; and then she would throw herself on the sofa and turn her back on him. He said nothing. He tiptoed around, terrified of upsetting her. After all, she had so much to deal with, and he wanted to be considerate.

Autumn arrived; October was dark and dense and rainy, November was freezing cold, windswept and sombre. On the eighteenth day of the month she returned to his flat. On this day she was in very bad shape, she was unable even to unlock the door on her own, she just leaned on the doorbell until he came out to let her in. He found her slumped against the wall, her knees trembling. She was pale and damp and her pupils filled her irises.

'Where have you been!' she screamed hysterically.

Alvar was alarmed. He glimpsed his own pallid reflection in the mirror above the chest of drawers, he held his breath as his thoughts raced around his head.

'I was waiting for you yesterday, on the sofa, I waited for hours! I needed a fix and I was broke!'

Alvar opened his mouth. His voice was feeble. 'I went to a late movie,' he explained, 'the movie finished at ten past one. I went to see *The Exorcism of Emily Rose*.'

She was trying to focus on his face, a little saliva trickled from the corner of her mouth.

'You went to the movies,' she said accusingly, 'and I was scared shitless because I thought you had gone away. To bloody Värmland or somewhere even worse. And I wouldn't be able to get any money and so I wouldn't be able to get a fix!'

She paused to catch her breath.

'You could have left me a note telling me when you would be back, Alvar! You can't do this to me! You're always here. You have to be here all the time!'

She collapsed again, she clung to the door frame. Alvar felt torn apart by distress.

'I feel bloody awful,' she gasped. 'Haven't had a fix for three days. I'm completely broke.'

He held the door open for her, but she did not move from the wall. His trip to the cinema seemed like a mortal sin and his knees felt weak.

'I can't walk,' she groaned. 'I can't stop shaking.'

Alvar was unaccustomed to physical contact with other human beings. He could barely remember the last time he had touched someone, he had never even escorted an old lady across the street. Now he held out an arm to support her as she came in. She staggered across the floor on her high heels and collapsed onto the sofa. The cat jumped up next to her, but she seemed unaware of it. Her eyes were watering and she kept curling up in a foetal position as if she was in pain.

'I've got no one but you!' she screamed. 'You can't just go out and not tell me!'

'I'm so sorry,' Alvar stuttered. 'I've always been on my own and I'm not used to thinking of other people. I'm so, so sorry!'

She stood up and swayed dangerously; it seemed as if she wanted to go to the bathroom. He had never seen her so wasted. She was slurring her words, wobbling, her arms were flailing as though she was pushing aside dense vegetation. Her body began to seize as though in the grip of fever, a sea of pain and discomfort he could not begin to imagine, but it took his breath away. Finally she closed the door behind her and Alvar stood horrified in the middle of the floor, his mind racing. Withdrawal, he thought, petrified. The poison was leaving her body, and now every cell was screaming out for more heroin. The true horror of the situation finally dawned on him. She could not be saved; she was heading for the abyss. His first impulse was to get her more drugs, he could not bear to see her like this, it hurt him too, and he was not used to feeling anyone else's pain. As soon as he had this thought a new fear overcame him. He started pacing the floor, while anxiously listening out for noises from the bathroom. What was she doing in there? It had gone very quiet. Finally he heard the sound of water running. She came out shortly afterwards, her fringe was wet and her mascara was smeared pathetically all down her cheeks. On her way back to the sofa she tripped over her own feet and fell flat on her face; she remained prostrate on the floor, struggling between the coffee table and the sofa.

'Oh God,' she slurred, 'oh God, oh God, I feel like shit!' Alvar rushed over. Again he was reluctant to touch her, but his heart was beating so fast, and he felt so distraught that he had to do something. He stuck his hands under her armpits and lifted her up. He dragged her over to the sofa and laid her down. She curled up in pain instantly. Then she started to shake again, the fits came and went.

'Can I get you a drink of water?' he asked anxiously. She did not reply, she just lay there shivering. A strange sound was coming from her mouth and he realised that her teeth were chattering. He quickly went into his bedroom and found a blanket. He returned and tucked her in, but she did not seem to notice and it made no difference either. He had never seen another human being in such distress and the sight of her terrified him. He collapsed into an armchair. There he remained while his heart pounded as he watched her being ripped apart. Soon she started sweating profusely, tiny beads formed on her upper lip and on her forehead. Suddenly she gagged violently, but nothing came up. She fell back onto the sofa and clasped her hand over her mouth.

'Why don't we go to see the doctor?' Alvar asked.

She still did not reply.

'I've taken out one thousand kroner, are you able to walk down to Bragernes Square?'

He was shocked at his own words, that he could even think along these lines. But seeing her like this was torture for him, so much so that he seriously contemplated going there himself, finding her dealer, buying her a hit and giving it to her so that she could get some relief. So that her hysterical body could calm down. Because he was feeling so distressed, he went out into the kitchen and poured her a glass of water which he placed in front of her. She took no notice of that either. She was shivering. She was shaking. She groaned, she wiped snot and tears away, she wiped away the sweat.

'A small sherry, perhaps?' he suggested out of sheer desperation.

He received no reply. Then he jumped up again and went out into the bathroom. Found a clean face cloth, dipped it in warm water, wrung it and returned.

'Look here,' he was practically pleading, 'you can wipe your face with this.' She did not take it. Then he pushed aside all his shyness, leaned forward and started cleaning her cheeks with the wet, warm cloth. She said nothing, she closed her eyes and Alvar let the cloth glide over her forehead, her nose and her chin, very lightly as though she was made of glass. He thought she began to relax a little. He stayed like this, bent over the sofa with the cloth in his hand, and he was filled by a strange sensation, it was something he had never experienced before. The satisfaction of easing another person's pain. Reaching out a hand and seeing how her features softened. If only she could fall asleep and sleep through it all, he thought, but she was unable to fall asleep. She started shivering and shaking again, it came in vicious fits. Suddenly she spoke in a laboured voice.

'My heart,' she said weakly.

Alvar pricked up his ears. 'Yes,' he said breathlessly, 'what about your heart?'

She groaned again, pressed both hands against her chest. 'It's going to burst out, I've got to keep it in place!'

He shook his head. 'No, it's not going to burst out,' he said quickly. 'It's not!'

'It feels that way,' she said hoarsely. 'I've got to keep it in place, it's going to explode. I can feel it oozing out between my ribs.'

'Do you want some paracetamol?' he asked helplessly.

She laughed a bitter laugh at his suggestion. 'Is that all you can offer me? Paracetamol?'

Her voice was brimming with pain and disdain.

He wrung his hands in desperation.

'What are we going to do?' he asked sheepishly. 'You can't lie here like this.'

She brushed her damp hair away from her face.

'I can't do this any more,' she said weakly. 'I haven't got the energy to live this life any longer.'

Alvar tore himself away and went over to the window. He stared down at the light-bulb factory and at the dome, which glowed. It competed with the grey November light.

'There's got to be someone who can help you,' he said.

'There are not enough places,' she replied from the sofa. 'I've tried lots of times. Not enough places, I don't get methadone, or subutex. Nothing. I haven't been using long enough.'

Alvar closed his eyes. Then she had another seizure and she howled into the sofa to cope with the pain. Every single fibre in Alvar's body tensed up.

'No one should have to feel like this!' he screamed into the glass. 'It's not right!'

He looked over at her thin body.

'Do you want me to go down to Bragernes Square?' he asked. 'Do you want me to try to get something for you?'

She was silent for a long time. Her breathing was irregular, he thought, her whole body fighting a huge battle.

'Do you think you could get me a fix?' she whispered. 'I'm shaking so badly that I don't think I can manage to go myself.'

Get her a fix? Was she asking him to inject her? He gasped at the thought.

'It's easy,' she whispered. 'I'll tell you what to do.'

He instinctively shook his head. There was no way he would inject drugs into another human being. Especially not a tiny girl, no matter how ill she might be. She had another fit, her voice was close to breaking point.

'Go find Roger,' she asked him, 'he usually hangs out by the quay at Skutebrygga. Long hair, green parka. Go now, please, Alvar, please! I'm begging you!'

221

Alvar clenched his fists. He felt a sudden urge to slap his own cheeks; he seemed unable to think straight. He ran out into the hall, driven by a mixture of desperation and determination. Put on his coat, snatched his keys from the key cupboard and left. Started the Mazda, drove down the hill and into Engene. Turned left at the fire station and then took another left so he had the river on his right. Pulled into a car park, locked the car and ran out. His eyes flashed in all directions, but there was no one on the quay, no dealer in a green parka. He checked the cars and the people in town, kids, old people, the cooing pigeons. The taxis lined up on Bragernes Square. But he could not see any drug dealers; it was as if they had all gone with the autumn wind. Helplessly he stood there looking around. He became aware that others were watching him. He probably had a look of panic in his eyes, a madness clear for all to see and everyone was wondering about him.

He began walking across the cobbled square, all the way to St Hallvard's fountain. There were some benches there; they were empty. He stared down the side streets, to see if there were any dealers there. But today, the eighteenth of November, only respectable people were out and about, the town's down-and-outs were nowhere to be seen. Exhausted, he let himself fall down on a bench. He rested his elbows on his knees, buried his face in his hands, hunched up to avoid the freezing wind. He had never in all his life felt as lost as he did now. He could see no way out of this mess, he could not return to her without something that would relieve her pain. Then he heard low voices. Someone had approached the bench, he was being watched.

'Having a bad day, mate?' a rusty male voice asked him. Alvar looked up. He saw a group of three people. Two men and a woman, dressed a little shabbily, were watching him.

'Are you Roger?' Alvar asked him hopefully, looking at the gangly man, who had long hair and was wearing a green parka.

'Who wants to know?' he replied, giving Alvar a doubtful look.

'Philippa needs heroin. She needs it now!'

They looked at him doubtfully, exchanged glances.

'We don't know anyone called Philippa.'

'She's blonde,' he said, touching his own bald head. 'She's very thin, her hair's almost white, she's ill, she's lying on my sofa and it's awful!'

They continued looking at him in a doubtful way.

'You mean Blondie?'

'Yes,' Alvar said swiftly. Of course she would tell them her name was Blondie, he was sure of that.

'I don't have any heroin,' the man said, 'but I've got something else.'

Alvar's heart sank.

'Will it help?' he asked anxiously.

The three people started to giggle as they sent each other telling glances. Roger dug his hand down into the parka's pocket.

'This works for everything,' he said, nodding. 'You got any money?'

Alvar fumbled to get his wallet out and showed them his money.

'All right,' Roger said. 'Come on, we're going down under the bridge.'

Together they walked across Bragernes Square. Alvar felt strange in such scruffy company; he trailed behind them like a little lost child, eyes fixed on the street, hands deep in his pockets. They gathered under the bridge, there was a walkway there, it was covered with syringes and other rubbish. A small sachet was shoved in Alvar's hand, he paid and thanked them. How easy it is, he thought, how easy it is to throw your life away if that's what you want. He put the small sachet in his pocket, followed the group with his eyes as they disappeared across the walkway. He ran back to the car park, all the time checking that the small sachet was safe in his pocket. He started the car and drove back to his flat. He had only one thing on his mind: getting her to a place of peace. He let himself in and went over to the sofa. She opened her eyes and looked at him.

'Find my gear,' she ordered him, 'it's in my pocket.'

Alvar bent over her and rummaged through the pockets of her grey jacket. In a leather purse he found a syringe and a rubber tube. Then he opened the small sachet and made a discovery. It contained a handful of tiny white pills. He put them on the table. She got up on her elbow and stared at them in surprise.

'What did he give you?'

'I don't know,' he cried, 'they didn't have anything else, but they said these work for everything. Perhaps you can take two?'

She shook her head in disbelief, sent him a wounded look and picked up the pills with trembling fingers. He thought he could hear her bones rattle, he thought he could see the red muscle of her heart force its way through her ribs. Before he had time to do anything, she had tipped all the pills into her mouth and was reaching for the glass of water.

'Oh no,' he exclaimed, 'you mustn't take them all at once! They might be strong and we don't know what they are!'

She had already swallowed them. She half fell back onto the sofa and stayed there without moving. Her mouth was half open, her face contorted. She finally closed her eyes. Alvar collapsed in his armchair from exhaustion, he watched the enormous transformation which slowly began to take place before his very eyes. After one minute she stopped moving, after two her breathing became more regular. It was as if her frail body sank into the sofa. A faint smile spread across her face. The smiled lasted, it was a beautiful smile and he saw clearly how lovely she was, fragile like an angel, he thought, and waves of relief washed over him, it was over now, for the time being anyway. And he hoped that wherever she had gone she would be there for a long time. The cat came creeping towards them and snuggled down next to her. Alvar let his head fall back onto the headrest and closed his eyes. He pushed aside anything the future might bring. At this very moment in time all he did was enjoy the silence, relieved that she was feeling fine, that her breathing was steady. There was something very reassuring about that, something that made him feel sleepy. Just a quick nap, he told himself. I'm exhausted.

Darkness outside, now. Silence.

He woke up and realised that he was cold.

The house rested heavily on its foundation, it was as if everything had ground to a halt. He imagined a machine which had suddenly been switched off and the steady hum he was used to had ceased.

He had been asleep for more than two hours.

With a jolt he jumped out of his chair, a half-strangled groan coming from his throat. He glanced over at the sofa where she lay motionless. Her eyes were half open. It seemed as though she was semi-rigid, her immobility was terrifying. He could not hear her breathing, there was something missing in the room. An absence. Her ice-blue eyes were vacant, covered, it seemed, by a film of frost. The cat had moved and was now lying in a corner of the room. Alvar rushed out into the bathroom and closed the door behind him. Now she was out of sight, he could convince himself it had all been a bad dream, a nightmare, he thought with his back to the door. He stayed there for a long time. Then he sneaked over to the mirror, and clung on to the sink. He blinked repeatedly, no, he was not dreaming, this was real, something dreadful had happened. No, he had to be mistaken. She'll wake up now, he thought, running back out again, she'll wake up if I shake her and call her name. But I don't know what her name is. He tiptoed over to the sofa. But shaking her was pointless, there was no life left in her frail body, no heartbeat, no pulse, no warmth. November, he suddenly realised. It's the month of November and it's an evil month.

He started pacing the flat with rasping breath, he went from room to room, he wrung his hands so hard his knuckles cracked, he saw that her face had contorted into an ugly grimace. Her jaws had locked, her eyes were raw and dry. Every now and then he would peek over at the sofa; he was waiting for her to wake up, he was waiting for his old life to return, the life he had always taken for granted. She continued to lie there. He went back to the bathroom and washed his face with cold water, his eyes were bloodshot. He came back out and she was still lying there. He went to the kitchen and poured himself a sherry with trembling hands, stood in the doorway, drinking it, she continued to lie there. She was a stranger now who had staggered into his home and then lay down to die on his sofa, that was what had happened, was it not? Death had turned her into a stranger and she was no longer any of his concern. But he had opened the door, he had gone down to Bragernes Square and bought the pills, put them in front of her, fetched water for her and sat there watching her as she swallowed them. His actions throughout the past year, his well-meaning and apparently good intentions, piled up in front of him and turned into a mountain of guilt. He, Alvar Eide, had displayed a degree of negligence which had led her right to her death. He started to sink onto the floor; he could never hold his head up high again, not after this. Imagine that this was how his life would end, tainted by guilt and shame and horror; why had he not been able to see where it was all leading? He lay prostrate on the floor digging, clawing his fingers into the parquet, trying to gather his scattered thoughts. And they gathered themselves and turned into a sly plan, which almost took his breath away, the ultimate proof that he had never been a good person. He realised that she had been right all the time, all he knew was pretence and cowardice, he had never been a hero. Merely spineless. Defensive, pathetic. And the vile plan which was slowly taking shape was all he had to cling to, it made his body obey, it made his heart beat at a normal rate.

I've got to get rid of her, he thought, I've got to carry her out of the house, I can't have her here, what will people say, what will they think? Will they put me away for this, will I be branded a criminal? I'll never be able to look anyone in the eye. I can't manage anything at all after this, he thought, why was I not tougher with her? If I'd been tough, she would have been alive now. Perhaps. He groaned in despair, his distress roared like a waterfall in his ears. What am I going to tell the police? I can't go to the police, it struck him, I can't tell them what has happened, they'll blame me. It was I who financed her addiction, I drove her to her death. It's all my fault. There is no God, there is no forgiveness. I was only trying to help her, I couldn't bear to see her in such pain, because I'm weak, I'm full of flaws and shame. Time will pass, he thought feverishly, time will pass, soon I'll be in another moment, an even worse one because she is still lying there with her gaping mouth and blind eyes. Why did she pick me? Can you tell from a distance that I'm a pushover; does it show in my pathetic eyes, am I betrayed by my nervous hands? Thoughts rained through his head like a shower of arrows. He concentrated on his plan. He put his palms on the floor and attempted to push himself up, but they were too weak. Blood rushed to his head, his pulse beat in his ears. A thought occurred to him, a wretched idea. He would put a blanket over her and cover her up. He pushed off again and stood up laboriously. Reluctantly he went over to the sofa, got hold of the blanket and arranged it so it covered her head and her body. But it offered him no relief, the contours of her thin body were still visible. Again he went over to the window. He stared out at the town, saw cars crawling through the streets, and the lights, yellow, red, green, people were heading home, it was rush hour. He stood there holding on to the trivial activities outside as the plan continued to grow in his head, slowly, from deep inside him: no one knows anything. No one can see into my living room, can see that there is a dead body on my sofa. Or that I'm responsible. That it is I, Alvar Eide, who pushed her into the abyss. I'll wait until night-time, he thought, then I'll carry her outside. I'll leave her somewhere, so she'll be found, and people can think what they like. I need to tidy my living room, I can't have things like that lying around.

A faint hope grew in him, a simple, cynical thought.

Perhaps I'll get away with it. After all, so many of them die, they call it an overdose, she's clearly one of them. She's been seen on Bragernes Square, the police will probably recognise her. They wouldn't make a big deal of it. I need to wait until later in the evening. When everyone has gone home. When will everyone be asleep? Between three and five in the morning. That's when I'll carry her outside and put her in the back of the car, I'll drive out into the woods with her, I'll cover her with the blanket. I never asked for this awful business to happen, I was just trying to help her. He forced himself to snap out of it and went to his bedroom where he lay down fully dressed on his bed. Turned over onto his side and pulled up his knees. He closed his eyes, but they opened again. He kept looking at the lamp on his bedside table, a cold glass dome.

He fell into a perplexing dream.

It was difficult to breathe.

He was crawling around on an ice-cold surface, on all fours, like a wounded animal, and the air was dense and raw, it was like inhaling thick porridge down his lungs. At the same time he sensed a cool breeze further ahead, a freezing draught from a hole in the ice. He struggled to find his way, fighting to breathe the whole time, it was like a lead weight on his chest, he had to use every muscle in his upper body to make his lungs open and take in air, every breath was a struggle. His hair and his cheeks were damp, and he worked out that he was in a thick fog, which was approaching from all sides, it surrounded him, made him invisible to the rest of the world. Still he crawled on, centimetre by centimetre, the cold breeze grew stronger and he thought he heard a faint murmur, a grinding sound, but he did not recognise the sound and it was too dark to see anything. Then his hand reached out into thin air. He stopped and froze, waved his hands in front of him in terror, there was nothing, he had reached the edge and a fierce, freezing cold wind hit from the void.

He woke up and gasped for air. There was still a weight on his chest, and breathing a sigh of relief, he finally realised what it was. Goya, his cat, was lying on his chest purring. He nudged him off and lay there staring at the ceiling.

At a quarter past three in the morning he got up and went into the living room.

His saliva tasted of blood and metal. There was not a sound coming from the house, the streets outside were empty. The yard was surrounded by a fence. Would Green hear him start his car? Would he turn over in his bed, check the time and wonder? He forced himself not to worry about that. He went out into the hall, put on his coat and shoes. Turned round, saw the tiny body under the blanket. Boot or back seat? he asked himself. It would have to be the back seat. He could hide her under the blanket. He sneaked out into the yard, unlocked the car, put the key in the ignition. Got out again and opened the door to the back seat, looked inside. There was plenty of room for her tiny body. Then something happened to his heart, it started beating violently and his legs buckled and he had to support himself against the car as the reality of his gruesome errand dawned on him. He automatically looked up at the sky, no stars were visible, it was cloudy and overcast.

He went back inside, stopped in the middle of the living room. Now he would have to touch her, hold her close. It felt like an insurmountable task. He did not want to feel her cold cheek against his own. He went over to the sofa, pulled the blanket off her and spread it out on the floor. Don't think, he decided, just act, be strong. Get her out of the living room once and for all. I should have done it a long time ago. He moved the coffee table to reach her more easily. Stood for a while stretching out his fingers as he often did.

She was lying flat on her back with her mouth open, her irises were starting to look cloudy. Alvar held his breath and prepared himself. Counted to three and lifted her. He froze. Her body was completely rigid. It was like lifting a log and one of her arms stuck out like the branch of a tree. He swayed violently for a moment, he nearly keeled over. Then he remembered that several hours had passed, and of course he had heard of rigor mortis. Nevertheless he felt paralysed; he stood holding her dead body for a long time as though his feet were nailed to the floor.

He finally pulled himself together. Reluctantly, with awkward, hesitant steps, he inched away from the sofa and over to the blanket. There he put her down. He wrapped her in the blanket, got up, wiped his brow. Then he went back out into the hall and jammed the door open with a shoe. Listened out into the darkness for sounds. It would take him a few seconds to settle her in his car, a few fateful seconds of his life. He breathed in and bent down again, lifted her up and started to walk. He was watching himself from afar. Here goes Alvar Eide with a dead body in his arms. It's three thirty in the morning, everyone is fast asleep. How did this happen, where did I go wrong? He walked with short, stumbling steps out into the hall and again sideways out through the front door. Then he walked as fast as he dared over to the car, bent forward and placed her inside head first, diagonally across the back seat. She lay like a wooden plank, her outstretched arm pointing accusingly at him. Carefully he closed the door without slamming it. Then he went back to close the front door and lock it. He felt revitalised now, it was nearly over. He quickly got in the car and started it, his hands were shaking so badly he almost couldn't turn the key in the ignition. Finally he got the car into gear, rolled past the letter boxes and out through the gate.

Down the hill he passed a car; it felt weird. It drove past him indifferently. Will I ever be able to sleep after this? he wondered. Will I be able to smile or laugh? Eat a meal, will I be able to swallow? He turned right at the Central Hospital. He drove further on, up towards the ridge, he intended to drive right to the top. Many tourists came there and there were always plenty of people; she would be found quickly, that was his plan. He could not bear to turn round and look at her, he drove quietly in the darkness, crouched over the wheel. To his right were a couple of houses with no lights on. Finally he reached the top. It was a viewpoint. He stayed in his car for a while, letting the engine run, staring out at the glittering town. A car had been abandoned in the car park, it worried him, but he could see no people. Then he drove into the car park and left the car as close as he could to the beginning of the path. A sign was visible in the beams of his headlights. *Åsa Pond, 11 kilometres.* It was a narrow path, but there was room for one car. He drove on for one hundred metres and then stopped. He sat there a few seconds to gather strength. Then he opened the car door and got out; he felt the cool November air on his face. The leaves were rustling, the trees murmured in a menacing breeze, he felt as though he was being watched. Then he walked round the car and opened the door to the back seat. Glanced frantically over his shoulder, got hold of her and pulled her out. Carried her a few metres before laying her down. He took a few steps back. The bundle was barely visible in the darkness, but the sun would rise soon and some unsuspecting person would walk by.

He drove away hastily.

Then he heard a low drumming.

The volume of the sound was increasing rapidly. The sound startled him, someone was coming through the woods, he sensed, and he clutched the wheel. In a flash he identified the sound. Sudden and violent raindrops started to splatter against his windscreen. The skies opened, rain came down like a grey, compact wall. It almost forced him off the road. Her tiny body would be soaked in a matter of minutes, the rain would go straight through the blanket, freezing cold and raw. He slammed on the brakes, buried his face in his hands. Was there no end to this misery? But she's dead, he thought, she won't feel anything. Nevertheless it was pouring down and he did not have the strength to push the thought out of his mind. Her skinny body at the side of the path and the rain washing down on her mercilessly. No one should lie like that, he thought, and it is I, Alvar Eide, who is responsible for all of this. He forced himself to drive on. He met no cars, the streets were empty now, he drove through them at a snail's pace, visibility was nearly zero.

Ten minutes later he rolled into his yard. He turned off the ignition and got out. The intensity of the rain had escalated. He carefully closed the car door and quickly entered his flat. He locked the door behind him and stopped. And then it all got to him, everything that had happened and the rain, which pelted the windows like a punishment from God. I can't bear it, he thought, she's lying out there getting wet. Someone else needs to take over now and help me. Then something occurred to him. He went over to the telephone, stopped and stared at it. He saw the yellow Post-it note with a number on it, which he himself had stuck to the telephone a long time ago. With his hand trembling he lifted the receiver and punched in the number. After three rings there was a reply.

'You're through to the Red Cross emergency helpline. This is Marie speaking, how can I help you?'

Alvar opened his mouth, supporting himself with one hand on the chest of drawers, his voice barely audible.

'I've done something truly awful,' he sobbed.

Silence. He could hear her breathing.

'Do you want to tell me about it?'

A female voice. So light and friendly. Alvar held his breath. He was overcome by fear of what was about to happen. Marie. Perhaps this really was her name, or perhaps she just called herself this when she was working, why should he trust her? Young women just made stuff up.

He carefully replaced the receiver.

CHAPTER 25

At this point in the story I lean back and sigh heavily.

I stare at the screen in despair. It's all my fault. I wanted to test Alvar and now I can see that he'll fail. So I imitate him. I get up and wander across the floor. I go over to the window and stare outside. I'm responsible; I have to get him through this. His despair is my despair, his shame is my shame, I don't know how it's going to end now. I begin to worry about his mental state and what he might end up doing, he has nowhere to go, no one who can help him. Yes, it was a difficult situation, but now he has made it worse, it's a disaster. The way things stand I don't see how he can avoid going to prison, and I don't think he can handle that. Then I think of his father who died at the age of fifty-three from a heart attack. I drift aimlessly through the rooms as I struggle to find a solution. Am I really omnipotent? That's not how it feels. There's only one way out, but I can't see it. How easy it is, I think, putting someone on a stage. Focusing a spotlight on them, getting them started, letting events unfold without a second thought. Suddenly you hit a wall and the audience waits expectantly like children, with their mouths hanging open waiting for the conclusion. I like to end my novels on a succinct, merciless remark.

My front door opens, I cease my restless wandering. I hear dragging footsteps in the hallway, a door slamming. Alvar Eide enters, grey-faced and with rings under his eyes. Without saying a word he collapses onto my sofa, then he slumps over the coffee table and hides his face in his hands. I watch him for a while as thoughts churn in my head. What does he need now, what am I going to say? He beats me to it. It's hard for me to make out what he's saying because his face is hidden.

'I can't find a way out. I'll have to kill myself.'

In the silence that follows I can feel my pulse throb in my throat. Alvar breathes heavily; he's rocking himself backwards and forwards. I'm standing there feeling I've been utterly cruel, but there is nothing else I can do.

'You can't,' I state calmly. 'Then there'll be no story.'

He does not reply. I go over to him, I place a hand on his shoulder.

'Marie,' I say. 'Marie who answered the helpline, she would have helped you. She would have told you what to do. But you didn't let her.'

I can hear some half-strangled sobs. I let myself fall into a chair, I watch his desperate figure and rack my brains for some words of hope and comfort.

'If I send someone to help you,' I ask him, 'will you let them?'

He finally looks up at me, he folds his hands on the table.

'As I see it,' he says, 'it's best that I remove myself from this earth once and for all. I can't handle this game, which life ultimately is, I don't understand the rules.'

'You can learn them,' I say, hurt.

He shakes his heavy head.

'I'm going to hook up a hose to the exhaust pipe and lie down in my car,' he groans. 'It'll be over in a few minutes.'

'Then you'll be letting down everyone who's followed you up until now,' I say, 'those who hope that you'll get through this.'

He looks at me darkly. 'Why should I care about them? I don't know them.'

'But they know you,' I reply, 'they've followed you every step of the way, you can't run off now.'

In the silence that follows I can hear the wind in the trees outside. A magpie lands on my veranda, it sits there bobbing its tail, a car drives past, the seconds tick away.

'I just want to sleep,' he says. 'It won't take very long and then I'll be gone.'

I sigh deeply at his words. 'Is that what you think will happen? You think you'll fall asleep and be dead in a few minutes?'

He looks up, he starts to waver. 'Exhaust fumes are very poisonous,' he says, 'I've always known that. I've heard they make you sleepy.'

I bite my lip. 'Yes, you're right. They're poisonous as well as deadly. But your death won't be that straightforward. It doesn't work like that.'

'Could it be simpler?' he asks, looking at me in disbelief. 'I'll be sitting in the car inhaling exhaust fumes, I'll sit very still with my hands in my lap.'

'You think you'll be able to sit completely still?'

He is growing more uncertain. He gives me a searching look.

'I'm not sure where you're going with this.'

I lean across the table and look at him sincerely.

'Everyone can flirt with the idea of suicide,' I say, 'but there's a big gap between thought and action. And even though you seem to think that it's a swift and easy death, I'm sorry to have to tell you that you're very much mistaken.'

'Why do you say that?'

'Because I know.'

'What do you know?'

I can't sit still any longer, I have to move. I walk softly up and down the room.

'True, exhaust fumes are very poisonous,' I say, 'but do you know how they kill?'

He shakes his head. He waits for me. His grey eyes are guarded.

'The fumes attach themselves to haemoglobin in your blood and prevent the blood from circulating oxygen. You will, in other words, suffocate from within. Literally.'

He is starting to look anxious.

'And it doesn't take a few minutes,' I say, 'it takes many hours. On your way to death you will need to go through several stages. Do you really want to know this, Alvar?'

He nods softly, he squeezes his hands in his lap.

'First you'll experience trouble breathing. You'll develop a severe migraine-like headache. Then you'll feel nauseous; your body will dispose of its stomach contents. Disorientation and hallucinations follow. Perhaps you'll start clawing at the door handle as your body desperately struggles. Before you finally pass out. Hours can pass between the time you faint and your actual death. When you're found your airways will be filled with foam. Your lungs will turn into two large oedemas, as will your brain. And you'll be found in your own vomit. There will not be much left of the imposing man you once were. In other words, you won't die in your sleep, you'll be fighting all the way until you die.'

He shakes his head in disbelief. His cheeks are pale.

'But how do you know these things?'

'I have been where you are now,' I reply.

He looks dubiously at me. 'You? Why?'

'I had my reasons,' I reply, 'and I thought they were valid. I'd done my homework carefully, I'd read all I could find on exhaust poisoning. I wanted to know how it happened, what I would have to go through. It was in March,' I continue. 'Everything stopped. I was overcome by fear, I couldn't manage anything. I couldn't eat, couldn't sleep, I couldn't even move. My fear came in violent attacks, like electric shocks.'

Alvar sits listening to me.

'I realised after a few days that I couldn't live like that, I wouldn't be able to handle it. So I got off the sofa and I went downstairs to the basement.'

'What were you keeping there?' he asks.

'A hose,' I explain. 'I brought the hose upstairs to the kitchen, where I kept a roll of parcel tape in a drawer. I went out into the garage to my Mercedes. Then I squatted down and examined the exhaust system. Inside the pipe itself were two smaller pipes and I went back inside and cut the hose into two equal parts of approximately three metres each. Then I went back to the car. I opened the window on the driver's side very slightly. I attached the hoses to the exhaust pipes, trailed them along the car and fed them through the gap in the window. Then I went about sealing every crack, so the inside of the car would be airtight. My plan was to achieve the highest concentration of the exhaust fumes in the shortest possible space of time. And given that the risk of vomiting is relatively high I decided to stop eating in the time I had left, because the thought of being found in a pool of my own vomit was unbearable. When the hoses were properly attached to the exhaust pipe and the window had been sealed, I went back into my house and upstairs to my bedroom. I took my duvet and my pillow and carried them to the car. I reclined both seats and arranged the bed linen as neatly as I could. I wanted to create the illusion that I was dying in my own bed. Because that's ultimately what we all want, isn't it?'

Alvar's eyes widened.

'Then I selected some music,' I told him. 'K. D. Lang would sing "Hallelujah". It was the most beautiful song I could think of. I inserted the CD into the player. Then I returned to the flat, it was late morning. I fixed a time,' I continued. 'My exit would be at three in the morning. In other words, it was only a matter of hours. The seconds ticked by quickly. I found a bottle of whisky and started drinking as I counted the minutes. It was so dark everywhere, in my mind, in my living room, I could barely see the furniture. I could see no future. It was like being in a tunnel that was growing more and more narrow. I took off my watch and put it on the coffee table. Next to it I put my credit cards, one Visa and one Mastercard. Then I let myself flop down again and drank more whisky. My fear was now so powerful that it occurred to me that I might have severe difficulties actually getting to the car because my legs would be unable to carry me. Ah, well, I thought, I'll just have to crawl. Crawl across the gravel on the drive to my final resting place. And because my fear came in bursts, I needed to act quickly. I had to leave the house between fits, if I was to get into the car at all.'

I stop speaking. Alvar looks at me across the table.

'But here you are,' he says. 'What happened?'

'I drank whisky all afternoon and evening,' I tell him. 'It dulled

237

some of my pain, but it strengthened my resolve to kill myself. Everything felt right and inevitable. I was committed to a course of action, I could not stop. I kept looking at the hands of the clock. When it was ten in the evening, I thought: now I've got five hours left. Three hundred minutes. They passed quickly, I tell you. The fear of death nearly suffocated me, I was so terrified I could taste blood in my mouth. And even though I was lying on this sofa, in this room,' I say, 'the room seemed as small as an attic.'

Alvar nods earnestly.

'Then,' I tell him, 'the telephone rang.' I nod in the direction of my desk, where the telephone is. 'The telephone rang, and I was so startled that I nearly ended up on the floor. It rang angrily as if it was urgent. I staggered over and stared at it. It rang a third time, a fourth, a fifth, I couldn't see who it was, the number was being withheld. But there is something about a ringing telephone, it's impossible not to answer it. I had the chance to hear a voice, be connected again to life and other people. So I answered it.'

'Who was calling you?' he asks breathlessly.

'A friend,' I say. 'A very dear friend. "How are you?" he asked.

'"I'm in a very bad way," I replied. "I'm going to end it all at three o'clock tonight."

'It went silent down the other end. I could hear he was thinking.

'"You can't stop me," I said. "I can't take it any more."

'He was still thinking because he is a wise man. He weighed his words.

"I can tell from your voice that you are serious," he said. "But there's something I want you to do for me."

'I held the telephone close to my ear and listened to his reassuring voice. "And what would that be?" I asked anxiously.

'"That you postpone it," he said. "That you grant yourself another day, and that you'll come over and see me tomorrow. We'll go for a walk in the woods. You ought to allow yourself that. You deserve another day."

'I clutched the telephone and thought about what he had said. A walk in the woods. I glanced out at the drive, towards the garage. Where my Mercedes had been turned into a gas chamber.

' "Are you there?" he asked.

' "Yes," I whispered.

' "Is that a promise?"

'I had to support myself on the desk with my other hand. "Yes, I'll be there."

' "I'm trying to get you to agree to something. Will you come over tomorrow?"

' "Yes," I said dully.

' "Are you sure?" he asked.

' "Absolutely," I replied. At that moment I felt that something had changed inside my chest. It felt as if a warm substance was trickling down it, as if something was melting.

' "Then I expect you to come," he said. "I'll be waiting for you. If you kill yourself tonight, I will feel that you have let me down. And you don't want to let down a good friend, do you?"

'I considered what he had just said. No, I didn't want to let him down. The feeling of warmth continued to spread through my body.

' "Then I'll see you tomorrow," he repeated.

' "Yes," I replied. "You'll see me. Thank you for calling. Goodnight." '

Alvar smiles a feeble smile.

'So what did you do once you had hung up?' he asks.

'I stood there for a long time trying to get my breathing under control,' I say. 'And my fear, which had held me in its vice for so long, finally let me go. Because I had avoided death by answering the telephone. I had given myself a rain check, I had plans. So I went to the garage. I tore loose the tubes, fetched my bedlinen and carried it upstairs. I lay down in my bed under the floral duvet. Whisky and exhaustion made me fall asleep instantly. And when I woke up the next morning everything felt strange.'

'In what way strange?' Alvar wants to know.

'The sun was so yellow,' I say. 'The light was so bright. It was an extra day, a very special day. A day I was not meant to have, and it felt wondrous. I had come back into the light after such a long time in the dark. I went out and started the car. K. D. Lang sang "Hallelujah", and it was entirely appropriate. And I walked with my friend in the woods. We talked about all sorts of things. And when we said goodbye, he wanted to fix another time, of course. And so it continued until I had returned to life completely.'

I look at Alvar across the table. 'And now,' I say, 'I want a promise from you. We can't say goodbye like this.'

'I don't have a friend who'll call me in the evening,' he says and looks down.

'But you have me,' I say. 'And I want to see you again. Come back to me when it's all over. We need to end this properly, we've known each other more than a year, I think I deserve that. With friendship,' I add, 'with friendship comes obligation; you, too, have to give something up when I ask you.'

Again he hides his face in his hands. But then he removes them and manages a brave smile.

'Alvar,' I say earnestly, 'you're not going to let me down, are you?'

out if she had been found, but he did not have the courage. He was hyperventilating and he felt dizzy. He also felt hungry, but he couldn't manage to eat anything. The doorbell would ring, he didn't know when, but the doorbell would ring soon and there would be someone outside who would point the finger at him.

The hours ticked by so slowly. Now and then he would doze off for a few minutes only to wake with a gasp. He kept seeing her, her tiny body by the path. Like a parcel someone has discarded, alone and abandoned in the rain. He curled up in agony. Pulled up his knees, tucked his hands under them and locked them; he lay like a convulsing knot of bones and muscles. How cruel life could be. What a coward he was, he could not take this like a man. All he felt was guilt and shame, and a degree of self-hatred that made him want to throw up. An inferior human being, that was what he was. Something pathetic, something worthless. Here he was lying curled up and whimpering like a baby, when what he ought to do was make a telephone call and get it over with. I need to rest, he thought, tossing and turning in his bed, I need to rest. I must gather strength for everything that's to come. I mustn't explain it away, I need to tell it like it is. Even though the truth is odious. How will I be able to carry this burden? I'm already broken. Someone who never pays their way, a stowaway, you could say. The world is filled with suffering and I've never done anything to alleviate it. Other people act, others rush in when disaster strikes. I stand in the wings and shudder. And he lay beating himself up the whole day, it was as if he was flagellating himself till his blood started flowing, he wanted to atone. The light faded and evening approached. The room was filled with shadows and whispering voices. Look, there's Alvar Eide, he's an idiot. They pointed their fingers at him, they snickered, they whispered nasty comments to each other, a swarm of accusations whirled around him from all directions. He fell asleep in the early-morning hours only to wake up with a scream after a series of nightmares. It grew light again, but he could not get out of bed. Today's Sunday, he thought, a day of rest. The worst day of my life.

Then the shrill sound of the doorbell pierced the rooms. Even though he had been expecting it, even though he was prepared, a jolt of fear, so forceful he could not help but call out, shot through him. They were here already, perhaps there were many of them. But he hadn't heard a car, he didn't understand that. He got out of bed and stumbled out into the hall. His shirt was crumpled and hung loosely over his trousers. His throat felt tight and he did not know for certain if he would be able to say anything. It's starting now, he thought. The nightmare. Then he opened the door. Green was outside waving the Sunday paper.

'Have you seen this?'

Alvar stared at the paper, which his neighbour was holding up in front of his face, a picture of a young, smiling girl with thin, blonde hair. She seemed familiar. Of course she was familiar. But in the picture she was happy, with round cheeks he had never seen her like this.

'Katrine Kjelland,' Green said, tapping the picture with his finger. 'Found dead up at the viewpoint yesterday morning. Wrapped in a blanket. Would you believe it?'

The newspaper flapped in Green's hand. Alvar swallowed hard.

'Katrine?' he asked, perplexed.

'She must have been murdered,' his neighbour went on. 'You know her, don't you? She was always coming to see you. The last time I saw her here was Friday, she came to your door.'

Green stood rocking backwards and forwards on the doorstep, his blue eyes sparkled with excitement.

Alvar was unable to reply. His knees started to tremble; he instinctively planted a hand on the wall to steady himself.

'You must call them,' Green said, his voice sounding a little too enthusiastic, 'the police are asking the public to help them. Have you phoned them?'

Alvar shook his head. He wanted to reply, but he still couldn't locate his voice.

'For God's sake, you have to ring them! They need all the information they can get, and she has been coming to see you for

243

months. What's wrong with you, are you ill? You're white as a sheet.'

Green lowered the newspaper and scrutinised him.

Alvar nodded. Yes, he was very ill. He had to concentrate very hard on staying on his feet.

'My guess is that someone gave her an overdose,' Green said in a businesslike way, 'and then they panicked. Wrapped her in a blanket and drove her up there. If I were you I'd call the police straight away. If you don't and they find out she's been coming to your flat, then they'll think it's suspicious that you haven't come forward. That's my advice.'

Green gave him a bossy look. Alvar nodded again. He was trying to collect his thoughts, articulate a reply, but he did not have the strength.

'Anyway, how did you get to know her?' Green asked nosily. 'She was not exactly your type. And so very young, only sixteen, would you believe it.'

Alvar swallowed a second time. 'Sixteen? I didn't know her,' he said weakly. 'Not really.'

'But she came here for a year. She even had her own key!'

Alvar was lost for words. He wanted to close his door, he did not want to explain anything to Green, whom he didn't even know well. Resolutely he reached for the door handle. His neighbour backed off.

'Well, I'm sorry to trouble you, but I do think this is very strange. I just wanted to make sure you knew what had happened. So I'll be expecting you to call. We need to call.'

He folded the newspaper. Retreated a little.

We? Alvar thought. He pulled the door so only a tiny gap was left.

'Yes,' he whispered. 'I'll make the call.' Then he closed the door completely, turned the key and went over to the telephone. He glared down at the numbers. How was he supposed to be able to call and explain anything? He could not even speak. He escaped to his bedroom again and fell onto his bed, exhausted and shivering. Again he felt hungry, but he did not want to eat. He did not deserve food, he did not deserve something to drink. He did not deserve sleep. The seconds ate their way through him, his agony grew hour by hour. Then it struck him that all the pain he was going through could be ended once and for all if only he would make that call. He would just have to stand there coughing and spluttering until they came to his door. Then the disaster would be a known fact, but he would also reach a different stage. He stared out into space with aching eyes. What was he going to say? Hello, my name's Alvar Eide. This Katrine Kjelland, she came to see me last Friday. She overdosed on my sofa and I panicked. I carried her out in the middle of the night and drove off with her. Because I couldn't handle the consequences. It was very stupid, but then I'm a very stupid man.

He reflected on these words, whether he would be able to say them out loud. Even he could hear how idiotic they sounded. What if they jail me? he wondered. Would I manage on my own in a cell? Am I now a criminal? How did this happen? Is there any hope of redemption for me? He lay on his bed struggling with these dark thoughts. Many hours passed, he slipped in and out of sleep. When the doorbell rang for the second time, he sat up dazed and confused, terrified and drowsy. He suddenly realised that Green would have called the police. Alvar planted his feet on the floor. He rubbed his tired face and staggered out into the hall. He opened the door quietly. There he was, the police officer. A mountain of a man, dark and broad, with dense, thick eyebrows. He took up the whole doorway and threw a menacing shadow into the hall.

'Alvar Eide?'

He nodded and clung to the door frame. His heart contracted and a rush of blood went to his cheeks.

'I'm a police officer. May I come in, please?'

Alvar still had no voice. He opened the door fully and walked ahead of him into the living room. Stood by the window looking down at the floor. The officer followed him, and stood calmly in the living room. An almost explosive silence followed.

It's happening now, Alvar thought. My entire miserable existence takes its revenge on me. My cowardice, my submissive nature, my total inability to take action. I thought I could live outside society, but that's impossible. Everyone gets involved sooner or later, in an incident, with another person.

'Do you know why I'm here?' the officer asked. He took a few steps forward, his voice was deep and authoritative.

'I think so,' Alvar stuttered.

'So you've seen today's paper?'

Alvar still had his back to him. He muttered against the pane. 'My neighbour came, he showed it to me. I suppose he was the one who called you?' He said this without turning.

The police officer took his time. He weighed his words carefully.

'Yes, we've received some information and now we're following it up. Is it the case that you knew Katrine Kjelland?'

'Yes, but not very well,' he mumbled. 'And she did not call herself Katrine. She called herself whatever she wanted to, every day it was something different.'

'When did you last see her?'

Alvar struggled to control his voice which was stuck at a very high pitch. 'Friday night. She was here. She lay on my sofa and slept.'

The police officer listened calmly.

'And when did she leave?'

Alvar bowed his head. The truth had become impossible.

'Well, I can't say for sure. She stayed quite a while,' he whispered.

'One hour. Two?'

'As I said, I'm not sure.'

'Was she under the influence of anything when she arrived?'

He half turned but avoided the other man's eyes. 'Yes, I suppose she was behaving strangely.'

'In what way strange?'

'Well, she was shaking somewhat.'

The police officer came up and stood next to him; now they were both staring out of the window.

'What was your relationship with her?'

'It wasn't a relationship,' he said swiftly. 'There was no relationship at all.'

'So she just came to visit you?'

Alvar grabbed hold of the windowsill with both hands.

'She came to borrow money.'

'Did you give her any?'

'Yes.'

The police officer pondered this for a while.

'Did anything unusual happen between you last Friday?'

'No.'

'When she left where was she going?'

'She never said, she just drifted. Around Bragernes Square.'

'You've got a cat, I see,' he said, diverting Alvar's attention.

'Yes, I've got a cat.' Alvar looked at Goya. The cat lay curled up on the sofa.

'He's very handsome. But he moults quite a lot, I can imagine?'

'I'm not bothered about that,' Alvar said, baffled by this question.

'You ought to be.' The police officer circled the floor, stuck his hands in his pockets.

'Katrine Kjelland was discovered up at the viewpoint yesterday. On a path, close to the car park. Dead, wrapped in a blanket. The blanket was covered in small, white hairs. If we can match them to your cat, then you've got a problem.'

CHAPTER 27

They told him he had a great deal to explain.

He crumbled instantly.

They told him his situation was serious and that he risked a custodial sentence, that there was much that warranted investigation and had to be examined in greater detail. They told him that Katrine was sixteen years old and that her family lived at Bragernes Ridge, her father was a dentist, she had two brothers; they knew she was a heroin addict and they had feared the worst. She rarely visited them and then she would talk about him, about Alvar Eide, about how she sometimes stayed with him. That he was a kind of friend, the only one she had.

They told him they found it hard to believe him, they kept asking him to repeat his story and there were many unanswered questions. But why, Eide, they asked him, baffled, why didn't you call us? Alvar was not used to explaining himself to others. He stuttered and stammered, he sat in the bare interrogation room looking at the floor. There were no windows here, just naked, cold walls. A camera was attached to the ceiling, there were a table and some chairs. The walls were painted white, there was a fluorescent tube in the ceiling giving out an almost blue-white light.

'That's just the way I am,' he ventured. 'I removed the problem from my house, my parents taught me to do this, it's the only way I know and I'm a useless man.'

Did he have any addictions?

He shook his head vigorously.

Had he ever suffered from mental health problems?

'No, no, I'm not one of those people, I just lost my head. It's only happened that one time!'

The two officers questioning him exchanged glances. As if they were not quite sure of what they were actually dealing with. They were calm, but very serious. Had he, at any point, wanted her out of his life?

Yes, there had been times. But as time passed, he had grown accustomed to her, she came and went as she pleased.

'Did she ever steal from you?'

'Only a key. I let her keep it, she carried it on a string around her neck.'

'Do you understand how serious it is, Eide? That the money you gave her led directly to her destruction?'

'It was like sliding,' he replied then. 'The speed accelerated and I couldn't slam on the brakes. I closed my eyes and let it happen. I waited for the big crash.'

'Now it's happened. She's dead,' they said.

'I've been expecting it,' he said. 'I knew it would end like this, she said it was what she wanted.'

'She was sixteen years old, she should have been saved. Did you try to get help for her?'

'She said that no one was prepared to help her, that there were no beds, that she was too young. I don't know much about these things, but I thought she wanted to be an outsider. She didn't enjoy being with other people and neither do I.'

'We don't completely understand your actions, Alvar Eide. It appears that you're intelligent and well adjusted.'

'It might seem like that. If you don't look too closely.'

'According to your boss, Ole Kristian Krantz, you're reliable and solid as a rock. You're brilliant at your job. Your flat is in good condition and well looked after and so are you.'

'Yes. I know. What I can't handle are the streets filled with people. There I have no control and anything can happen. How badly can this end?' he blurted out.

They cited the Penal Code.

'Section two hundred and thirty-nine. "Anyone who by means of threats, or in a motor vehicle, or by any other means causes the death of another," we repeat, "by any other means causes the death of another, will be punished by up to three years' imprisonment, or in aggravating circumstances up to six years. If mitigating circumstances exist a fine may be imposed."'

He placed his hands on the bare table.

'I'm actually a good person,' he said. 'You've got it all wrong.'

'They all say that,' they replied. 'We deal with facts. You were the last person to see her alive, you carried her out of your flat. The postmortem will tell us how she died, and we will then decide what to charge you with. You never called for help, you never resuscitated her.'

He looked at them in disbelief.

'Her eyes were covered by a film. I could see at once that it was too late. I was scared that I would be blamed.'

'And you think you shouldn't be?'

This silenced Alvar for a long time.

'Have you ever witnessed withdrawal close up?' he asked eventually.

Yes, they had seen it. A lot of screaming and shouting, they admitted, but nothing that they couldn't handle.

'I can't bear to see others suffer,' Alvar said, 'and that's why I keep everyone at a distance.'

'Katrine was an exception?'

'She got a hold over me, I've never experienced anything like it.'

'We're talking about a sixteen-year-old girl,' they stated.

'Oh,' he burst out, 'but she had so much power, such will! If she was in the room with us now, you would have felt her force, like a magnetic field.'

The two officers exchanged looks.

'Did the two of you ever share the same bed?' they asked suddenly.

Alvar's jaw dropped.

'I wouldn't have dreamt of it. I'm sorry to have to say this, but you're barking up the wrong tree completely.'

'You say that you gave her money. Didn't you ask for anything in return?'

'No.'

'Do you expect us to believe that?'

'I ask you to believe it because it's true.'

'And she never came on to you?'

'Never.'

'Would you have said yes? If she'd suggested something like that?'

'No.'

A long pause followed. Alvar tried to breathe calmly, he was scared of walking into a trap. He had heard that the police might try to entrap you.

'You seem very sure of this. Even though you've just told us that she was like a magnetic field.'

Alvar looked them in the eye. There was nothing left to lose. He quickly glanced up at the ceiling, he noticed the camera in the corner. The camera, which would capture his face and his voice right now, capture a few simple words he had never said out loud. The lens would capture his final confession.

'The thing is,' he said quietly, 'I prefer men.'

Again they exchanged glances. But his remark did not lead to scorn or contempt, they just shrugged, that was all. Left it there and changed the subject. Alvar was beginning to wonder if he had any rights at all. A lawyer. Was it not the case that he could simply refuse to answer any questions unless his lawyer was present? He was not entirely sure. He supposed they would have told him if this was the case, surely they were obliged to read him his rights.

'If it's true,' they asked, 'that you keep away from other people and that you're a shy man, then why did you pick a heroin addict when you finally made contact with someone?'

'She picked me,' Alvar said. 'She said she was all alone in the world, that her mother had committed suicide, that her father had left the country. I thought she was telling the truth. I'm not used to people lying. Now I've learned my lesson,' he added.

'And what about you. Are you telling the truth?'

'Every single word.'

'We hear what you're saying, we believe the actual circumstances, but we find it hard to understand them.'

'When it comes to being with other people, then I'm unfit,' he said quietly. 'I accepted that a long time ago and I have to live with the consequences. Everything that has happened is incomprehensible to me too. It's as if forces outside me have taken control, it's like heading for disaster. I won't shirk my guilt. Nor will I blame her, she was a helpless victim, she needed a strong man. She did not get that, she got me.'

'The tablets that you gave her. You never asked what they were. Can you explain that?'

'They told me they would fix everything, that was all I needed to know. I don't take drugs, I'm not interested. It was best not to know, was what I thought. Besides, I didn't have the time, her heart was about to jump out of her chest!'

At this they exchanged a very long look.

'But one thing I can tell you,' he added. 'No matter what I'd come back with, she would have taken it, she was unstoppable, she was desperate. No one would ever have stopped Katrine, she had made up her mind.'

'What about responsibility, Eide?' they said darkly. 'Do you consider yourself to be a responsible person?'

'I always have done. Now I don't know any more, perhaps I don't even know what being responsible means. The way I saw it, I was the one keeping her alive. How could I have been so wrong!'

CHAPTER 28

His defence counsel entered.

It happened so elegantly that Alvar thought he could hear a fanfare in the distance. Benedict Josef Lind entered the room with a spring in his step. Dressed in a dark suit and a snow-white shirt with a narrow bottle-green tie which matched his eyes. He was slim and long-limbed, about the same age as Alvar, and he carried a black briefcase. He stopped. Took a good look at Alvar. His gaze was steadfast, his handshake firm and warm. Then he held up the briefcase and pressed the locks. A sharp snapping sound was heard as they both sprang open at the same time, a carefully studied gesture, a ritual. He took out some papers. Stood for a while peering at the words, put the papers back in his briefcase.

'Eide. Delighted to meet you. How are you?' he asked with authority. His voice was powerful and deep. 'Have they given you something to eat?'

Alvar shook his head, he was confused. He could not remember the last time he ate, but he did not feel hungry. Only giddy, it felt as if he was floating.

'I'll take you downstairs to the canteen,' Lind said resolutely. 'If you're going to get through this, you'll need a decent meal.'

'But,' Alvar faltered, 'I need to explain myself! It's such a long story, you see, I need time!'

Lind looked at him.

'You'll have all the time in the world, Eide, I give you my word, but you need to take care of yourself. You look exhausted, you've ended up in a difficult situation.'

There was no point in protesting. Alvar closed his mouth.

Suddenly it felt good that someone else was taking charge. He, who up until now had never wanted to let go, now surrendered completely to his commanding, confident lawyer in the dark suit. It was a totally new sensation, a feeling of falling, of melting like butter, becoming pliable. Because could it get any worse? He had a vision of himself lying on a bed with his hands behind his head. A small window with bars in front of it. A desk, a simple chair, a shuttered door. Uprooted from the community. Though it occurred to him then that he had never been part of the community.

'The canteen makes first-class sandwiches,' Lind said. 'And Magda, the cook, can make a cup of coffee that will wake us both up. Come on, let's go. We can talk while we eat.' Lind nodded in the direction of the door; Alvar got up from his chair and followed him. Together they went down the corridor, Alvar with his head bowed, Lind with his chin up. They took the lift, they stood close to each other. A faint smell of aftershave filled the tiny space.

'Everything can be explained,' Lind said. 'There's a logical explanation for even the most incomprehensible action.'

'Exactly!' Alvar burst out. 'If only they'll believe me. If only they can understand!'

'It's my job to make sure they believe you, but I'll obviously need your help.'

Alvar nodded. The lift had stopped, they exited. Lind strode into the canteen, he knew his way around and was completely at ease. Alvar trailed after him, while he looked fearfully at the other diners. But no one even glanced at him twice, they had their own problems to contend with, he thought.

'Here, Eide. By the window,' said Lind, pointing.

He had stopped at a table for four; now he pulled a chair out for Alvar. This tiny gesture moved him, he had never been attended to in this way. It made him study Lind furtively.

'What can I tempt you with, Eide?' Lind asked. 'Rissoles? Prawns? Roast beef?'

'Rissoles, please,' Alvar said modestly. Suddenly he felt starving.

He remained at the table while Lind went over to the well-stocked sandwich counter. He poured two cups of coffee, paid, and returned. Carried the laden tray with the greatest of ease. Alvar stayed in his seat, staring at Lind's well-groomed hands; his fingers were long, his nails completely clean. No ring on his finger, though that meant nothing, the man was probably married and had children like everyone else. No, a little voice told him, not this man. He is different. His feelings took him by surprise; he stared down at the table. Grabbed his knife and fork, he could not think of anything to say.

Lind sat down. His manners were exquisite, as though he had been a winner his entire life, someone who could cope with anything life threw at him.

'So this Katrine Kjelland,' he said, 'whom it appears you knew, if I've understood it correctly, for a whole year. Do you blame her?'

Alvar looked up. He shook his head fiercely.

'Oh, no,' he said sincerely, 'I don't blame her for a second. She was a lost soul. She was trapped in the mire and she couldn't get out. That's how I look at it.'

Lind kept watching him. Alvar felt that his bare head shone like a bowling ball. Lind frowned.

'But she put you in a very difficult situation, surely we can agree on that?'

While he waited for Alvar to reply, he cut off the corner of his open prawn sandwich and put it in his mouth. His teeth were white and flawless.

'Well,' Alvar pondered, 'I suppose it takes two. I was naive. I always have been.' He stuck his knife into the rissole, it was very tender.

'That's not a crime,' Lind said with emphasis. He washed down the prawn with a mouthful of coffee. 'And your intentions were probably good.'

'Good intentions?' Alvar looked at him across the table. Every time he looked into those green eyes, he felt perplexed. Because everything about this man seemed so familiar. He sensed a kind of trust, as if they were on the same side. And so they were, but there was something more than that, something that made him blush.

'You bought drugs for her,' Lind said, 'because you couldn't bear to see her suffer. That's a good intention, don't you think?'

Alvar nodded. He drank his coffee and wiped his mouth with a napkin.

'I've always kept people at a distance,' he admitted. 'I can't bear it if they suffer. I can't bear the responsibility. I'm a coward deep down. The mess I'm in now stems from my own cowardice. It's my only explanation, my only excuse.'

Lind studied him closely. His green eyes grew sharp.

'Why don't you blame her at all?' he asked directly. 'She forced her way into your life, she exploited all your weaknesses. She manipulated you, emptied your bank account, slept in your bed, drank your coffee, died on your sofa?'

Alvar dropped his knife and fork.

'But she had no proper control over herself,' he said, trying to make excuses for her. 'Everything she did was controlled by heroin. Addicts are not themselves, you know that.'

Lind listened, resting his chin on his hand.

'True,' he conceded. 'In a way you were victims of each other. You both did something right, you both did something wrong. I want the blame shared, Eide, what do you say to that?'

Alvar hesitated. 'Sharing the blame? Only one of us is alive, surely that says it all?' Suddenly he felt utterly despondent. Lind chatted on undisturbed.

'Her family doesn't hold you responsible; they could see where she was heading. They don't blame you,' he said softly.

'I don't understand,' Alvar said. 'How can they be so magnanimous given what's happened?'

Lind looked at him sternly. 'It was her lifestyle that killed her,' he stated. 'Not you, Alvar Eide. Don't you see?'

'I contributed,' he argued weakly. 'I went to Bragernes Square and I was careless. I should have checked what it was I bought for her.

Suspected that it might be harmful. I was just trying to ease my own discomfort, I'm actually very selfish.'

'But she took the pills herself,' Lind said. 'She grabbed them and washed them down with water.'

'While I was watching her,' Alvar said. 'Passively. Terrified. And what happened afterwards is unforgivable.'

'Tell me about it,' Lind asked him.

Alvar looked down. 'I felt deeply ashamed. It's a well-known feeling for me, I grew up with it. It's in my veins, let me put it that way. It was like being dragged along by the current. The feeling that I could never hold my head up high again.'

Lind pushed his plate aside and kept listening to him.

'How people would gossip, the story splashed all over the front pages. Suggestions that I might have been taking advantage of her, but I didn't!'

'I know,' Lind said calmly.

'But worst of all was the fear. As I sat in the car driving through town with her dead body on the back seat, I suddenly had the feeling that I didn't know myself at all. That I had a cunning and devious side to me that I had never known about until then.'

'You're not cunning and devious,' Lind said softly.

Alvar folded his hands in his lap. 'I probably won't manage very well in prison,' he said feebly.

'If you're convicted, I'll make sure it's a suspended sentence. We will claim mitigating circumstances.'

'No,' Alvar shook his head in despair. 'You won't be able to get me off this one. I'm touched that you have faith in me, but I'm a grown man of forty-two and she was a sixteen-year-old girl. The jury will expect a certain degree of maturity, which I clearly don't possess. And that's humiliating, it's unbearable.'

Lind leaned forward. His voice was low and sincere.

'But you had your reasons for acting the way you did,' he said. 'We need to tell the jury what they were. We will show them in such a way that the whole sequence of events seems inevitable and logical.

You took her in for a whole year. She considered you to be her friend, her family will testify to that. The way I look at it, your chances are good, but you have to believe that, too. I'll be with you all the way.'

His last sentence echoed in Alvar's head. *I'll be with you all the way.*

'There's a story behind this tragedy,' Lind said. 'Twelve long months when she was a part of your life. You need to tell this story, Eide, right down to the last detail. What you thought, what you felt, how you were. How she got this hold over you, which she clearly had. She did have a hold on you, didn't she?'

'I can't stand up in court and speak ill of her,' Alvar said quickly. 'I've no right to do that and you can't make me.'

'You don't need to speak ill of her, but you need to tell it like it was. That she was stronger than you. I presume that she was?'

'She wasn't scared of anything,' he said in a tired voice. 'Not until that Friday when she turned up in withdrawal. I think of her as a brave soldier, she went to war every single day. While I, big coward that I am, sat safe and sound in my own comfortable castle.'

'You're very hard on yourself,' Lind said. 'Why is that?'

Alvar relaxed his shoulders. 'I should have seen where it was going. I should have turned her away, then she would still be alive.'

'No,' Lind said calmly. 'She was already on her way down and she took you with her.'

Then he folded his arms and rested them on the table. 'Tell me this,' he asked. 'Will you miss her?'

A wounded smile escaped from Alvar's lips. 'Yes,' he said, 'I will miss her. No one else comes to my flat.'

This revelation made him blush a second time.

'If you've had enough to eat,' Lind said, 'I suggest we start work. Is there anything else you want to tell me, anything that's important?'

'My cat,' Alvar said suddenly. 'My cat's probably sitting on my doorstep waiting to be let in. I'm sure he's hungry.'

'You have a cat?' Lind smiled. His white teeth sparkled. 'I'll look after your cat. Give me your keys, I'll stop by your house when we've finished.'

Alvar rummaged through his pocket for the key. He got up and pushed his chair. Lind gestured in the direction of the lift.

'Together we'll build a defence,' he said. 'You need to do your part. Do you understand?'

Alvar stared at the floor.

'Those who will be judging you need to know who you are. This means that you need to make yourself vulnerable and tell them all those things, it means you've got to trust me, you must believe that I want what's best for you.'

Alvar swallowed hard. 'I've never been in the habit of talking about myself in great detail,' he said quietly.

'What are you scared of?' Lind wanted to know.

'That they'll laugh, I think. That they'll despise me. That they'll call me a pathetic loner.'

'Don't be so negative,' Lind said firmly, 'chin up! Talk about yourself, start giving people a chance. People are much better than their reputation. Now you've got the opportunity to make a new discovery.'

'Perhaps they'll reject me,' Alvar said, deeply worried.

'Perhaps they'll find you not guilty,' Lind said.

The lift door closed. The space felt intimate.

'How did it start?' Lind asked. 'When did you first meet her?'

Alvar closed his eyes and remembered. Suddenly it all became clear to him. His first, but oh-so-fateful mistake.

'It was late last November, and it was cold. She came into the gallery where I work, staggering on her high-heeled boots, and she was freezing cold. I've never in all my life seen anyone so cold. Someone had to do something,' he said. 'For once in my life I decided that it was going to be me. So,' he sighed, 'I went up to the kitchen and got her a cup of coffee.'

CHAPTER 29

A man jumped the queue.

He was second in line, but he could not wait. He came into my house, all the way to my bedroom, he demanded to be heard. I carried him for twelve months. He has been in my thoughts every single day. His despair was my despair, I have felt responsible for him every single minute. Now I am standing by my window looking out at the world, the world I forget about for long periods of time when I am preoccupied with my writing. The azalea by my front door sways in the wind. Every now and then there is a sudden and forceful gust. It looks as if the whole crown of the tree is dancing a mournful dance, it bends, it surrenders. It has been standing there for more years than I have been alive, and it will still be there the day I die. That day may not be far away, I live a hard life. One day my teeth will be grinning in my skull, while the azalea dances.

The wide Lier Valley spreads out in all its glory. I can see farms, cows out to pasture, and now and then I can hear lowing, mild, woeful complaints in the stillness. I let the cat in, he goes to the kitchen for some food. I stroke his head lightly, feel his small skull underneath his fur. It is autumn, it is dark November. This season which I love most of all, the time when everything settles down. The outer landscape matches my inner one, it is gloomy and windswept. I go over to the computer, pull out my chair and sit down, pondering in the blue light. I have left Alvar Eide in the care of Benedict Lind. He does not need me any more, he can manage the remainder of the race himself, but I have given him some tools. He has been given his own story and he needs to tell it to those who will judge him. I hope they don't judge him harshly, I certainly don't. Yet there is one more detail before we finish. I feel that it belongs in the story. I want to give Alvar a final, friendly send-off. So I make myself comfortable and type, swiftly and fluently, a last important page. Just then I hear a sound from the corridor. Cautious steps, a door creaks. Alvar enters in his usual, shy way. He stops, he folds his hands. Looks at me across the room with mild eyes.

'Why are you still writing? I thought we'd finished?'

His eyes are unusually bright. I don't comment, I don't want to embarrass him.

'Yes,' I reply, 'but I have one important thing left to do.'

'What is it?'

He is intrigued

'I thought you might be interested,' I say. 'It's the post-mortem report.'

At this he goes white as a sheet.

'I don't know if I will be able to make sense of it,' he says, embarrassed. His grey eyes start to flicker, he shrugs helplessly.

'Then let me explain.'

I continue typing, my fingers run briskly across the keyboard. Alvar waits, I can hear his breathing.

'According to the pathologist Katrine Kjelland died from a cerebral haemorrhage,' I declare.

He gives me a frightened look.

'And what does that mean?'

'Bleeding in her brain,' I reply. 'What happens is that a vein bursts. It can occur in young people and can be caused by high blood pressure, or stress. In other words, she didn't die as a result of the pills you gave her, it was not a fatal dose, but they made her fall asleep. Thus you are not to blame for the death of Katrine Kjelland.'

Alvar cries out in relief. He buries his face in his hands, his knees look as if they might buckle.

'It that possible?'

'It says so here in black and white.'

The colour starts to return to his cheeks.

'But what did I give her then?' he asks quickly.

'Morphine,' I reply. 'She was probably experiencing some sort of blissful state when her heart stopped beating. And in her last moments someone wiped her brow with a warm cloth. She died on the sofa of a good friend,' I add. 'I might not be that lucky.'

He circles the floor. He clearly wants to shout for joy, but controls himself as always.

'But I drove off with her,' he recalls, 'that's unforgivable, what will people think?'

'I've got an old copy of the Penal Code here,' I say. 'If you like I can read it out to you.'

He nods silently. He waits.

'Section three hundred and forty-one. "Anyone who unlawfully or secretively either destroys the body of a deceased person or disposes of it so that it cannot be examined appropriately, or who refuses to inform the authorities of the whereabouts of a child or other incapacitated person they have in their care or who participates in so doing will be punished by a fine or up to six months' imprisonment."'

'Six months' imprisonment?'

He turns pale again.

'Let's hope they let you off with a fine,' I say. 'Now give people a chance.'

He nods again. Looks at me kindly as if he is seeing me for the first time.

'And what about you?' he asks. 'How are you doing? You've reached the end of the road. Are you happy?'

I shake my head. 'I haven't reached the end, Alvar, the worst is yet to come.'

'What's that?' he asks quickly.

'The book needs to reach an audience. I can barely find the courage. So I'll go over it a few more times. Adding, deleting a sentence here and there. And I still have to read the proofs, that's pure torture. Is that really all I did? I think, battling hard with myself, while I plan my next book. The book where I'll finally succeed once and for all.'

'Are you saying that you're disappointed with this one?' he asks nervously.

'Well,' I say, 'I'm not ecstatic. But that's the way life is. My dissatisfaction drives me to act, to write another book.'

I look up at him. I smile.

He nods. 'Do you wish me luck?'

'That goes without saying. You're on your own now. Trust those who will be judging you. Believe that they are compassionate people who'll understand.'

'I'll do my utmost,' he says. 'I want to thank you, you've been very generous.'

'You paid a high price,' I say, 'for the events you're about to face. But friendship is never free, you have to do your share.'

'It was worth it,' he says firmly. 'Besides, I'm wiser now.'

'How about Ole Krantz?' I ask. 'Have you spoken to him?'

'Yes. Benedict helped me explain. Krantz doesn't blame me and the job in the gallery is still mine.'

'What about the severed bridge?' I ask.

He smiles. He tilts his head. 'The bridge has been sold,' he says calmly.

'Is that right?' I say, giving him a big blue-eyed look of innocence. 'How do you feel about that?'

He juts out his chin. 'I don't need the bridge any more, not for anything. Because I have finally connected with another person. Benedict Josef Lind will be a friend for life.'

He walks quietly towards the door. I know that I'll never see him again and I'm filled with a sudden surge of grief. The door will never creak again, he'll never return to the room we shared for so long. Then he is gone and it goes very quiet. I switch off my computer, get up from my chair. I stand in the empty living room, left to my own devices, to a reality which is almost unbearable. Dear God, this silence, all I can hear is my own heart and I no longer have a destiny to cling to. My hands are empty. Who can I turn to, where can I go? I walk softly over to the window. I look out at the long queue of people still waiting on my drive. The woman with the dead child is still at the front. I watch her for a while, she doesn't move. She doesn't appear to have noticed me, she seems paralysed. I go out into the corridor, I put my shoes on, I open the front door. I walk down the drive, crunching the gravel. For a while I stand underneath the porch light studying them one by one. A couple of them look up at me hopefully. Some poke at the gravel with their shoes. They stand there with all their problems, all their guilt and shame. They stand there with hope of happiness and true love. I take the last few steps towards the woman with the child. I stop in front of her and give her a kind look.

'Hello. Do you want to come inside?'

She does not reply. Her eyes are apathetic. There is no doubt that her child has died, his small face is lightly marbled, his eyes are sunken.

'What happened?' I ask, trying to get her to look me in the eye. 'Did you find your child dead?'

Still no reply. Only silence, only her vacant eyes.

'I really want to help you,' I say, 'but you need to talk. If you don't talk, I won't be able to help you. Do you understand what I'm saying?'